All the Water I've Seen Is Running

All the
Water
I've Seen
Is Running

A Novel

Elias Rodriques

W. W. NORTON & COMPANY
Independent Publishers Since 1923

For information about permission to reproduce selections from this book, write to Permissions, W. W. Norton & Company, Inc., 500 Fifth Avenue, New York, NY 10110

For information about special discounts for bulk purchases, please contact W. W. Norton Special Sales at specialsales@wwnorton.com or 800-233-4830

Manufacturing by LSC Harrisonburg
Book design by Lovedog Studio
Production manager: Julia Druskin

Library of Congress Cataloging-in-Publication Data

Names: Rodriques, Elias, author.
Title: All the water I've seen is running : a novel / Elias Rodriques.
Description: First edition. | New York : W. W. Norton & Company, [2021]
Identifiers: LCCN 2020053069 | ISBN 9780393540796 (hardcover) |
     ISBN 9780393540802 (epub)
Classification: LCC PS3618.O3596 A79 2021 | DDC 813/.6—dc23
LC record available at https://lccn.loc.gov/2020053069

W. W. Norton & Company, Inc.,
500 Fifth Avenue, New York, N.Y. 10110
www.wwnorton.com

W. W. Norton & Company Ltd.,
15 Carlisle Street, London W1D 3BS

1 2 3 4 5 6 7 8 9 0

To my mother and brother

Geography is not fate but fatal.

—Ishion Hutchinson,
"The Mariner's Progress"

Waters

Back then, we body surfed until saltwater rushed into our sinuses and pushed liquid mucus out our noses. When we tired of trying to catch the tide, we waded out, stopping to dive under incoming waves. Above us, the rushing water sounded like wind heard from within a plane landing. We surfaced and continued out to where we could not touch. We treaded and bobbed in the tide and congregated on sand bars. When that exhausted us, we swam back to shore and baked in the sun until the day turned to a haze of half sleep.

We lived for water, salt, fresh, and brackish. We waited out schooldays for the weekends and school years for the summers to return to it. We stood on our river's mud shores and cast lines, hoping to catch something big, only ever reeling in catfish. We wriggled our hands into their mouths, unhooked their slimy insides, and tossed them back into our brackish river. After sweat and spray coated our faces, we kicked off our flipflops and swam in murky waters. When the sun stole our shade, we moved on to the next shore or pier or dock or dinghy. We were all waiting for life after high school, after our no nametown in North Florida, so we figured we'd wait by the water.

On the best nights, we saw the glint of moonlight rippling on a current. I spent many evenings with the girl I loved in high school, Aubrey, trying to touch the moon's reflection, our hands plunging through cold waters as if digging in the sky. I liked to stand in the glow and pretend we were characters in some fantasy book carrying out a ritual, my hair standing on end as the magic took hold. But I think it was just the feel of Aubrey's eyes on me, a Black boy on the wrong side of skinny, who never thought anyone would want him, least of all her.

The longest night we spent on the biggest river that runs through Palm Coast, the Intracoastal, was when I was seventeen and Aubrey was eighteen. We made plans at lunch. She was waiting at our table and I hoped to rush through the free-lunch line at school, but it was longer than normal. The growing number of middle-class kids in line, all of whose parents worked in real estate or landscaping, suggested something was changing. But I wouldn't learn what until the 2008 housing crash gave my county the highest unemployment rate in the state that had the highest in the nation.

By the time I retrieved my lukewarm burger and french fries and joined Aubrey, a dark-haired white girl standing to about five-six, lunch was almost over. After we shot the breeze, I asked what her weekend plans were. She said she didn't have any. I said we didn't have a track meet tomorrow, Saturday. She said we were going fishing that evening.

Lost in daydreams about the night to come during my classes and at practice, the day passed by in a blur. On the school bus home, Des asked if I wanted to kick it; I said I was hanging with Aubrey. He extended his hand, dapped me up, and didn't say anything else. When I got home, I told Mom

I was spending the night at my friend Twig's house. An hour later, she dropped me off and, after she left, I drove Twig's car to Aubrey's house. In her neighborhood, every street name started with a B—Bird of Paradise Drive, Buffalo Bill Place, Brushwood Lane—so everyone called it the B section. The houses there were bigger and the lawns better kept than in my part of town, but Aubrey's driveway seemed poorly paved for the neighborhood.

I knocked on her window and she came out. Her hair was up in a ponytail and her teal Abercrombie shirt was just short enough that it exposed the seabass tattoo on her waist. I tried not to stare, but I kept glancing at the curve her hip bone drew.

You could've rang, she said.

It's late.

I didn't ring because I worried Aubrey's sister would answer. A few weeks earlier, I stood behind her sister in line at Walmart. She was buying alcohol. When she reached the front, the white cashier with a buzz cut and goatee asked for her ID. She handed it over. He held it up to the light. She shook her head as she stared at his fake diamond earring. When he finally returned it and rang her up, she walked away and said, Fucking nigger. I wondered what Aubrey would have said to her sister if she was there.

They don't care, Aubrey said.

She opened the garage. We hooked her dinghy up to a red truck as I tried to avoid looking at the Confederate flag bumper sticker that I assumed was her sister's. Then we got in the car and drove to Bing's Landing. As we pulled in, shadowy Spanish moss swayed from the branches overhead. We passed the one-room barbecue joint and the small grass square that made up the park. At the river's edge, silhouettes swung and

I heard a hook splash into the Intracoastal. I was trying to distinguish the line from the night when Aubrey reversed the truck down the ramp and the dinghy into the water. We got out, detached the boat, and held it still.

Get in, Aubrey said, barely more visible than the shadow people in the distance.

Where are you going?

To park. Can't bring it with us.

What if I float away?

Hold on to the dock. As she walked away, she muttered, All them book smarts and not a lick of common sense.

I got in and grabbed its rough wood beams, which felt like they might splinter into my hand. The water bobbed beneath and I worried I would fall. Moments later, a gray-blue hue to her skin, Aubrey returned with the spear, the bucket, and the lamps.

Can we turn the lights on? I asked.

Got to wait till they're in the water, she said.

I can't see anything.

You afraid of the dark?

Aubrey got in the boat, shoved off, and guided us out with a pole. Then she turned the motor on and propelled us downstream. The front tipped up a few inches. The bow carved a V-shaped line into the water that would become our wake. Beyond it, no one else was on the river. Overhead, the stars were scattered across the blue-black sky like spilled glitter.

This good? Aubrey asked, turning the motor off.

It's good, I said.

Aubrey plunged the pole to the riverbed and steered us closer to the bank. The shore ran in a soft incline up to a dark-gray forest where tree shadows faded into one another. She passed me the lamps and I dropped them in the river. They bounced on the surface. She turned them on, and they lit the bottom gray like the surface of the moon. Reedy, seaweed-like plants waved from below. Pebbles littered the dirt-sand, which looked softer than any beach I had ever set foot on. A thin fish floated off the floor and Aubrey yelled, Flounder.

Aubrey stabbed the spear through it. A ribbon of pink curled out. Then a sand cloud rushed up from where Aubrey hit the bed and blotted out the blood.

That's what you're looking for, she said, pulling the flounder out of the river and tossing it into the bucket. Sometimes they look like rocks. Only way to know is to stab.

You go first. I'll watch.

Aubrey and I switched places. I steered the boat from the back, pushing the pole to the bottom, leaning my weight on it and pulling it loose from the sticky earth. The dirt shores on our right gave way to short cement walls that I assumed the river overcame during hurricanes. Above them, long wood docks lit by lamps led to waterfront houses. How often did they drain floodwaters from their floors?

Go slower, Aubrey said. Can't see anything if you don't go slowly.

As she peered over the side, my eyes adjusting to the night, I could almost see her bony shoulders through her shirt. It crept up to reveal a thin line of vertebrae. I tried to count them, imagined what they would feel like.

Slowly now.

She let her dark-brown, almost-black hair down. I was surprised to see it fall so far below her shoulders. It was straight. She must have just straightened it. When she leaned to stab at the floor, her hair swung a long arc, blurring in the dim light before settling in front of her shoulders, a thicket hiding her face.

Slowly. They get scared if you don't go slowly.

She had curled her hair for homecoming. Her pink ruffled dress almost matched the shape of her dark curls. The picture was so clear in my mind that I must have stared when I saw her.

Slowly, she said. Then she stabbed. I pushed a few more times and she speared again. When she hit rocks, she laughed as if mocking someone.

Slowly.

I am going slowly.

You're going faster than you think.

Show me then.

We switched. Up front, I stabbed at every gray disk on this moon's surface. At first, I cut through the water. Then my shoulders began to burn. The spear moved slower. My arms ached. I stabbed less than Aubrey did. How did she get so strong?

Can't believe you've never been gigging, she said.

Not something my friends do.

All rednecks do it.

Don't hang with any rednecks.

We're hanging right now, she said.

You're not a redneck.

Sure am. Daddy's from the Panhandle.

I looked at the shore. The large houses with sprawling lawns began to look like miniature plantations. I could almost see the enslaved people, just now leaving the master's house for their homes.

Still don't think you're a redneck, I said.

I go mudding. Wear camo.

No accent.

Only when you're around.

We passed a clearing where there were RVs, trailers hooked up to trucks, and six or so rectangular trailer homes. The light was on in one. Two shadows stood opposite each other, then came together until they overlapped in an inhuman shape. Worried Aubrey would notice me watching them, I turned. At the clearing's edge, instead of a wall, the earth crumbled into the Intracoastal.

You're not like the others, I said.

What's that supposed to mean?

I didn't say anything. Aubrey asked to switch spots. As we tried to step around each other in the small boat, I smelled the river on her. Her body brushed against mine and it was softer than expected. She looked me in the eyes. My cheeks burned at our contact, at being close enough to catch her scent, and I turned away. I stepped to the back of the boat, pushed for a little, and then stopped to watch the bed. The mud floor looked soft enough to fall asleep in.

Tired already? she asked.

It's hard work, I said.

Ain't you Mr. Track Star?

That what they call me?

What my sister called you, when I told her what I was doing tonight. Probably shouldn't have told you. Don't want it to go to your head. She paused and looked up at the sky. Think you're going to miss all this when you get that scholarship?

If I get a scholarship.

You going to get one.

Tell the truth, I don't think much about that. Just think about getting on out of here.

You scared of ending up like your brother?

I didn't say anything. In the distance, the river was black. As we got closer, it yellowed. Then it turned gray and transparent. If we went on for long enough, we would travel the path debris takes when it follows the current out to sea. We would stall where the river fought the ocean.

Beautiful out here, I said.

Nothing like it.

Quiet.

Sure is.

Never heard your voice so clear, I said.

What you mean?

School's so loud. Out here you sound different. I never noticed your voice was so, and then I trailed off into silence.

Shrill?

Airy.

We were quiet as a big boat motored by. In its wake, we bobbed, and it felt like I was standing on the waves. The bank looked like it was floating, the plantation-style houses and trailers like they might rock off the shore. Aubrey cussed under her breath. But when the bobbing stopped, even though our boat was small, it felt firm.

You good? she asked.

I'm good.

I was quiet as I looked at Aubrey, a gleam to her face from some mixture of sweat, river, and moonlight. Shorter than me but seeming to stand at eye level, she wasn't smiling or scowling, as she so often was. Her dark hair framing her face, her large brown eyes wide open, she just let me watch her and watched me back. No one had ever stood so still in my gaze nor had I done the same for anyone else. I didn't worry about my nose's acne as I often did when I noticed other people looking at me at school. I didn't feel a need to fill the quiet. As the frogs droned and the water slapping against the shores sounded like a dog lapping from a bowl, I didn't fret about my crooked teeth and I smiled.

I'd ride down this forever if I could, I said.

We'd hit the inlet eventually, she said.

We could keep going.

Into the sea?

Across the world.

We stopped pushing and coasted in the current. Unoccupied by anything but watching the shore pass by and counting the silent seconds, we felt the weight of all the things we had not shared becoming too heavy. Believing love to be defined by mentioning every unmentionable, we spilled our secrets in jumbled words, sentences without periods. (I can't bring myself to share them here, now.) We touched. We turned around, headed back to land. We waited out the moon on shore. We parted as the birds awakened around us.

Histories

I'm thinking of that night and our waterlogged days, now seven years ago and a thousand miles away, as I lie in bed next to my boyfriend, Virgil, in New York in 2015. He knows little of that time—when words drawled out of my mouth, when I thought I would never make it out of our conservative town. He doesn't know the news that I have just read.

Phone cradled in front of my face, brightness low so I don't wake Virgil, I read the *Flagler Live* headline again: ONE DEAD IN CRASH OFF US-1. According to the article, Aubrey was riding shotgun when her ex-boyfriend, Brandon, swerved off US-1 between Daytona and Palm Coast. Aubrey wasn't wearing a seat belt. She flew through the windshield and landed in the woods amid the untamed brush and longleaf pines. She died before the paramedics arrived. In the picture above the article, her dark eyes shine, her pale skin glistens, and her pink lips crack a bright smile in front of the sky-blue background of her graduation photo. She looks just as I remember her. The memories come rushing. The dark turns to a theater; a montage plays: sunlit Florida days scored by a melancholic soundtrack.

When reliving the past becomes too hard, I turn to Virgil. Still asleep, the comforter covering most of his nude body, he is the color of tea mixed with milk. His long limbs stretch across the bed, an arm tucked beneath my pillow from when he cradled me last night. Lying still, he looks like another fold of fabric in the morning dark. If it weren't for his rising chest, I might think him a corpse.

I run a hand behind his ear and he curls into me without opening his eyes, burying his face against my side. His words are muffled when he says, You been up long?

A bit.

Something on your mind?

For a moment, I consider telling him. If I do, will he be awake enough to listen?

No, I say. Just work.

He tries to pull me into him, but I resist.

I have to get ready, I say.

Already?

I kiss him on the forehead and get out of bed. The cold of his underheated Crown Heights apartment in March makes me shiver. Dazed, I shower in water so hot, mist blankets his windowless bathroom. After, I squint through the steam at the mirror to fasten my tie and try to lesson plan for my tenth-grade class in my head, but the memories of Aubrey keep interrupting. I'm shaking my head at the low knot when Virgil kisses me on the cheek and steps into the shower. I start over on my tie. When he is done, I'm still trying to get the knot right, though I have done this every workday for years now.

You all right? Virgil asks.

Fine. Why?

You're usually gone by the time I'm done showering.

I look at my watch. I'm late. I grab my things and run out the door without kissing him goodbye. I speed down the stairs, throw the front door open, and jog for the same train that I have caught every morning for a long time. The cold March air burns my chest. The sidewalk hits hard against my soles, pain shooting up my legs. By the time I rush through the turnstile, down the platform, and onto the train, the shin splints that I developed in high school still burn. When I sit, I'm breathing heavily. Eventually, my lungs slow, the commuters and the train fade away, and Aubrey returns. I'm there with her, a teen in Florida once more. As she walks by my side, books clutched to her chest, my stomach flutters and I still love her, though we haven't talked in years, though I haven't loved a girl in years.

The train ride and the time before first period passes without me realizing it, so I'm surprised when students start filing into my room. During my first class, the boy I suspect is currently homeless is absent, and the two girls who fought are still suspended. I try to keep the attention of the ones who remain, but I can't even keep my own; we're doing practice questions for the upcoming state tests, which bore me and the students on a good day, let alone today, when I'm still thinking about Aubrey. For the rest of the day, I fight my memories to focus on teaching, struggling to remain patient enough to answer the same question multiple times. During last period, I lose my temper on a girl talking to her friend, yell at her for never paying attention, and tell everyone that I'm doing this for their benefit. When they leave, I'm ashamed. Today was a wash, I think to myself, but I'll make up for it tomorrow.

I sit at my computer and search for more news about Aubrey.

All I find is her picture in a mug-shot database. I didn't know she had been arrested. I scroll through the photos. One for a charge of breaking and entering in 2010, a charge for unlawfully occupying a home in 2011, and a probation violation in 2012. Over the years, her skin grows paler and her cheeks sink inward. In the final mug shot, her makeup-free eyes are dull and a frown creases her face. She looks nothing like the girl I loved in high school.

Then again, Aubrey was bad in high school. She cut class, smoked, drank. I might've expected her to get a DUI or a drunk in public. I might even have expected her to get arrested for fighting at a bar. But breaking into someone's home was planned. I never knew her to go out of her way to hurt someone. What else didn't I know?

When I look at the clock, it's almost four. School's been over for an hour. If I keep this up, I'll stay in my classroom staring at her all night. I gather my things, go to Virgil's apartment, and let myself in, dropping my bag at the door. On the navy two-person couch in the living room, I watch a sitcom, trying to lose myself in problems so inconsequential that they have no bearing on the next episode. The screen's blue glow and the bright square window, which looks out onto another building, barely light the dark room. The sun has almost entirely gone when Virgil comes home.

I didn't think I was going to see you today, he says. My eyes burn as the water comes and I blink quickly. What's wrong?

Aubrey passed.

Who's Aubrey?

My high school girlfriend.

I'm so sorry, he says, sitting down and stretching an arm

around me. He tries to pull me into his chest, but I don't budge, so he pats my shoulder. Were you close?

She was basically my best friend in high school, but I haven't talked to her in years.

What was she like?

Different. Probably wouldn't be friends if we met today. But the first day I got to school after we moved to Florida, I didn't know anyone. Sat at an empty table outside the cafeteria. Next day, she was just there. Asked her if I could sit down and she said go ahead. Figured she ain't had no friends neither. Turned out she was arguing with her best friend so she was just looking for somewhere to be alone. Either way, we kept sitting together.

I look at Virgil, expecting him to say something. He sits quietly, as if waiting for me to say more.

To tell the truth, I continue, she was kind of mean. One time, she threw a pencil at a teacher and got suspended and told me she wished she had taken his eye out. But she was always nice to me. She was a bad girl and I was just this nerdy, poor kid who only cared about school and track.

Was she white? I shoot him a look and he puts his hands up, as if backing away from a fight. No judgment. Just curious.

Yeah, she was white, I say. But honestly, I don't care about any of the fucked-up shit that she did or the ways I fucked up anymore.

Virgil nods and watches me for so long that I look away. My knee is bobbing up and down. I don't know when that started.

Grieving's hard, he says. You're allowed to be sad.

Am I really though? If I really cared, wouldn't I have called?

Maybe, he says, and then inhales audibly and looks around the room. I don't respond and the silence sits for a little. Then someone stomps around the apartment above us, kids scream unintelligibly outside, and a car roars down the street. We never get even one quiet minute in this overgrown city.

When's the funeral? Virgil asks.

This weekend.

Are you going?

I have work.

They'll find a sub, he says.

Flights are too expensive.

I can chip in.

I don't want to go, I say.

Virgil scratches the back of his head and then says, So what you want to do?

I don't want to talk anymore.

Virgil nods, goes to the kitchen, and begins preparing dinner. As usual, I halfheartedly offer to help and he tells me to relax. I can do the dishes. I consider watching more TV, but the thought bores me. Instead, I walk into Virgil's bedroom, step around the clothes on the floor, and climb onto the rusty fire escape overlooking overflowing trash cans. Their sour scent wrinkles my nose for a moment and then dissipates. I sit and watch the occasional person carry out a large black bag of garbage and birds perched in a tree, taking flight every few moments and then returning to a different branch. After some minutes, my phone buzzes. Mom's calling. I pick up.

I was wondering when I was going to hear your voice, Mom says.

Sorry I haven't called in so long, I say, trying to think of the last time we spoke; it's been about a month, maybe longer. I've been busy.

I know, she says. Them kids driving you crazy?

They're all right, I say. Lost my temper today though.

What happened?

Usual stuff. I was in a bad mood. Got some bad news. Aubrey died.

Which one's Aubrey? Mom asks.

White girl I went to high school with, I say.

Don't think I remember her, but I'm sorry, she says. I'm quiet for long enough to hear the birds chirp and cars passing by. Mom continues, A friend of mine died recently too. Went to school with him at St. Jago. Him and his wife were killed at home. He was fifty-five. Too young.

When was the last time you saw him?

Years ago. Lots of deaths these days in Jamaica. Always makes me think of Junior.

Junior was my mom's younger brother. He was found with a bullet in his head in an abandoned warehouse in East Flatbush before I was born, almost three decades ago. He was twenty-five.

Been so long, Mom says, but I'm still thinking about him.

Sorry, I say.

It's okay, you know. Just the price of surviving. We let the quiet sit a minute, and then Mom asks, When are you moving back to Jamaica?

I haven't lived there, I think to myself, since I was ten. I haven't set foot on the island since 1999.

I don't know, I say. I have to go, Mom. I have something on the stove.

Well, I don't want to keep you, she says. I know you're busy. Just make sure to take some time to rest.

Thanks. I'll call you soon.

After we hang up, I sit on the fire escape until Virgil calls me in for dinner. As we eat, he asks questions that I respond to in a few words, leaving little room for conversation. The silences last too long. As he watches me, I can tell that he's trying to think of the right thing to say, but I'm still thinking of Aubrey. After dinner, we do the dishes and watch TV until I feel exhausted and climb into bed. Virgil stays up for a little and then joins me. He kisses me. His hands roam my body, trying to pull us into something passionate, but I pull away, give him a peck on the forehead, and turn over.

In the night, I dream I am lying in bed with Aubrey. The room is golden, sunrise or sunset. I'm sitting up on white sheets, back against a mahogany headboard, looking down at her, lying in pale ripped jeans and a white T-shirt, looking back up at me. In her light brown eyes, I see my reflection, the high school, short-haired Daniel wearing a shirt from the Bob Hayes track meet. I can see all of myself in her eyes. She props herself up on her elbows. She cracks a smile, wrinkling the corners of her eyes, and just watches me. We're together. We're finally together. We're finally in love again.

I open my eyes. Half-asleep, the glee lingering, I think for a minute that I'm still in high school, that the body next to me is hers, that she's still alive. Virgil shifts and I look around my room and she's not there. I roll onto my back and stare at the ceiling for a little. When I fall back asleep, I'm in the dream again, lying with Aubrey. Part of me knows she's dead, so I'm half-excited that she's here, half-worried I'm having a psychotic break. Fear grips my chest, though I can't move, can't stop looking at Aubrey. Ecstasy and panic mix, until I wake with a start in Virgil's room. It's morning now. I don't need to be at work for a while, but I get out of bed, get ready, and leave before he wakes.

During the day, as the dream keeps coming to mind, the city blurs before me. None of the few trees catch my eye. The buildings all look the same, as do the small patches of overcast sky that I glimpse between them. I can't tell one pigeon apart from another. Even my students, whose parents and voices and lives I once knew, start to look alike. I'm too lost in thought, in the dream that won't stop returning. I felt so strongly about Aubrey when I was younger, I keep thinking. I felt so strongly this morning. Did I ever feel that way about Virgil?

In the evening, I meet Virgil at a bar equidistant from our apartments. It's new, so the bar is mostly empty. It looks like all the other tiny bars opening up around here that play anodyne, once edgy songs from the 2000s. Aside from the large window on the front wall, it's barely lit. A white bartender with tattoo sleeves pours our drinks and then we sit at a corner table, dark beers between us. Virgil talks about the band practice he just came from. He plays the bass in a jazz ensemble. They're booking some gigs, mostly weddings, but it's not as fun as it used to be, he says. I nod along.

You've been quiet, he says. What's on your mind?

I inhale deeply. A voice tells me, You don't love Virgil, not like you loved Aubrey. You still love Aubrey.

Finally, I say, I think we should break up.

What?

I can't do this right now.

You don't want to break up, Daniel, Virgil says, reaching across the table, putting his hand on mine, which lies limp.

You're just sad. I look down at the table and sit quietly for a while. So that's it? You don't have anything to say to me?

Virgil, I told you what I want.

Fuck you, Daniel, he says, getting up and walking out of the bar.

I sit until I finish both beers and then leave. The buzz numbing my face and loosening my limbs, I walk toward my apartment past indistinguishable people. About halfway, tired of the old brownstones abutting boxy new buildings, I text one of my closest friends from high school, Twig, who always kept me laughing, who dropped me off at home every day after track practice and who I spent many days riding around with, looking for something to do. I ask if he's going to the funeral and if I can stay with him if I go. He replies, Of course. He's always got a bed for me. I look at flights. They're even more expensive than before. I don't know if I should spend the money. I call Mom.

Two days in a row, she says when she picks up. Lucky me.

After we tell each other how we are, she says, Did I ever tell you about Granville?

Your cousin, right?

Yeah. He was always working. He'd bag groceries during the day and then run to whatever restaurant he worked in at night. Always said he wanted to be a chef. He was getting close too. Think he was about to get a loan when he had that stroke while he was driving and crashed.

Mom talks for a little longer about Granville and then about her day. I tell her I have to go when I get to my apartment. Later that night, as I'm washing dishes, Twig texts, asking about my flight. I look again and the prices have risen even higher. I don't text back.

I call Mom again the next day and then every night after that. She keeps talking about our family, about whom she has learned more since returning to Jamaica. She tells tales she whispered to her sisters when I was young and they thought I could not hear, tales of ancestors enslaved or indentured, of men getting women pregnant and then fleeing their partners, of childhood squabbles that turned to adult fistfights and finally years without talking. She sketches the lives of relatives who appeared and disappeared from her stories. In time, she begins to piece together patches of histories that once went missing without explanation. She tells me these things, she says, so I can keep our story alive. So we are not forgotten.

As the nights pass, I feel like a child again, listening to Mom tell me fables about Anansi, the trickster spider who lied to keep himself alive. (Anansi, Mom said back then, stole the stories the Sky God hoarded to preserve our history.) I'm doing as Mom did when she was young and sitting in the shade of a lime tree in New Monklands in Jamaica, listening to her grandfather's family history. As the stories accumulate, the similarities between my family's experiences and my own make me feel like I am living parallel lives, at one moment my own and at the next my kin's.

Since returning to Jamaica, Mom has learned so much about our people by talking to the folks she knew or who knew our relatives. She has remembered moments long forgotten by revisiting the places where she grew up. She has heard the other sides of stories that made her life what it was, what it is.

If I go home like her, if I try to learn more about what happened to Aubrey after we fell out of touch, I'll have to face

Brandon. My stomach clenches. I imagine asking him why he got in the car that night and him deflecting, claiming it wasn't his fault. Then I picture my hands around his throat, shaking him until his eyes roll back and his neck turns limp. Though the image only ever riles me up, I never let it go; I keep picturing myself dropping him to the ground. Finally, when the airline prices drop two weeks later, I book a flight home.

Names

I land in Jacksonville, rent a car, and drive south. I have some time to kill before meeting up with my friends, so I head to the beach. I exit the highway into Bunnell, equidistant from St. Augustine and Daytona. A sign names it the Crossroads of Flagler County, a relic from when railroads made it a boomtown. Its high school was one of the last to be desegregated in Florida.

Today, this four-lane road divided by a grass median is flanked by strip malls, cleared lots, and wild clusters of trees. There are more empty parking spaces than I remember. I wonder if anyone I know is in those buildings, shopping or working, and if they would recognize me if I stopped by.

After I pass the park and one of many identical housing communities, I ascend the bridge over the river that Aubrey and I traveled down years ago. Running parallel to the ocean, it was dredged up and widened, we were told, by the Army Corps of Engineers during World War II. Its waters still separate the beach towns from the mainland. I roll my windows down, hoping to smell the ocean, but it's still too far. Instead, an earthy, oily funk flares my nose. I glance left and right. Boats travel downstream, leaving white wakes. People stand on docks and cast lines. Then the river disappears around a bend. Its name changes depending on the region. Around here, maps call it the Matanzas, named for the sixteenth-century Spanish massacre, but we called it the Intracoastal.

✂

When we were in high school, everyone had a nickname. Aubrey had at least a dozen for me. When I first met her, I introduced myself as Daniel, but she called me Dan. I didn't correct her.

About a month later, when my hair grew unruly because I had not yet found a barber, she called me Bum Head. When she found out I was in honors classes, she called me Einstein. When I talked about how I could not wait to get out of Palm Coast, she called me Big-Time. When I took her tinfoil gum wrapper and put it on my teeth, pretending I had a grill, she called me Muckmouth. And my junior year, when I became captain of the track team and she overheard my teammates call me TC, she repeated the nickname with a sneer.

Now that you leading the troops and whatnot, she said that day, you going to get all full of yourself and start bossing me around?

Even if I did, you wouldn't listen.

You don't know. I could be a good soldier.

You ain't got the discipline.

Oh, so I'm soft? she said, eyebrow creeping up. She leaned over the table, her hair drawing forward with her, as if waiting to pounce.

I ain't say all that, I said, leaning back, hands up.

You think you tougher than me. Is that it, TC? she said, lightly punching my arm. Think you can beat me up?

Aubrey, I was just playing.

No, if you think you tougher than me, then prove it.

Aubrey hit me again. I put my hands between us and she boxed them. I weaved my head back and forth, mimicking the boxing scenes I saw in movies. Aubrey stood up and I did too. She exaggerated leaning into her jabs and I backpedaled, pretending to give her instructions. Jab. Jab. Right hook. Uppercut. She swung harder, her fist and my palms connecting in louder and louder claps, until one of the teachers told us to stop horsing around. Not wanting to be punished, I dropped my hands. Aubrey's left hook connected with my arm, drawing pain along the bone. The teacher yelled again, Aubrey rolled her eyes, and we returned to our table. Though I pretended I didn't feel anything, my bicep stung for a while.

For real though, Aubrey said, her voice quiet as she caught her breath, I'm proud of you, Daniel.

※

On the few occasions she said my full name in her Southern accent, the syllables drawling into the surrounding words, she always looked me in the eyes, made me feel like no one else was around. Thinking about the times that her voice got so low that I had to lean in to hear her call me Daniel brings me back to that cafeteria where we ate lunch together every day. The memories are so strong that, somehow, it feels like I could knock on her front door and Aubrey would answer. We would look like we were both in high school, her looking at me straight-on and me looking at the floor. Before I could say anything, she would jokingly complain—You must think you're mighty special, she'd say, to show up here after so long—and I would apologize until she shrugged it off and let me in.

But she's not here. I never came back to see her when she was alive. I haven't returned in seven years. Since I moved to New York, I lost myself in a new life and fell out of touch with my old friends and much of my family. Maybe if I hadn't, I would have a right to grieve. Instead, I'm feeling sorry for myself.

My hands are shaky as I park in the ten-car lot just south of the pier. I turn around to see if anyone is behind me, but on this late March day the lot is empty. When a single car passes by on A1A, it almost looks fake.

My mind wandered for longer than I thought. I drove over the bridge and through an intersection without paying attention. I could've hit someone.

I step out of the car, knees creaking from overuse on the track. It's colder than I expect as I cross the street onto the walkway above the beach and peer down. Scattered green brush grows at the top of the hill and thins as the shore slopes. The sand is orange. The shore is short. High tide. A film of skim rolls back into the inky sea. A riptide, I think, hides where the water turns opaque.

I scan the near-empty beach for a face I recognize. On my left, three young white men wearing wetsuits wax shortboards. On my right, two teenagers hide beneath a blanket, their bodies mashing into each other. One rolls on top of the other as though they're in a bedroom with the curtains drawn and the door closed. I look away and notice someone approaching. He's wearing a black shirt and khaki pants, the uniform for the pizzeria opposite the pier. He walks close enough that he blocks the wind. When he cranes his neck to get a look, I meet his pale-green eyes, the color of a sea much farther south than here.

Though his jaw is squarer and his body leaner now, I recognize him: Peter. I wonder if he spent much time with Aubrey after we graduated. After a few paces, he turns around and passes by again. This time I follow. His hips switch when he walks. He was the only male dancer in high school. Everyone made fun of him for being gay, myself included. He swore that he was straight. We didn't care.

Peter walks to the pier bathroom. Sand cakes in the shape of a spiral, like a dried-up Milky Way, around the drain in the urine-soaked floor. He walks into the handicapped stall and leaves the door open. As he watches from beneath thick, dark eyebrows, I follow and lock the door behind me.

Later, he zips up his pants while I do the same. My belt buckle clanks as I tighten it. I stare at the tiled wall where dark grime covers the grout. In the corner of my eyes, I see him watching me.

Daniel, right? he asks. How long you around for?

Couple days.

Am I going to see you before you go? he says. He pulls out his phone and hands it to me. He's creating a new contact. My first name is filled in but not my last. He does not know it. It is my mother's: Henriquez.

✳

I didn't know much about the Henriquezes until recently, when Mom began telling me more about our family history. Henriquez, she said, comes from her biological father, but she rarely talks about his side of the family and mostly tells stories about her mother's relatives. Her mother's father, Richard, was the son of Indian indentured servants, born in a hut on the outskirts of the coffee plantation where the man who purchased their debt lived. His birth certificate, which Mom tracked down along with other documents of our family history, labels him a Coolie.

Richard married a light-skinned Black woman, Sylvia, my great-grandmother, a descendant of enslaved Africans. (I don't know what their wedding was like. Did they jump a broom; did the Indian relatives speak their home language, and if so, which one?) Shortly thereafter, they had six girls, including Velma, my grandmother. I assume they gave them his last name. When Grandma married, she, like all her sisters, took the name of her husband and gave his name to their children. Even after Grandma left him, she kept his name: Henriquez.

My mother was born Joyce Henriquez, but she barely knew her biological father. When Mom was young, Grandma left him, married another man, and moved in with him. He worked on a coffee farm in New Monklands, a small village in the island's southern hills. Whenever I ask about them, Mom tells the same story: Grandma grew up during the 1930s strikes and hunger marches, so she always wanted to escape Jamaica. About a week after Independence Day, she finally did, leaving behind Mom's stepfather and her two children. The next morning, as Mom's older sister did her own hair, their stepfather sat Mom down between his legs. He held her still with his knees. One calloused hand gripped her head. The other drove the comb, scraping the skin and ripping kinks. It was a plow tilling her scalp, uprooting weeds until he left for the fields.

They followed that routine for months. Then Grandma saved enough money to send for her daughters. Mom left her stepfather for Spanish Town, and eventually the States.

✳

Mom says her stepfather is the closest thing to a father she ever had, but she never took his name. I don't remember it, or Grandma's family name. I wouldn't even know how to find the name the Indians had before they arrived in Jamaica, though people saw enough of them in me to call me Coolie when I was growing up on the island.

Despite going to high school with me, Peter knows nothing of the history of my name, the name of Mom's biological father, a man who did not raise her, whom I have never met. I don't want to give it to him. I just want to leave.

I enter a fake name and a fake number. I run my hand along the back of my neck, where fuzz has long since overgrown my lineup.

What're you doing back? Peter asks.

He leans against the paint-chipped stall, standing between me and the door. He smiles when we make eye contact. His crooked front tooth leans over the other in the way dancers cross their legs.

When Aubrey died, I say, I wanted to come back for the funeral, but I couldn't swing it. Bought a flight for the day I could afford. Figured I been gone too long.

Peter shifts from side to side. I wonder if he knew her, if her passing still hurts.

You hung out with Aubrey?

Not really, Peter says.

Never talked?

She was in one of my classes. Called me fag a few times, but you know.

Everyone in high school was homophobic. She was meaner than most. Our classmates said she kept her daddy's pistol in her glove compartment, even when she parked at school. The whole cafeteria saw her rip a fistful of hair out of the head of her onetime best friend, Jess, who stole her boyfriend, and watched as the school security officer bent Aubrey's arm behind her back and paraded her to the dean's office. But the girl I knew wasn't heartless.

The slaps of flip-flops against heels echo in the bathroom. Peter looks through the crack between the stall door and its wall. Behind him, I see a silhouette of a tall man moving toward the urinal. Peter's reddened neck beads with sweat. He motions to me to keep quiet. When the man leaves, Peter tucks in his shirt, its black cloth wrinkled from my hands.

I peek through the gap to see if anyone else is there. It's empty. I turn around, meet Peter's glance, and then look away.

Would've thought y'all hung out after high school, I say.

You ain't been back in a while, he says, if you thought everyone was cool with each other after we graduated.

I been gone a minute.

Folks still call me fag when I see them. I'm guessing you still closeted?

Been out since college.

Anybody down here know?

Ain't keep it a secret, I say. I just ain't talk to nobody.

Peter shrugs and then says, I'll just say this: Aubrey wasn't the type of person who'd hang with me.

No rumors, no small-town gossip about Aubrey. Not totally surprising. Last I heard from a friend, she moved up north to Maryland after high school. I saw on Facebook that she got engaged. As far as I could tell, she had finally escaped our shit town. So what was she doing back here in her ex's car at three a.m.?

I check the time. I'm late. I hope my friends know more than Peter does. I return his phone and open the stall door. He says something behind me, but I don't hear him. I rush out of the bathroom. The sun overhead is so bright now that it makes me squint. My eyes scrunched, I see the contours of the wood planks on which I walk and the boxy buildings to my right. Mostly, I see the sky, blue and pale as though painted with a light brushstroke.

I think I hear Peter's footsteps behind me, but I don't turn around. I need to get to the bar to ask my friends what they know about Aubrey. If they find out that I want to track down Brandon, they'll tell me dogs who stick their noses where they don't belong get hit.

❈

That saying always reminds me of my father. He's Trinidadian. His father was middle-class and Lebanese. His mother was poor and Black. I don't think they married, but my father spoke so highly of his father that I assume he knew him. I imagine he came by once a year in late December after Boxing Day. He stood at the entrance to my father's home and passed them unwrapped presents. They were hand-me-downs from his lighter-skinned family. My father held tight the gifted clothes his mother couldn't afford. He looked up at his father, silhouetted by the sun and wearing a shirt whiter than the one in his hands. My father must have hated his mother and her hut for keeping him from his Lebanese siblings. He must have hated her last name and donned his father's: Ali.

My father left Trinidad to go to the University of the West Indies in Jamaica. There, he met my mother, who had longed for home throughout her years in the States and eventually returned when she was in her mid-twenties with her first son, my brother. She found work as a secretary in the Life Sciences Building.

I imagine my father looked at Mom twice because her hair was curlier than it was nappy. According to Mom, he asked her out and she said no. The next week, he asked again and she said she was too busy taking care of her son Junior, who mom named after her younger brother. The third week, she realized he wouldn't leave until she said yes. They began dating when he was an undergraduate. He told her that when he graduated, he would take care of her son as if he were his own. Mom got pregnant before that happened. They married. Unlike Grandma, Mom kept her last name.

When I was born, they named me Daniel Ali. They walked me in a stroller at the Mona dam every Sunday. My father always kept his distance from my brother and criticized Mom for not caring for me correctly. He often told her to cover me from the sun. Otherwise I would get too dark. She always protested. He always told her that the Alis were not dark-skinned people. They were not, he implied, like my brother.

They separated when I was too young to remember. Mom moved to a house in Liguanea by the university, and my father lived somewhere on the other side of Sovereign Centre. I spent every other weekend at my father's house.

The first time my father beat me, he squeezed my wrist at the mall till my dark-brown skin bruised purple. The next time, he backhanded me and his watch scratched my face and blood pearled on my cheek. The next time, he threw a bowl of cornflakes at me. He missed and the bowl shattered against the wall of his home. Then he punched me and my nose bled. The next time, he tried to throw me into his car. My forehead hit the doorframe and I landed half-in, half-out. When I came to, he told me he was sorry. He loved me. The last time, he picked me up and threw me into the mirror. The glass broke into shards and sliced my side. I went to the hospital.

I later learned that, in the following months, Mom applied for a green card, saved what money she could, and hid her travel documents in a plastic bag in the freezer. One June morning in the late '90s, when I was seven, I stepped out of my bedroom and saw suitcases piled by the front door. Mom told me to get my three favorite toys. I brought her a spinning top, a sack of marbles, and a LEGO car my brother and I built. We took a taxi to the airport. On the ride, I asked where we were going. She said to America. I asked for how long. She didn't reply.

On the flight, I sat between Mom and Junior. After take-off, Mom fell asleep and Junior stared out the window at the clouds. I spun my top on the seatback table. When it fell under the seat, I poked Mom's arm. She stirred awake. I poked her again. She said stop. I asked how long we'd be gone. She said for good. I asked if Daddy was coming. She said we were starting over. I left the top on the floor.

At first, I continued to write Daniel Ali on my homework. Every time my brother saw it, he told me my father didn't love me.

When Mom overheard him, she asked me to use her last name. She told me stories about beatings that I had forgotten. After a year, I gave in and started using my mother's name: Henriquez.

I kept my father's last name as a middle name. I was Daniel Ali Henriquez. Sometimes I hyphenated them: Henriquez-Ali or Ali-Henriquez. Sometimes, when I remembered the night he threw me into the mirror, when he told me that I was special because all the Caribbean's people came together to make me, I reverted to Ali.

When I was in high school, I asked Mom if he beat her. She said he never touched her. I said I didn't believe her. She told me she scared him one night when she was nursing me and he wanted to argue. He curled his fingers into a fist. Mom grabbed a kitchen knife and pointed it at him. After that, he never tried to hit her again.

The night Mom told me that, I lay awake in bed, staring at the too-close ceiling. The Florida night tinted it blue and its rough grain looked like carvings of waves. As I lay in bed, I recalled the way my father looked when he tucked me in at night. The night and shadows of my father's house tinted him the same color as my ceiling. Looking down at me, he was the tallest person I had ever seen, but the darkness made it hard to tell just how tall he was or if he was there at all.

The next day, I dropped my father's middle name and took the name Mom kept throughout their marriage. I became Daniel Henriquez.

On this beach, where I once knew most high schoolers strolling by, I expect to hear someone call out my name. But no one knows me. They're all teens who were children when I was in high school or adults who must have moved here after I left. A town of strangers where my home once stood.

I turn down the street and look over my shoulder to see if anyone is following. No one. I turn back around. The two teens who were making out on the beach walk toward me. Sand falls from them with each step. Red-and-blue bruises spot their necks, but they don't seem to care. They grin and watch each other, and I wonder if Aubrey and I looked at each other in the same way before we knew we had feelings for each other, when we were too young to read the signals that we sent each other, too inexperienced to ask or act. Their stare holds for so long and with such an intensity that I think I have not looked at anyone in that way in a long time, maybe since I was last looking at Aubrey.

When I pass them, the blond boy turns toward me. His eyes narrow and his brow tenses. I cross the street. One of the wet-suited surfers walks toward me. I look down at the ground but feel his eyes on me. Does he smell the bathroom? Or does he smell Peter? I pick up my pace.

When I make it back to the car, I slam the door shut and lock it. I turn around and still no one stalks me in the lot. I face the road and watch the people pass by. The clothes look the same, but the brands are different from the ones we wore. They don't look back at me. They probably don't notice me. I press my fingers hard into my palm, breathe deep, and face the water. In the distance, the sky's blue pales, as though faded, and the ocean matches it. I look for the line separating the two but can't see it.

Beds

On my way out of Flagler Beach, I worry about seeing my old cross-country team. When I last saw them, just before I left for college, we drank in Twig's backyard, filling the time by searching for someone to laugh at. When someone slipped up, we cracked on him and insults came raining. A voice raised, protesting and fighting back until someone else made a fool of himself and all eyes turned to him and we began all over again. Just remembering all those offensive jokes embarrasses me. When I see them today, if one of them calls me a fag, will I avert my eyes? Or, worse, will I laugh with them as though nothing has changed?

I sigh as I cross the Intracoastal. The sea's salty scent gives way to overgrown grass. On my right lies the paved trail through marsh where alligators occasionally sunbathe. I keep driving, merge onto 95. There are more cars than I expected. No matter how hard I push down on the gas, everyone seems to fly by. Where are they rushing to through this no-man's-land?

After a few miles, I exit onto Palm Coast Parkway, near equidistant from where they killed Trayvon and from where they locked up Marissa. The four-lane road, tall streetlights, and winding sidewalk belong in some bigger Florida city. I turn down Old Kings, drive to the bowling alley, and enter its bar at midafternoon. A twangy guitar and a country singer's deep voice fill the room, lamenting a lost truck or dog or wife. All the people I knew who loved country in high school were self-professed rednecks. My cross-country team preferred pop punk and metalcore. The runners I knew never would've listened to this.

My teammates circle around beer pitchers at the U-shaped bar. In the red light, their faces look pink. Jason has grown jowls, Mack a belly, and Rob both. Ben and Steve gained muscle, so their biceps bulge out of too-small sleeves. But their eyes mimic those of the skinny boys with whom I once ran across this county.

For a moment, I watch them. It has been a long time since I've been the only Black person in a white crowd. Twig turns around and yells my name. The rest join in. They slap my hand, my back, my head. By the time they're done, I'm holding a cup of beer and a shot of whiskey.

I'm driving, I say.

Mr. High School English Teacher got soft? Jason says.

Shit, you could drive a straight line after two drinks, Ben says.

Maybe you could, I say, passing the drinks back. I sit next to Twig. He has several new tattoos and a brown-red, thickly settled beard now. He looks down at his cup and asks where I've been. As I answer, I inspect the ridge above his cheek, where there's a line of freckles like a crooked Orion's belt and a dark color collecting like recently fallen ash.

Quit being fags, Mack yells from the end of the bar, and get over here.

Twig laughs and we turn to them. They try to shove another cup into my hands and I refuse again. Then someone tells a story about the time so-and-so drank so much in class he fell asleep and pissed his pants. The time so-and-so got slapped by his ex-girlfriend in the stairwell. The time so-and-so pulled a knife on so-and-so in the hallway.

When our laughter settles, I ask, Anybody go to Aubrey's funeral?

They shake their heads.

Anyone hang with her after we graduated?

They look away.

Anyone see her around?

Twig puts a hand on my shoulder and says, We ain't really keep in touch with her. Ain't even see each other much recently.

Always figured y'all still kicked it, I say.

Life gets busy, Twig says. Half of us moved. The other half just working.

I take the beer and everyone but Twig cheers. They talk and I drink until my head and my stomach warm. The beer loses its sour. I keep drinking and my body keeps loosening and I don't notice the time passing until Twig says it's late. We stumble into the parking lot. Twig takes my keys and drives us both home. He says his parents are sleeping and we whisper and stifle laughter as we ascend the stairs. He tells me good night as I enter his brother's room. The twin bed is hard and the sheets are scratchy, but I'm grateful it isn't a couch. I have spent many nights in sleeping bags on floors and in the fetal position on small couches.

When I was young, sleeping at my father's house on the weekends, I hated nighttime. That began one evening when my father and I watched Jamaica play in the World Cup. After all the excitement at the Reggae Boyz finally qualifying, they lost their first games. The one we watched, their final, was against Japan. After my father finished his Heineken, he told me to go to bed. I didn't want to. If the Reggae Boyz lost, we might finish in last place. I told my father I'd go to bed after the game ended. I was watching a midfielder run at one of Japan's forwards when my father grabbed my chin and turned me to him. He said he would not tell me a second time.

I went upstairs to my room. The white walls and hardwood floors were bare. One dresser drawer lay open with my clothes for the weekend. The rest were empty. I looked out the window. My father sat on the hood of his car and smoked a cigarette.

The room was hot and the air smelled stale. I opened the window. It squeaked long and loud, and my father turned around. I rushed to bed and closed my eyes. When he threw the door open, it crashed against the wall. I pretended to be asleep. He hit me open-handed from my shoulders to my hips. Minutes after he left, my skin still stung. That night, the pain, the sheets sticking to my body, and the lumpy mattress kept me awake.

The next day, when my father dressed me, he inspected my chest. It bruised purple and red. He told me to keep my shirt on in front of my mother.

The next weekend I was with him, about twenty minutes after he sent me to bed, he opened the door. Sometime later, I heard it open again. Every time the house creaked, I worried that he was coming, that he would see me pretend to sleep, and that he would hit me.

�֍

My father told me he loved me every night before he put me to bed, and then I lay awake afraid of him. I didn't know the border between love and fear. Perhaps I still don't.

My college classes and friends taught me that Southern conservatives would kill me. But here I am once more, back with the Floridians I loved when I was in high school, lying in the bed of Twig's younger brother, who, Twig told me, joined the military and become a self-professed redneck. I don't know how I ever felt so safe here.

Before I know I'm asleep, I surface in a nightmare. I'm trying to close the door to a bathroom. On the other side, someone tries to push it open. I scream for help when I hear something like a voice at the end of a tunnel. Everything darkens. I half realize I am asleep, but I do not know if I am the dreamer or the being-dreamt. The sound again. I'm underwater and the voice is above. I swim upward, surface, and gasp for air as light teems through my now-open eyes. Twig stands over me, his eyes pale blue.

You okay? he asks.

What time is it?

Nine.

Let me sleep, I say.

Twig reaches over me. The gray-ink anchor on the back

of his hand is close enough to kiss. He pulls the pillow from under me, my head hits the mattress, and the fake floral scent of detergent fills my nose.

Get up, Twig says. Got things to do.

His voice sounds like he has picked up smoking. I roll over.

Surprised you could sleep that long on my brother's tiny bed, he says.

I'm used to it.

✳

Mom says all Jamaicans spend some of their childhood in someone else's home. During Michael Manley's first term as prime minister, she shared a bed with her sister, Auntie B, in her stepfather's home. A few months after Grandma moved to the States, she sent money to move them to Spanish Town to live with a family friend whom Mom calls That Woman.

That Woman cleaned houses for a living. After she returned from work, That Woman made Mom and Auntie B scrub their school uniforms with bleach in the sink. The smell made Mom nauseous. Once, Mom refused. That Woman called her a boar-faced Coolie. Mom called her a dutty old Nega. That Woman unplugged her iron and whipped Mom's back with the cord's end. Mom cried, and her tears fell into the sink and stirred the marbleized soap film.

After, Mom went to her room, where Auntie B sat in front of the mirror, fixing her hair. She was going somewhere. Mom asked if she could come. Auntie B said she was too young. Then Auntie B put on a shirt Mom washed earlier that day. Mom told her she was going to get it dirty. Auntie B didn't respond. Mom told Auntie B she couldn't wear it. Auntie B grabbed her comb, jabbed it into Mom's forehead, and carved a cut to her brow. Blood dripped into her eye, stinging it shut.

By the time Mom got a rag from the bathroom to press against the wound, Auntie B had left. Mom got into bed, turned onto her side to keep her weight off the welts, and put the cloth between her forehead and the pillow to keep her blood off the sheets. Hours later, she heard the window shake. Auntie B climbed through the window and into bed next to her.

�֍

After Grandma saved up enough money to buy them tickets, Mom and Auntie B joined her in the States. There, they became Black because Coolies didn't exist, not in the same way. Mom says she never used the N-word derogatorily again, but every time she tells the story about That Woman, she repeats the slur and I don't know if I should feel embarrassed or angry. Then I recall my silence through the slurs dropped last night and think that I am no better. In some ways, I am worse.

I exhale and my shoulders drop. I look around the room. Science-fiction novels fill the bookshelf. Red-inked posters for bands like Killswitch Engage and Avenged Sevenfold cover the walls. At the center of each are drawings of bats and skulls. Twig's younger brother's drum set sits in the corner: two high-hats, two snares, and a bass with a gray towel in it. Behind them, Twig sits on the black stool, resting a cup of coffee on his knee. He's wearing a camouflage-patterned Jaguars hat.

You a good-ol' boy now? I ask.

Something like that.

Wasn't too long ago you were a Boston boy, I say. Never thought I would've seen the day you'd wear camo.

You been gone a long time.

I sit up and liquid sloshes in my stomach. I balance my forehead on my palms, though it's almost too heavy for them. The blinds are drawn, but it's still too bright. I rub my eyes and breathe deep. My lungs struggle to fill.

What you want to do today? Twig asks. Figure we could hit up Captains. Get some barbecue.

Got to shower first, I say. And I need to visit my grandmother.

I told Mom I would visit Grandma at the old-folks' home. After that, I want to talk to someone who spent time with Aubrey, someone who can tell me about her life. If anyone would know, it'd be Desmond. During track season, he was a sprinter, like me. In high school, he talked a lot of shit and got into a lot of fights. After we became friends, he stood up for me when other people tried to punk me; once, he swung on a runner for cutting me off in the 4x400 and got kicked out of the meet. If he's anywhere near as impulsive as he was back when he tried to start brawls with other teams because someone took the wrong tone with him, I don't know what trouble we might get into.

I crack my knuckles, walk to the bathroom, and shower. When the hot water runs through my scalp, I exhale deeply and bow my head. The water warms like the ocean at Flagler Beach on a late August day. The door creaks. On the other side of the curtain, Twig's bulky shadow moves. The faucet runs and the shower turns cold.

What're you doing? I ask.

Brushing my teeth.

What if I was naked?

I waited till the shower turned on, he says.

I'm saying though.

You got a curtain.

I pick up a bar of soap covered in small curly hairs and put it down. Then I squeeze the bodywash's blue liquid into my hand. As I lather, it smells like a teenage boy's spray deodorant. When I'm done, I run my hands through my hair, which still feels oily.

Ain't nobody trying to look at you, Twig says.

Ain't that private, I say. Just wasn't expecting you.

Twig finishes brushing his teeth and leaves the bathroom, and I shut off the water. Then I dry myself with a towel softer and thicker than the ones I'm used to. It smells fresh, the touch of Mama Twig, who does all the housework, even though she works full-time.

Your parents at work? I yell to Twig.

Yeah, he says from outside the bathroom. How's your mom?

She's good. Moved back to Jamaica a few years ago.

Tell her I say hello. After a pause, he adds, What happened to your house?

Foreclosed.

Sorry to hear that.

I put on my clothes but avoid the mirror. My hair will look unkempt, my face unshaven, and my eyes sagged down. Instead, I stare at the sink as I try to brush away the syrupy remnants of whiskey and beer on my teeth. When I finish, the film they left is gone, but my burps still taste of both.

Baby D, what're you really doing in Palm Coast?

Damn, I say, ain't nobody called me Baby D in a minute.

Don't change the subject.

Seeing friends.

You ain't come home once in about eight years, Twig says, but all of a sudden you just wanted to show your face and see the town?

�֎

I live in New York now, but I haven't returned to Flatbush, where we lived when we first moved to the States. The first time I set foot there was my first night in America, after Uncle Winston picked us up at the airport. He was a jet-black man with a square jaw and a thick mustache that Mom said he had not cut since he was a teen. He wore dark-brown Clarks, the same boots men wore on the island, a love affair I later heard began when the British sent Jamaican soldiers home from World War II with Desert Trek boots. Wearing those shoes, Uncle Winston looked like he had never left the island.

He drove us to Flatbush. As we rode on Nostrand with the windows rolled down, I heard so many familiar accents that it felt like we had not left Jamaica so much as found a town on the island with much taller buildings. After he parked, we entered a building whose lighting tinted the chipped walls yellow and then walked into his cramped, dark first-floor apartment. In their living room, Auntie B hugged me. She was brown-skinned and wore close-cropped red hair. As she pulled away, I saw a mole sprouting hair where laugh lines creased her mouth. I stood by Mom as they spoke, while Junior sat on the couch next to our cousins. Their hair was nappier, their shirts larger, and their sneakers more colorful than ours. Mom told me to join them.

As we sat on the floor, the older boys took turns on a video-game and I watched. The adults sat on the couches and talked to each other. At some point, I heard a loud popping noise outside. Mom asked what it was. Without taking his eyes off the TV, my oldest cousin said, Gunshots.

That night, everyone but Mom slept in the same bedroom. Auntie B and Uncle Winston shared the queen-size bed by the window. Against the opposite wall, my cousins slept in the bottom bunk and my brother and I in the top bunk. The snores and still bodies suggested everyone fell asleep quickly. The heat and smell kept me up.

Hours later, angry mumbling woke me. I didn't know if it was in the bedroom or outside. I crawled down the ladder and rushed to the living room, where Mom slept on the plastic-wrapped couch. I stepped on a creaky floorboard and her eyes sprang open. Blood-red spiderwebbed around her black pupils.

What time is it? she asked.

I don't know.

Mom turned onto her side and pulled me onto the couch. My body was inches from its edge, but her arm held me in place.

After we moved out of Flatbush, I thought of it as the nights on the couch with Mom, the people I didn't recognize on the streets, and the gunshots. I'm sure we had good times—days at the park learning how to play basketball and American football buying bootleg movies on Flatbush Ave, and so many meals—but I mostly remember the fear.

❈

This ain't got nothing to do with Aubrey?

I turn the faucet on and pretend I don't hear Twig as I wash

my face. When I finish, I run my fingers against the rough
stubble collecting under my chin, which feels like sandpaper,
and step out of the bathroom. Twig stands by an open window.
He holds a lit cigarette and tries his best to blow smoke out the
window, but fails and turns the room hazy. On the TV behind
him, two heads scream about Obamacare's death panels.

Thought we said no politics, I say.

You said no politics.

I ain't going to make it through the weekend with this on.

You don't watch the news?

This ain't news.

I walk into his brother's room and pile my dirty clothes on
the floor. I consider asking for a plastic bag to contain the scent
but don't bother. Even after the shower, I can still smell the
sweat in my armpits. The TV in the next room quiets. When
Twig walks in, I rummage through my backpack, though I'm
not looking for anything.

Left Florida and got all sensitive?

Something like that.

I give up the ruse that I'm looking for something, and sit on
the bed. Twig leans against the wall.

Why you miss Aubrey's funeral? Twig asks. I ain't hear from
you in, like, five years. Then all of a sudden, you text me out
the blue talking about how you want to fly down and you
need a ride.

I was drunk.

I texted about your flight. You ain't hit me back.

I was busy.

Then I ain't hear from you for a minute.

What you want me to do? I say. Shit, man, it's embarrassing. Couldn't afford to fly down for the funeral, so I ain't hit you back. Then I try to talk to folks about it up north but they ain't get it. So I come down here thinking that'd make me feel better, and y'all ain't get it.

Twig lets out a big exhale, his cheeks puffing out as he does, and lets his head hang limp-necked. He's looking at the ground when he asks, So what you want to do?

Past the beard and Twig's new weight, I still see that bony-faced boy whom I depended on to fill the silence in his car with jokes. I felt safe here once, I think to myself. He walks back to the living room and I follow. He picks up the remote. I shoot him a look. He puts it down and turns to the window.

Can't go to no grave, Twig says. She was cremated. They scattered her. You say you want to feel better, so come out with me and the boys. We'll get some beers, go fishing.

I ain't here for old times.

Far as I can tell, says Twig, you ain't got nothing else around here.

✷

When I first got to Palm Coast, everyone already had their crew of friends because they went to middle school together, but I didn't know anyone. Twig was one of the first people I befriended.

We moved to Palm Coast because Mom was having a hard time paying New York rent and food prices. She had started working as a temp at a skyscraper in midtown and we moved out of Auntie B's to an apartment west of the park, where the block was safer, the schools were better, and my classmates asked how a Jamaican got a Spanish last name but looked like me.

In our new apartment, Junior slept on a futon. Mom and I shared her bed. When the company she worked for extended her contract, Mom bought me my own. A year later, they told her they didn't need her anymore. Mom returned to the temp agency, which sent her to work as a receptionist in skyscrapers all over midtown, never for more than three months at a time, for years. Then the agency went bankrupt. Mom tried to find work through others, but they all said they couldn't place an uneducated older woman. Mom started getting unemployment, but eventually that ran out. Some months later, our landlord evicted us.

We flew to Jacksonville, where Aunt Shirley picked us up. We drove south to Palm Coast and stopped at what I would later learn was the town's first stoplight. We passed the McDonald's and the Cracker Barrel and turned into a housing community named the Woodlands. There, we parked at a red-roofed, one floor, white box of a house, where Mom said Grandma watched my great-grandmother live the last years of her life. When we opened the front door, Mom complained about the smell of cigarettes, the smoke of which stained the carpets and the walls yellow. We walked to the sliding-glass door and stepped out onto a screened-in back porch. From there, I looked down at the sandy soil that extended back to a small decline into the nature preserve, a forest encroaching on our home.

In the fall, while Junior was at college, I began my freshman year at the local high school. Aside from Aubrey, nobody really talked to me. After a semester with few friends and little to do after school, I decided to do a sport. My science teacher, who was also the distance-running coach for the track team, encouraged me to join. Because Mom was a top sprinter at St.

Jago, I figured I would be good at it too. Besides, it was cheaper than the other sports—all I needed were shoes—so I figured we could afford it.

At the first practice, we separated into sprinters and distance runners. The distance runners, including Twig, were lanky and white and wore short shorts. The sprinters, including Desmond, were stocky and Black and wore basketball shorts. Our coach, a light-skinned Black man who had been a top sprinter at the University of Florida, lined us up at the starting line.

For our workout, we did a step-down: 350 meters, then 300, and so on. The most experienced sprinters went first. I waited until the last heat. When Coach said go, I ran at top speed and struggled to stay in my lane. The wind whistled as I entered the straightaway, leading my heat. I was fast, I thought, faster than everyone else. I surged ahead again, hips switching faster, wanting to prove that I was the team's best. Before I reached the second curve, my legs slowed. My knees sank. My chest burned. Trying to pull in enough air was like shoveling water out of a sinking ship. My teammates passed me. By the time I entered the final stretch, I was barely jogging. I walked across the finish line. Coach said I died. Then he turned away and focused on the faster runners.

I hobbled onto the infield and sank into a crouch. Head cast down, I tasted iron and worried my throat was bleeding. A wind blew and almost knocked me over. North Florida in February was cold, but I was sweating, so I couldn't tell if I was going to shiver or overheat. Trying to catch my breath, I berated myself: I gave up on the race. I looked around. The other runners paced with their hands on their heads. They weren't tougher than me. They didn't know what it was like to go to bed hungry. They hadn't survived my father. Anger carried me back to the starting line and washed away the pain through the next heat's beginning. For the rest of practice, I alternated between belittling and aggrandizing myself, the two voices spurring each other on until I couldn't hear anything else.

In time, I learned that sprinting after dying was normal for Florida track. When we didn't vomit, coaches said we weren't working hard enough. When stomach acid turned our throats tender, they said the burn was how we knew we wanted to win. And when we placed at meets, we proved their strategies worked. They said little about the time spent at the trainer's, taking ice baths or applying heating pads to soothe our shin splints, tendonitis, hip-flexor strains, pulled quads, torn calves, knee problems, weak ankles. They never discussed the injuries their runners developed in high school that prematurely ended their collegiate careers. And they didn't mention the people whose bodies gave out before the season's end. Instead, they reminded those who remained that track was a fight between yourself and your pain. The toughest runner came out on top.

That day, when I finished last in every heat, was my initiation into our struggle with dying. After Coach dismissed us, I stepped off the track, kneeled over the nearby gutter, and stared into yesterday's rain. I vomited brown-orange mucusy bile into the dark waters. Coach patted me on the back, congratulated me for working hard, and walked off as I retched again. When I finished, I walked toward the school bus. My calf cramped, my right leg clipped my left, and I fell. On the ground, I told myself I was never coming back.

Need some help?

A distance runner wearing a Boston Red Sox shirt held out a hand slippery with sweat. He helped me up, tucked his arm under mine, and walked me to my bus. His name was Will, but everyone called him Twig.

That night, when I lay down to sleep, my throat felt like sandpaper had rubbed it raw. My sheets felt like they were trying to smother me. But when my mind drifted to Twig, I fell asleep. My bed was wet in the morning. In the summer, I joined the cross-country team with him. After our summer practices, when I lay down for a nap, I slept easily.

Soon I started hanging out with Twig and his friends, the other distance runners. We mostly played videogames and cards or drove around looking for something to do. Throughout it all, we repeated jokes we had heard, the raunchier the better. A bit Jason often repeated: What do you call the kid of a Black man and a white woman? An abomination. In response, I joked about white boys having small dicks, and so on. We hoped to prove we were funny without caring who we hurt, stopping only to talk about all the things we were going to do when we left this boring town.

Even Aubrey got serious when she and I talked about the future. We mostly hung out at lunch because track and cross-country occupied my non-school hours during the year and because she spent her summers hanging out with her sister and her best friend, Jess. Over our meals, she often talked about what we were going to do when we finally did see each other outside of school. She was going to take me mudding or hunting. I never pointed out that the folks who did those things didn't want someone who looked like me around. Instead, I said I wished I could come. She said I'd love it. But even when I was free, she never invited me.

One afternoon, in the fall of my senior year, Coach canceled practice. Aubrey said we were hanging out. I said I had homework due the next day. She said I could do it at her place. After school, she drove us home in her Ford sedan. She wore a teal hoodie with a maroon dove on her chest. Her lips shone pink from a thin coat of gloss. Her eyeliner made her light-brown eyes look large and dark. She turned to me and I turned away. Gray clouds lay low in the sky. It would rain soon.

Aubrey rolled down the window and lit a cigarette. She turned on Skynyrd, who played something like a Southern-rock version of a funeral arrangement. Above a guitar's high-pitched whine and an organ, a nasally man sang, telling his girl he had to go, but he hoped she would remember him. As the singer compared himself to a bird, Aubrey talked about her weekend plans: drinking, fishing, hunting.

After twenty minutes, we arrived at her home in the B section. Her sister and parents were out. Aubrey parked and we entered her house, one of the only ones I had seen that was not carpeted. She led me to her bedroom in the back. Garth Brooks and Toby Keith looked down from posters on her wall. Her bed was three times the size of mine, her light-blue sheets unruffled and uniform in color as though never washed. I put my backpack in the corner and sat on the dark wood desk. She opened her closet. Shirts and jeans, identical except for color. She separated the teal shirts from the light-gray ones to reach the lone empty hanger and hung her Hollister hoodie up. I wondered how much her wardrobe cost.

Why're you sitting on the desk? Aubrey asked.

I made a corny joke about preferring tables. She didn't laugh. Tapping on the window announced the rain outside. Aubrey kept watching me expectantly until I sat next to her. I had never sat on a girl's bed before. The mattress was firm, sturdy. Her sheets were soft but didn't stick. My stomach fluttered. I scanned her shelves.

Ain't know you read that much, I said. You should be in the honors class with me.

I don't like reading like that, she said. Just murder mysteries, the bloody ones.

You're creepy as all hell, I said.

Aubrey slapped my arm. I said we better start our homework, took out my honors English textbook, and flipped to the night's reading. She asked what it was. I told her it was a selection from the first novel ever: *The Odyssey*. She said she hadn't heard of it.

Y'all will get there, I said.

We use a different textbook than y'all brainy kids.

Aubrey asked what *The Odyssey* was about. I said it was about a man trying to get home. She said that was a silly thing to write a book about. Everyone goes home every day. I said it's different after years on the road. She said she slept in her bed every night. Everyone in Palm Coast did. She wished she could've slept anywhere else. She was so unlike my rootless family, who rarely had beds of their own, so unlike me.

⚜

I stare at the ground and blink fast, breathing deep in the way coaches taught us to do when we finished a heat. After I clear my throat, I look up at Twig and ask, How she end up in his car?

I don't know, bro.

She hated this place. She ain't even like Brandon that much.

According to you, Twig says.

According to her. She said it. If she would've just been somewhere else, she'd still be alive. I don't get it, man. She was so young. She ain't even live here no more. How'd it happen to her?

Don't really get it myself, Twig says. I mean, I know she's gone, but I don't really believe it.

I got to talk to him. Maybe if I hear a little bit more, it'll really sink in. Maybe I'll feel better.

And, I think to myself, Brandon and I both loved her. We share a kind of bond. He's the only one who will really know what I'm going through.

Twig shakes his head. Then he says, You lying.

How I'm lying?

You ain't want to talk to him. You want to fuck Brandon up now that you ain't the skinny boy you was back then.

You don't want to swing on him?

After a pause, Twig says with a shrug, Even if I did, ain't nobody seen him since the crash.

I know where his daddy stay. Pretty sure he still lives there.

Brandon's crazy. You go out there, you might never come back.

I ain't no punk.

Ain't nobody calling you soft, says Twig, but there ain't no reason to come back and get yourself killed.

Rivers

After I gather my things, I get Twig to drop me at my car at the bowling alley, claiming I need to get a start on the day. When I turn the engine on, I realize I haven't eaten anything. Though I haven't touched fast food in years, I drive to McDonald's. I consider sitting inside until I see the plastic tables, where we ate off the dollar menu for many evenings after Junior dropped out of college and his student loans defaulted, leaving Mom to struggle to pay his debt and our bills. Once, after we finished our meal, Mom stopped at the counter as we were exiting. She ordered three caramel sundaes: a treat for our walk home. I yelled at her for spending money we didn't have on something we didn't need. The people around us stopped to look. The cashier and Junior turned away. Mom's face tightened. I worried she might cry. Then she said softly that she deserved nice things too. I was so obsessed with money, so angry at Mom for bringing me into a world she couldn't afford.

My cheeks warm with embarrassment. I join the drive-through line, order a meal, and pull up to the window. An acne-faced teenager hands me my bag and I speed away.

I should go to Grandma's nursing home, but I'm not ready

yet. I call the place, let them know I'm running late, and eat while driving to Linear Park. On the way, I see the private health center, a sandstone building with a California-style red roof, where Twig's family moved his grandmother after she fell and broke her hip. I wonder if she died there. I pass the building, drive down the narrowing road crowded by thin-trunked trees, and park in the crowded oval lot.

Years ago, Twig and I sat here in his car, waiting for cross-country practice when an August thunderstorm rolled in. The rain covered our windshield with rivers. Our team pulled up next to us, but no one stepped outside. Twig's air conditioner didn't work and the car insulated us from the storm's cool. The heat hung thick in the air, as did the funk of our trainers. Sweat pasted my clothes to my skin. It was too hot to run. Besides, I only joined cross-country to stay in shape for track season and to hang with Twig, and as a sprinter, I never knew how to pace myself, so I always started out too fast and then struggled through practice. Our runs were always difficult for me, but with today's heat, this one would be miserable. I asked Twig if Coach would cancel practice. He said Coach wouldn't cancel practice for a tornado. I said I preferred the rain. It made the heat bearable.

When the storm slowed to a light drizzle, we exited our cars and jogged down the gravel pathway into the woods as the shower became a mist. We crossed the bridge over a stream bulging brown. The rain stopped. Bright-yellow lights spotted the path and the woods where the sun pierced the canopy. The air was heavy with rich soil. When I inhaled, I still felt out of breath. Sweat covered my body. Thin gray wisps of steam rose from the pavement like clouds returning home. We were running in a sauna. Today was going to be hell.

In the distance, sunlight reflected on the river where the silt-fed stream poured into it. As we approached, the Intracoastal's brown-gray waters spread out in front of us. Twig surged ahead and pulled his shirt off. His arms were thin enough to wrap a hand around, but muscles carved valleys in his freckled back. He ran down the gray dock and past the boats owned by the people who lived in the nearby condos, all of whom seemed rich to me then. He stopped, kicked his shoes off, and leapt. I followed him into our cold man-made river.

Underwater, I opened my eyes and saw a yellow screen. The river stung my eyes shut. I surfaced gasping for breath and saw Twig grinning. We treaded water as teammates surfaced, tadpoles born from the river. From the path, Coach yelled at us. We turned around. When the river was shallow enough to stand, its mucky bed clung to my feet. I walked onto the shore, where oily waters coated me like a film of mist. That evening, my body itched. Light pink swelled below my brown skin. I sprouted hives.

It was so hard not to scratch myself, I remember, a grin starting to spread across my face, as I get out of the car and walk down the path. I struggle to stifle it for fear of what others might think of a lone black man smiling to himself. Every half minute or so, a bicycle or a mother running with a stroller passes. As I near the river, there are more and more people walking. I stop at the fork. Left is European Village, its cluster of apartment buildings sharing a courtyard lined with restaurants. In front is the river. On its edge, a black man stands ankle-deep in a faded denim bucket hat and a Nautica tall tee, casting a line.

Caught anything? I ask.

The man turns around. Patches of a scraggly beard cluster on his cheek. His skin shines with sweat.

Not yet.

What you fishing for?

Anything that bites, he says. I ain't selling nothing though.

I ain't buying.

All right now, he says, turning to face the water.

All right.

He doesn't want to talk. Maybe he doesn't read me as Black. Maybe he thinks I'm not from here, my accent Northern. Or maybe he just wants to fish in peace.

I walk away from him and from European Village and cross a small bridge. On my right, pale-green grass extends into trees that seem to go on forever. On my left, motorboats coast down the gray river. The path swivels out to a man-made bluff no more than four feet above the water. I climb down the incline and onto a sand-dirt shore. As the river travels up it, the water turns transparent and white froth bubbles on its surface. It stops and then returns. A thin film follows, some of which descends into the dirt-sand's cracks with a slurping sound.

I visited this small shore often after Junior dropped out of college and money got tight. Whenever my friends wanted to drive to Five Guys for a burger, I never had money for gas, let alone a meal. I declined their invitations and spent my evenings wandering Linear Park's not-yet-paved path to this beach. I sat on the shore and watched the brackish tide climb.

Sometimes, when Aubrey wasn't out drinking with her friends and when I had minutes on my Virgin Mobile phone, I called her and she joined me. On warm nights, we waded into the water, splashed each other occasionally. On colder nights, we sat cross-legged and watched the oily smelling river pass. She joked about alligators and snakes stalking us until she tired of tormenting me. Then we lay on our backs and looked up at the stars or the fast-moving clouds overhead. I tried to ignore the fear of some reptile ambushing us. Aubrey talked about whatever bothered her, which seemed to come easier when we weren't looking at each other.

After a while, she trailed off, stood up, and skipped rocks. I joined her, but I wasn't very good, so she always made fun of me. She said I was the only boy in town who ain't know how to throw. No wonder I ran track. Couldn't do any other sport. Sooner or later, I asked her to show me what to do and, eventually, her advice took hold. I learned to bounce them seven or eight times before they sank. I hoped one day we would get one all the way to the other side of the river that kept us company. We never did.

Since I left for college, I have not set foot on anything like these spits of dirt. I didn't know it until seeing them now, but I've missed them.

✄

I didn't realize how many of my high school memories took place by the Intracoastal until recently, when Mom said that there is a river in every Jamaican's life. Mom and Grandma shared a river, the Negro in New Monklands. (I don't know the origins of the river's name, nor does Mom.) There are no pictures of Grandma from back then, so I imagine her as she looked when I was young: a stout caramel-complexioned woman, hair densely settled at the scalp that thinned as it grew, and a nose that spread at its base like a tree's roots. Mom says that, every morning, Grandma walked to where the goats grazed on Guinea grass. In the early hours' cool, she approached cautiously until one let her pet its back. Then she placed a bucket beneath its belly and ran a hand from the top of the swollen udder to its tip.

When Grandma filled the bucket, she set it to cool on the Negro's bank. Then she waded shin-deep into the river and stopped where the current slowed. She pulled a cheesecloth from the riverbed: her goat cheese, which the Negro kept cool because they didn't own an icebox. A few paces down, other women from the village left their buckets on the bank and followed suit. When they finished, they stopped for a moment to share guesses about what the morning sky portended for the day's weather or to complain about the white people whose homes they cleaned after they cooked for their families. Grandma never said much, according to Mom, but she laughed a lot before everyone returned home to finish cooking for their husbands and sons, who would soon leave for the fields. When she was young, Mom thought that if she put her ear to the Negro, she could hear the women laugh.

When she got older, in the mornings after Grandma left for work, Mom fished there every day. When that bored her, she waded to its center and sat on a half-submerged rock. She dipped her feet in its cool waters and sat there until the sun became too hot. Then she forded the river once more to return home.

One summer day, Mom sat on her throne when a drizzle started. She was too busy watching raindrops ripple the moving surface, and the occasional fish, to notice the rain picking up and the river growing. The water browned from the banks washed into the stream. By the time the summer shower pelting the stream sounded like a stampede, the Negro was too high to cross. She pulled her feet out and clutched her knees to her chest.

After some time, she saw a tall dark-skinned man with fraying, graying hair on the riverbank. The man yelled for help. No one came. He looked over his shoulder and then at her. He stepped into the Negro. Once waist-deep, he tilted. When he caught his footing, he waded forward in fits and starts, pausing only to secure his balance, until he reached the rock. He grabbed hold. Mom inched toward him. He pulled her to his chest, and she clung to him. The current tugged as he carried her through the rain-gorged stream until they reached the shore.

That man caught a fever and died soon after. Mom went to his service in the church that was little more than a room. When it was her turn, she approached the coffin and told him she would never cross the Negro again.

✴

Although I spent much of my life on a riverbank, like Mom and Grandma, I dreamt of escaping it in high school. I wanted to run away from this town where we couldn't afford dessert at McDonald's, where fights broke out in the cafeteria, where I grew callous to white folk calling people niggers. I did as Mom and Grandma did and left my river in search of safety. I'm not sure I found it. I don't know that they did either. I don't know that we could have.

Maybe if I'd listened to Mom or Grandma more, maybe if I'd returned Mom's calls more often, I wouldn't have had to learn the hollowness of those dreams the hard way. Even now, I'm wandering the park instead of seeing Grandma. I should be ashamed of myself. I don't know how many more chances I'll get to see her. Mom said she's been forgetting a lot. She's having a harder and harder time walking. I hurry back to my car and drive to Grandma's nursing home, which looks like a large house. The lawn is perfectly kept. Behind the home, just below the cement wall, I catch a glimpse of the canal's bobbing waters. I walk in and up to the front desk, where a brown-skinned woman stares at her computer. When she finishes typing, she looks up, her glasses shifting as she tilts her head.

I'm here to see my grandmother, I say.

Daniel?

Yes, ma'am.

What took you so long? she says in a thick Jamaican accent.

Sorry. Something came up.

Hurry up, she says. Day's almost over.

She walks me back to a carpeted room with fluorescent lights. Grandma sits in a leather chair too large for her. She looks out the window at the dark canal waterway. Her brown skin glistens, as if oily. Her thinning hair frizzes as if no one has combed it in a week. She doesn't see me, and I watch her quietly for a moment. She wanted to be independent, I remember Mom saying, ever since she was a child. She trained to become a seamstress until she was fifteen, when my mother's father asked her to marry him. When Grandma told her mother about the proposal, her mother said, Hog say, first dirty water me catch, me wash. Grandma heeded her advice, gave up her dreams, and birthed our family. And now she lives alone in a nursing home.

I close the door. Grandma's head turns and she asks, Who are you?

Your grandson.

Grandma's thick brows hunch down on her eyes and she shakes her head.

You're too old, she says.

I'm Janet's son.

You're too old, she says, her voice rising.

I nod slowly, sit down in the chair opposite her, and lean my elbows onto my knees. Grandma's pupils dart around, as if scared. My heart speeds up. I don't want to upset her. I hope my visit isn't doing more harm than good.

Okay, I say, softer now, chewing on the inside of my lip. I'm Daniel.

Do I know you?

No. The nursing home asked me to come.

Why?

To talk, I say. My name is Daniel. What's your name?

Tara.

Nice to meet you, Tara.

I hold out my hand. She looks at it for a moment and then places hers in mine. Her skin is folded and thick, but her knobby knuckles prod. She feels so different from the Grandma whose hugs pulled me into her soft body. She pulls away, places both hands in her lap, and flattens out the creases on her dark maroon frock.

Know what we're doing today? she asks.

No, I say. Don't you?

She kisses her teeth and turns back to the river.

They never tell us anything, she says.

What do you want to do?

I want to go fishing.

We might be able to do that.

Grandma nods and slides out of her chair but leaves one hand on its armrest to lean against it. I jump up and offer the crook of my elbow. She ignores me and reaches for her cane. Then she walks to the window. Her hair blurs in my peripherals as I stand behind her, watching a small boy wearing a baseball cap standing at the end of a dock, throwing something into it.

Turning to face me, Grandma asks, Can we go to the Negro?

Where does she think we are? If I tell her we're in Palm Coast, will she freak out? I've never interacted with anyone forgetting everything before. From what I've seen on TV, I worry disagreeing may send her into a fit. She might start yelling. Worse, she might get up, try to rush out, knock stuff over. They would restrain her, my grandmother, as old and weak as she is.

After a pause, I say, No. It's too far.

I want to go to the Negro.

I'm sorry.

I don't want to go fishing, she says with a huff. She returns to her chair, which squeaks as she shifts, moving her legs and adjusting her back until she's comfortable. Then she looks down at the floor.

I'm sorry, I say, which makes her jump. She faces me and surprise shines in her eyes.

Who are you?

Daniel.

Grandma leans in.

Daniel, she says, as if feeling my name with her mouth. You look like my father. You have Coolie in you?

I'm a Coolie, I say. Did your father take you fishing in the Negro?

You know the Negro?

I've heard of it.

※

If my brain deteriorates, will I still remember enough to tell the young about my rivers? About Aubrey and me sailing the Intracoastal or skipping rocks at night? About the summer before my senior year of high school, when a hurricane flooded the B section, turning streets into streams?

During the storm, the clouds never broke. Twilight hovered every day. On the second afternoon, the electricity went out. The third morning, after the boombox ran out of batteries, I read *The Lord of the Rings* until the dim light strained my eyes. Then I sat on the back porch, felt the moist wind waft through the screen, and watched the rain. When strong gusts blew, palm trees bent over until their fronds swept the floor. I worried they would break. They didn't. They had lived through far more storms than I, and they would survive many more.

After Mom stopped cleaning and trying to get me to join her in doing so, she read on the living-room couch. We spent most of the remaining day in silence. Then the storm broke. A few hours later, the lights and cell service returned. Aubrey called me. She said the rain flooded the retention pond by her home. The water was too deep to pass, even in her truck. Could I bring some jugs of water?

How am I going to get through the flood? I asked.

I'll take the boat.

I borrowed Mom's car and drove to the Publix. The aisles were mostly empty of other shoppers or employees. No one had restocked the water. The occasional jug or case remained on the shelves, which looked much larger than I had realized with so little on them. The crinkling sound of a bottle rolling on the warped tile floor drew my eye. I shivered. Then I bought a case and left.

On that midday drive to the B section, I passed few cars. The wind pushed debris down the street. Pools of water filled the gutters lining the road. In the middle of a four-way intersection, a downed limb frayed into woodchips. I drove around it and pulled over to let ambulances, fire trucks, and cops pass by. Then I turned down Aubrey's street. From its entrance, I saw a gleaming sheet of silver extending where the road once was. I drove less than fifty feet before I had to stop. I got out of the car. A skim ambled toward me and back into the stream like water up a bank. Farther back, it turned dark. An eddy stirred. Small branches floated away from me and toward wherever the water was draining.

In the distance, I saw Aubrey, a skinny silhouette, gliding above the water on a dinghy that she propelled by pole. She was wearing torn jean shorts and a plain white shirt. Her hair was up. When she got close enough for me to make out her face, I saw that she was smiling. Once she reached transparent floodwater, she jumped out.

Ain't that supposed to be dangerous? I say.

You see another way for me to get to you? Come on and help me pull.

Frowning, I kicked off my flip-flops and waded shin-deep into the flood. It was cold and made my hair stand on end. We pulled the boat onto our gravel shore. I shook my legs off like a dog, but an oily slime remained. God only knew if I was going to catch an infection.

Quit your complaining, she said. You get the water?

I nodded and popped the trunk. Aubrey and I unloaded the case onto the boat. Then she ran her arm across her forehead, which was pink from the sun, though I didn't see any sweat.

Crazy out here, I said. How deep does it get?

Pretty bad in some parts.

Your house flood? I asked.

Water ain't make it up the driveway. Guess we lucky. Heard this ain't nothing compared to when Andrew hit.

Aubrey shrugged and sat on the hood. I joined her. Then she lit a cigarette.

Been craving one of these something awful, she said.

Your mom don't know?

I think she knows, but we don't talk about it.

Aubrey exhaled a plume of smoke and ran her hand across her forehead again. Her fingers left a white imprint for a moment until the pink filled it in.

My mom barely let me out the house, I say.

She got on you bad?

She been on my case. It's raining like the world's about to end and she trying to get me to clean.

And if a branch crashed through the window, first thing she'd say is get the broom.

Aubrey threw her cigarette into the river. The yellow filter bobbed for a moment. Then it drifted off with the current.

Don't much feel like going home, Aubrey said.

Me neither.

Let's float for a bit.

Before I could respond, Aubrey grabbed me by the wrist. She pulled me into the water and to the boat. By the time I was in, I still felt her soft, smooth fingers on my arm. Then Aubrey shoved off and I stumbled. The boat rocked from side to side.

Steady now, she said.

I'm getting there.

Don't look like it.

Could've given me a warning.

You thought we was going to sit still?

Aubrey pushed until we caught a light current. She let go and we rode downstream. On our sides, the flood flowed through gutters into lawns and lapped at the bases of driveways. The occasional house's garage was open and a generator ran. A few people stood outside smoking or watching the water. Aubrey began pushing again and yelled hello to someone, who yelled hello back. What did we look like to them? A black boy and a white girl on a boat in the flood, a case of water between them, the boy sitting at the front as though being ferried, the girl standing in the back as though in control.

The current strengthened and the boat slid along with ease.

The farther into the neighborhood we got, the higher the water climbed up lawns and driveways. We must've been nearing where the water stormed the banks. I watched the homes and the people and the water pass by, feeling like I was looking at something far away, as if I were watching the evening news. At one house, a man in a white tank and cargo shorts sat on his front step, his head in his palms. Through the open door and past the sandbags behind him, I saw two young children rolling around on the floor. Neither children nor parent seemed to notice each other. Then the floodwater swept us on and they escaped my sight.

As we continued, we saw a few boats: some middle schoolers in camo hats steering an inflatable raft, a man wearing a bucket hat with a cooler on a dinghy, and a young couple in a kayak. Aubrey waved at them all and they waved back. We followed the water to where it was deepest and curved around a home turned into an island. On our left, a doe watched us from muddy land amid the woods on an undeveloped lot. Then it turned around and returned to the forest. We floated into the center of the retention pond, which was lined by tall thin trees on three sides. When I faced away from the way we came, it looked like we were in the wilderness.

The water was calmer here, almost still. Aubrey sat down and looked up. The shadow of the lingering storm had almost entirely gone. The sky was nearing blue now. I heard the click of Aubrey's lighter. When I turned to her, smoke shrouded her face.

Jess's house flooded too? I asked.

No, she's all right.

So why'd you call me?

You mad?

I chuckled and said, You always think someone's mad at you. You always surprised people lean on you.

The boat began to turn clockwise. I looked over the edge. The surface was dark, brown. Grass and pine needles floated near us. A black garbage bag bobbed a little farther off. Beyond it, large and small branches circled us, the water staining them a dark color.

Even when Jess and I wasn't talking because I was dating Brandon, she said, you came to lunch, kept talking to me. Even if I skipped four days of school, you was there on the fifth. Figured you would've brought the water even if you had to walk all the way here.

Figure you're right.

A rustle gathered in the forest. A crowd of birds emerged. They called to each other with shrill, high-pitched sounds, traveling across the sky until they flew in front of the sun and disappeared. Its light made me squint then shut my eyes. When I opened them again, black dots scattered across my vision as I watched Aubrey drink from one of the water bottles. She burped long and deep, and even above the earthy, moist scent in the air, it smelled sour.

Gross, I said.

She laughed and punched my arm lightly.

So easy to get a rise out of you, she said. Everybody else stopped reacting to my burps.

I ain't everybody else.

She rolled her eyes and said, Tell the truth, we ain't need the water.

Thought you might be lying.

Aubrey punched me again. Then it was so quiet that I heard her cigarette sizzle when it hit the pond and the distant trickle of water coming home.

Wanted to get out the house, she said. Mama been getting on my nerves since my sister left for her boyfriend's. Soon as she walked out the door, Mama said she was leaving us in an emergency.

Like you ain't never been in a hurricane before.

And Mama just kept talking about how everyone left her. Husband's in jail. Daughter's at her boyfriend's. She got to take care of herself and me, even though she ain't know what to do if it floods. Then, maybe the second day or the third, she got quiet. Barely talked to me even when we was eating canned food cold for dinner after the power went out. So I was just alone. Spent the time just sitting, hearing the rain coming so steady I stopped noticing it. Looked out the window and watched it till it got boring. Then I laid on the couch and stared at the ceiling. Went to my room and did the same there. Thought maybe it'd look different. It didn't. Just lay there waiting for the rain to stop. Then the street started filling up and the water was coming up our driveway and Mama got loud again. Started talking about how she got a bum man and raised a bum daughter who done left and got to take care of the other one with no help.

A dry, almost warm breeze passed by. Aubrey downed the rest of the water and threw the bottle into the pond. It splashed dark drops into the air. When it settled, it rotated in the same direction we did.

Moment the rain left, Aubrey said, I got in the boat. Been riding around till I called you. Figured you'd have something on your mind other than what's going on at my house. Something to say about school or track.

Boring, dependable Daniel.

It's kind of boring sometimes. But it's something else to talk about. All the other stuff gets old.

What you mean old? You the one doing all the drinking and smoking. Going to parties. Cutting school.

I do that all the time though, she said. Got the rest of my life to fish and mud and get drunk. Everybody I know doing the same. Just something to pass the time.

You don't like drinking?

Everybody likes getting drunk, Daniel. Don't be stupid. But when you come in all excited about putting on your short shorts, that's new to me. You all excited to run round that circle, trying to run your way on up out of here.

When I'm on the track, ain't nothing else matter.

When you do good, Aubrey said, you get to talking about where you going to go and what you going to do when you get out of here. And when you do bad, you got this fire in you for days can't no joke of mine put out.

Ain't know you noticed.

Then Aubrey leaned forward, her hands on the case of water as she closed the distance between us, and said, Bet you miss it.

Lord knows I been feeling restless.

You excited to get back to practice? Get so fast you get you a scholarship and get out this no-name town.

Can't wait till I set foot on dry land again.

Oh, you can't wait huh?

A smirk creeped in at the corner of Aubrey's lips, but her look remained steady. A light wind blew and her hair rustled with it, the air made visible as a chestnut wave. Some of the loose strands reached out to me but didn't make it all the way. When the wind passed, as her hair fell slowly, I smelled her sweat, warm but not unpleasant, for a moment, and then the floodwater covered her scent.

I can wait a little longer.

�֍

The time we shared passed quickly. The sun went down shortly thereafter. I had to be back before the hurricane curfew started. The months to come, that afternoon, I didn't savor it enough. I was too busy dreaming about leaving our town. I spent all my free hours on track and homework so I could go to a good college and find a job where I could make enough money to go out with my friends, instead of sitting on the riverbank at night, and live in a big city with a name people recognized instead of a place where the rain ruined people's homes. I never worried about what I was leaving behind.

As I close the door to Grandma's room behind me, I worry that I didn't make the most of my visit. I don't know how to talk to a woman who no longer knows we have a history. With a sigh, I lean onto the windowsill and look at the canal that feeds into the river that Twig and I swam in, that I sat in front of when we had no money, and that I went gigging on with Aubrey, with whom I escaped from my home to the water, who found an escape in me. I rub my eyes with my fist and walk to the front desk.

Good visit? asks the receptionist who signed me in earlier.

Think so.

She looked happy.

Hard to tell.

I ask her where the restroom is and walk down a small hallway. I enter a windowless, dark-gray room. The light buzzes. A metal bar runs along the wall by the toilet and one runs along the shower in the corner, where a metal bench hangs. The room smells of urine. I turn the faucet on and splash ice-cold water on my face. I scrub at the sweat on my cheeks, but my skin still feels slimy.

As I dry my face with the scratchy paper towels, I wonder when the last time I saw my grandmother was. I was in high school. There were no grays in my hair. Baby fat still rounded my hairless cheeks and jaw. Whiskers sprouted on my face in patches. It's no surprise she didn't recognize me.

Someone knocks at the door. I exit and walk to the front, which the midafternoon sun tints yellow. The nurse sits behind her desk, opens a binder, and asks me to sign out.

She don't smile much these days, she says.

I figured.

The nurse looks down at a small gold watch.

You coming back?

Not sure.

It's good for them, you know. Having someone to talk to. Even if they don't remember it.

My flight is early tomorrow morning, I reply, realizing I may not see Grandma again. Then I walk to the door, ready to drive to Desmond's, where I'm long overdue.

Lies

I ride down Florida Park, a street lined by some of the only sidewalks in Palm Coast. As a teenager, when I could not sleep at night, the sticky Florida heat keeping me up, I imagined all the things Aubrey and I would do when we graduated high school, and when my dreams turned farfetched, I pictured us living in a house on this street. Over the canal in the back, we would build a mahogany dock and keep a small boat for gigging and a large one to take out with friends. On cool summer evenings, we would sit on the canal's cement wall, legs dangling over the edge, and drink Shock Tops until the moon rose. We would wave to our neighbors' silhouettes on their back porch. They would wave back. Or we would invite our friends over, drink too much, and fall asleep on the couch next to each other, not because we couldn't make it back to our bed but because we were still too reckless to control ourselves. The teenage fantasies of a boy with no money and little sense of the world beyond his suburbs and even less experience dating come rushing back, their images blotting out the town around me.

A car honks. I turn into the F section and pull into a driveway where green reeds push through its cracks. Desmond sits on the step in front of his door and smokes. His plumlike skin is dark, tinged with purple. He wears a white tank, mustard Timberland boots, and black basketball shorts with a white Nike sign. He still dresses the same. He doesn't light up with recognition when we make eye contact through the windshield; he waits as though this is just another Saturday and I a regular visitor.

I step out of the car, make a square with my fingers, and hold the fake camera to my eyes. He stands up, turns to what he used to call his good side, and crosses his arms. Then he crouches and turns the camera to me. I point my two arms diagonally to the sky like an archer aiming for the sun.

Damn you hit them with the Usain Bolt, he says.

With the paparazzi out here? I got to do it for the streets.

My voice sounds deeper than usual. The words move quicker and drawl.

For the island, he says.

Put it on my back.

Put the Coolies on the map.

My voice and his fall into the same rhythm like rappers trading lines over the same beat.

Damn, Brown, he says. Been a long time since I seen you.

I'm saying though. When the last time they seen Black and Brown?

Des holds his hand out and I grab it without thinking. Our fingers clasp. We shake. His arm circles my back and mine his. Our chests touch. I smell cocoa in his lotion. Then we separate and snap. Moments later, I still feel his hand on my back.

So what you doing in town? he asks.

Man, you already know.

Missed the funeral.

Couldn't get off work.

When I look at Des, the folds in his forehead like waves viewed from above, I wonder if he thinks I'm lying. I wonder if he thinks I didn't come because I've lied about my relationship with Aubrey.

�֎

Mom says that all Jamaican men, myself and Des included, love to lie. She said that when she returned to New Monklands as an adult, all the women told her my Coolie great-grandfather was a liar. A woman named Beatrice told Mom he spent many afternoons in her home after his wife left. She spoke to Mom from a chair outside her house. In the picture Mom took, she wore loose fabrics that billowed out over her body and age ridged her face like a dry valley seen from a plane.

Beatrice said my great-grandfather always came by when she was cooking supper, while her husband worked in the fields. The stew was not yet thickened from hours of heat and the salt pork's fat, but my great-grandfather always asked for a taste. She passed him a spoonful. He joked it would taste better with a hunk of meat. She told him to let her know where to find some. Then he told her stories his parents told him about India until it neared the time for her husband to return.

After his first few visits, Beatrice asked what his wife thought of him visiting other women when no one else was around. He told her his wife thought Jamaica wasn't good enough for her, so she left him. She moved to the States to find a rich man where the streets were paved with gold.

Mom told me that wasn't true. His wife, my great-grandmother, moved to Flatbush, where she shared a bed with her cousin and took care of a white woman's children. She wrote letters every week. Because he was illiterate, Grandma read them aloud to him. He always asked her to write back that he would join her soon, but he never did.

After my great-grandfather passed, Grandma fulfilled his promise and moved to the States to live with my great-grandmother in Flatbush. Some years after arriving, Grandma went to church with her mother and bumped into a man she grew up with in New Monklands. He had just arrived from the island with his daughter. They reminisced about their childhood—the look of spring, so unlike the one they were living through in New York, and the games they played—and he confessed that, when they were teenagers, he told the local boys they dated in secret. Grandma laughed. He continued as if he didn't hear her, saying that he always had a thing for her, that they should go out now that he was here, that they should make good on the stories he told. Grandma tried to tell him that she was too busy, and he said he was flexible. Eventually, Grandma told him she didn't want to go out with him. He said she hadn't changed. She always thought she was too good for her own kind.

❋

As I watch Des, I want to tell him the truth but can't look him in the eyes. Head cast down, I run my hand with the grain of my hair. Des coughs loud enough to stir me from my daydream. He stubs his cigarette out on the front step. The burning end streaks black on the gray concrete. Then he tucks what remains behind his ear. The creased paper smells even more of smoke than it did when lit.

We step inside. In the front room, a worn leather sectional sits next to a coffee table covered with remotes, *Essence* magazines from the '90s, and a King James Bible. Against the front wall, next to the blinds yellowed from dust, is a TV and several videogame consoles that they don't make games for anymore. On a bookshelf, a framed picture of Des at his kindergarten graduation sits next to one of him in his high school cap and gown. Between them is an empty frame for a college graduation picture.

Ain't a thing change round here, I say.

Cleaner than it used to be.

How you figure?

Remember when we had that fish tank? asks Des.

The one with no fish in it?

Made Ma throw it out.

Des slides open the glass door and steps onto the screened-in back porch. The carpet is dark blue and rough. We sit on white rocking chairs with floral-patterned cushions. He lights his stubbed-out cigarette, inhales, and then perches it in the ashtray on the coffee table.

You mind? he asks.

I shake my head. You go to the funeral?

Yeah, he says. I mean, Aubrey's people weren't my people, but I went. Must've been the only nigga there. Walked in a little late and everyone turned to look at me. All white. When they turned around, bro, I thought they were going to rush me. But ain't nobody do nothing. They turned back around and I seen what they was looking at. Her face on the projector. Her big old brown eyes looking back at us.

That look, I say.

That look though.

That look like she knows what you ain't even thought yet.

Looking at me like that at her funeral, he says. He picks up the cigarette and drags. In the backyard, grass grows long in patches. The brown-yellow soil rises in inch-high hills and falls in divots like a windswept beach shore. In the distance, dark-barked longleaf pines cluster together in an undeveloped lot.

Can't believe you ain't go, Des says.

Me neither, I say. But I'm glad you went. I know y'all weren't close, but I'm glad you went for me.

Nigga ain't nobody go for you.

My fault, I say. I ain't know you know her like that.

I ain't say all that, but she treated me good ever since we did community service the summer after junior year. Des shakes his head. So dumb, bro. We're about a month from summer and I got to bring the water bottle with vodka to school.

In the distance, thunder rumbles. The reedy grass leans to the right in a cool wind, then returns upright. A shadow falls over the backyard.

Hot out there, Des says. We was out there on the movie theater road. Wearing bright vests so cars could see us coming. Pants to be safe. I think I could've worn shorts and been fine, but we ain't have no choice. So we was out there in pants in the summer and, you know, by eight a.m. it's already ninety degrees so we was sweating out there. Walking up and down that road, picking up trash. Man, I would've died if Aubrey wasn't there.

Forgot she got community service after scrapping with Becky in the cafeteria, I say. Y'all talk a lot out there?

Bro, tell me why she was the only person I talked to. Everyone else had beef from back in the day or ain't like Black folks or I don't know what. But Aubrey, bro, we talked every day. At first we just cracked on you. She made fun of your voice a lot. Talking about how, when you started talking to her, your voice would get high-pitched and shit. That puberty middle school shit, you know what I'm saying?

I don't remember none of that.

I bet you don't, Des says. Shoot, I don't think I could live with myself if I remembered my voice cracking every time I talked to the girl I was feeling.

How you know she ain't lying?

Ain't no use lying.

The wind picks up, coming steadily, cool and moist. The clouds roll in above and the backyard turns gray.

At first, he says, we cracked on you. Then we cracked on the people we were with. Especially the big old bald-headed white dude telling us what to do. He was way too big to be out there in that heat. Aubrey kept saying she thought he was going to pass out one day and she wasn't going to help him neither. She was just going to watch him bake.

Man, she was ice-cold.

Something cracks loudly in the distance, like a far-off explosion.

Ain't it early in the year for a summer storm? I say.

They been coming later and later and earlier and earlier.

Forgot what this feels like, I say. It don't rain up north.

It don't rain in New York?

Just drizzles. What they call rain, we call drizzle.

The wind blows harder now, and that along with the clouds' shadow cools the day. In small scattered spots, the soil darkens, but I still can't see the water.

Came in one morning quiet as hell, Des says. I mean, she was always quiet at first because it was early and hot and sometimes she was still drunk from the night before. But this was different. I cracked on the bald dude when he walked by and she ain't even hear it. She was so in her head she ain't know what was going on. I ain't say nothing about it because I ain't want to pry or nothing like that.

She wouldn't tell you anyway, I say.

You're probably right, he says. But then, out of the blue, she looks up at me and asks, What you going to do when you get out of here? So I say, If I get out of here. Hit her with the slickness, you know what I'm saying? Let her know the kid's deep and hears her words and shit, but I can speak her language too. So I'm thinking she's going to be impressed when she says, Ain't no use talking about no ifs. That's how you get stuck here. I should've said, You can get stuck here even if you think you going to get out, but I ain't say nothing. So she says it again. How you getting out?

The falling water thickens a little, resembling barely visible glass shards. Larger clumps of the soil darken.

What'd you say? I ask as Des lights another cigarette.

I'm getting to that, bro. You always rushing niggas.

Man, you out here trying to smoke a whole pack and still not tell the story.

All right, bro, all right, he says, laughing. I said I wanted to build cars. Wanted to be there from start to finish. Not just put the engine in or design the body but draw what it looks like. Make prototypes. Go back after seeing it and draw it again. Fix what's wrong. Do that a million times till the car is lean with fierce eyes and enough room under the hood for a fat engine. A spoiler if it looks right. That's what I told her. Said I wanted to get out by making the flyest cars.

That's the dream.

Cars would be mad expensive too. Can't just have any old person rolling through in a Desmond original. That's what I told her. And she looks at me and says, I can get one for free though, right? I should've said, Yeah, but I said, I'll give you a discount. She laughed so I figured she was feeling better. Then I look at her and ask, How you getting out?

With a heavy gust of wind, the rain picks up, sounding like the steady pitter-patter of a crowd walking down the street.

She looks at me and says she don't know. Her daddy just got back from jail. Parole violation. Second time in her life he came home from upstate and had to go right back to jail. Second time she went to jail to visit him and heard him talk about how he's going to do everything by the book when he gets out. Second time he gets home and says it's going to be different this time and before you know it, it's back to the same old shit.

The falling water thickens, casting a veil over the backyard that seems to rush the day to dusk.

She told me about that night, I say. Never said what her dad was doing that got him in a cell. I ain't ask. Enough Henriquezes been to jail for me to know better than to ask. Folks always say they ain't done nothing.

Niggas in the pen stay tight-lipped, man, Des says. Probably ain't matter to her anyway. All that matters is that whatever dirt he doing took him away from her.

Right, I say. And she been mad at him all these years. She been talking about how she was going to tell him off and all the shit she going to say to him when he got out. But then he made it home and she seen his dumb face smiling, not wearing no jumpsuit or nothing, and she couldn't help but being happy. Gave him a big old hug when he came in. Then everybody's getting beers out the fridge. He gives one to Aubrey too even though she underage. They go to the back porch, drink, celebrate. But soon enough her daddy and her mom start yelling at each other. Her sister tries to calm them down and then they start yelling at her. She ain't having none of it. Gets in her car and goes to her boyfriend's. Aubrey gets mad and starts arguing with them, talking about, Why y'all chase her off? Then her parents start yelling at her. Aubrey ain't have nowhere to go so she walked outside and lay on the hood of her car and looked at the stars. Her dad came out and asked her what she was doing and she ain't say nothing. Just got in and drove. Said she drove to my house and sat in the driveway. Turned the lights off so she wouldn't wake up my mom. Thought about knocking on my window but ain't want to wake me up. Wish to God she would've knocked.

The moist soil is so thick in the air it feels like we're rolling around in mud.

I ain't know all that, Des says. She just told me her dad was being an asshole. Said it was typical but she ain't got to be there. Said she ain't know how she was going to get out, but she was good as gone. She'd go to Gainesville or Orlando or Jacksonville. Hell, she'd move up north and live with her grandma in Maryland if she had to. All she knew was she wasn't staying here.

With a crack of thunder, a bright streak of lightning, and steady gusts of wind, the rain swells.

Aubrey wanted to run away from her father, but she remained here longer than she planned. Even when she did escape, she moved in with her mother's relatives up north. I doubt she could ever completely cut off contact with her mother.

My own father's words followed us across borders. When Mom was pregnant with me, Grandma and Auntie B returned to Jamaica for a funeral and stayed with Mom, my father, and my brother. According to Mom, one day at dinner, he blamed dishes left in the sink on her. Then he turned to Grandma and Auntie B and complained that he did all the housework and took care of my brother. (He rarely cleaned, almost never watched Junior, and never cooked.) He paid the bills. If it wasn't for him, Mom and Junior would be homeless. Before Mom could respond, Auntie B cut her eyes at him and asked him who shared whose blood? My father was slow to respond. Auntie B asked again whose relatives they were; Mom's or his? When he didn't say anything, Auntie B told him not to forget who belonged to whom.

Even after we left Jamaica, my father talked about us to Mom's friends and family. When we lived in New York, Mom occasionally heard from relatives that my father told them she was addicted to drugs, she beat me and Junior senseless, and she was too crazy to take care of the kids. Once, he got Grandma's number and told her Mom abandoned him and kidnapped his children. When Grandma and Mom talked about it, Grandma said she didn't know why she let that Trini run Mom out of her home.

When I was in high school, I didn't talk to my father, though Mom said he found her email and sent her many messages. If classmates or teachers asked about my parents, I said that I didn't grow up with my father. It was easier to fall into the stereotype than to explain what happened. I even lied about my father to Aubrey for a long time.

After I left for college, my father contacted me. One Saturday afternoon during my freshman year, my eyes sore from sleeping too little, I saw that he emailed me. He said congratulations on my college acceptance but I should have gone to Harvard. Then he told a story about seeing a childhood friend of mine at Sovereign Centre. The friend asked how I was. My father said I was fine. He said I had no idea how painful it was to pretend that your son was talking to you. He knew Mom lied about him being a bad father, but that wasn't true. If only I would respond, he would tell me the truth.

I stopped reading and deleted the email. I searched my name online. My email and college came up. I didn't realize the school listed them publicly. I had them taken down and filtered his emails to spam. But my father continued to email—usually telling me that I was hurting him by not replying—and I still read them.

�֎

I chew on the inside of my lip. The occasional gust blows a cool mist through the screen. As I wipe the beading water from my forehead, I say, Heard she had a few bad years after we graduated.

You talking about the B and E?

You know what happened?

Des shakes his head. Heard stories, but hard to tell who's keeping it real, who's bullshitting, and who's talking about something they don't know nothing about.

Still, never expected it. Never thought she'd stick around for so long. The silence sits for a second. I continue, You see her much?

Not really.

In the rain clouds' shadow, the leaves and tree trunks darken, fading into each other in the distance. Thunder cracks and sounds like a branch breaking.

Bumped into her at the Publix once, Des says. I was waiting for a sandwich when out the aisle comes Aubrey with the Vanilla Coke. Before I even said a word, she hugged me. It was one of them hugs that you ain't prepared for so your heads bump and your arms ain't around her. Then she said she heard my mom got fired. I asked where she heard that and she said she was working part-time in customer service at Palm Coast Data. Said my mom was good. Ain't deserve it.

They play them games over there, I say. Had my mom working thirty-five hours for the longest.

I'm saying though. But what choice my mom got? No degree. Even if she had one, ain't nowhere else to work. Des drags on his cigarette long and deep. His eyes droop as he pulls and then open as he holds the smoke in. He continues, She asked how you were. I said you were good. I mean, I ain't heard from you in a minute.

My fault.

I ain't tripping over that now. At the time, I made up something about how you was wilding out in Cali. Tried to get her jealous.

That's cold, Des.

Man you know she ain't get jealous. She ain't pay me no mind. Shrugged it off, said she was glad, asked about my mom. When my sandwich came out, she offered to pay. Said she figured money was tight at home since my mom lost her job.

You let her pay?

Hell no I ain't let her pay, he says. Couldn't let her know we was broke.

✳

When we were in high school, we wore our best sneakers to school and made up stories about what we did on the weekend. We hoped no one called our bluffs, though we suspected everyone who knew how to listen could tell we were lying.

The only thing we lied about more than money was girls. The first time I lied about Aubrey was the day after I saw her bedroom. I was at track practice. Des and I had just run our fourth 200; he edged me out by the length of his head. When we stepped off the track and onto the grass by the starting line, we walked in circles with our hands on our heads, trying to keep from bending over, hoping to catch our breath and slow our pounding hearts. My dry tongue and throat felt swollen. Des took his tank off and dropped it on the ground.

When we could finally breathe enough to talk, Des asked, What happened with Aubrey?

Nothing, I said.

Nothing? Ain't you tell me you couldn't come through because you was kicking it with her? Because you was at her house?

The other sprinters from our heat looked at us, though they were too focused on breathing to say anything. Many of them had already had girlfriends. Those who didn't said they had hooked up with several girls. I was the only one who had never dated or hooked up with anyone. Several teammates joked I was gay. They all watched intently now, ready to crack.

Ain't nothing happen, I said. I was tired.

Beyond Des, past the chain-link fence surrounding the school, the distance runners were jogging back. Twig led the shirtless pack. His pale skin contrasted with the untamed greens and browns of the overgrown lot beyond him.

You was tired? said Des. So what? I'm tired right now, but if my girl rolled up, it'd be a different story.

Not practice tired, I said. Sleepy tired. Chilling on her bed and falling asleep tired.

You fell asleep?

My dumb ass fell asleep.

Then Des and the boys cracked on me. Des said I wasn't a closer. That's why I lost that heat. Someone else said I had no game. Someone else said I wouldn't know what to do even if I had game. They cracked on me, calling me gay until the next heat began.

After that day, Des and I didn't talk about Aubrey for a long time. Then he came to my house to give me a haircut in my bathroom. I sat shirtless on a chair facing the mirror, watching Des behind me. He walked around the room in his tank, rifling through clipper attachments. He plugged them in and they buzzed loudly.

Why you let your hair get so long? he asked.

Ain't nobody cut my hair right.

Who fucked your head up a couple months ago?

This dude in the Publix strip mall.

That's because he cut your hair like a white dude, Des said, squatting to look at the back of my head. He seen you and your hair and he ain't know what to think. Next time someone cuts your hair, you let them know. Tell them, Bitch I'm Coolie.

This nigga said, Bitch I'm Coolie.

Little Coolie boy, Des said, putting on his best Jamaican accent, the *t*'s turned to *k*'s, sounding like two glass bottles clinking together.

Des put the clippers to the back of my head. They vibrated as they moved up my scalp. They caught a knot and pulled the hair out. The pain made me cringe.

That hurt? Des asked.

I'm good, I say.

So what happened with old girl yesterday? Seen you and Aubrey talking in the hallway. She was crying.

Hair landed on my shoulders and pricked my skin.

She asked about prom, I said. Told her I couldn't go because it's the same night as States.

Twig's going with his girl. Leaving after his race.

Yeah, but I don't want to go.

Des's warm hands brushed the hair off my shoulders. I wondered what he would think of me not going to prom with the only girl he had seen me alone with, what he would say about me at practice.

So you just not going to go? Des said.

I ain't trying to go with her. We broke up.

Broke up? I ain't realize y'all were dating.

Wasn't nothing serious.

But you ain't tell your boys? That's cold, Brown.

Des's hand gripped the back of my head and pushed me forward. I looked at the ground. He pulled out his liner. Its loud buzz gave me a moment to think. I had to keep my story straight. I couldn't renege on any details.

Man, it ain't got nothing to do with y'all, I said.

Des's liner singed the back of my neck and I cringed.

Sit still, he said.

My fault, I said.

You hit?

Been hitting.

And you ain't tell me?

We wasn't official or nothing like that, I said. Just fucking. Then we broke it off.

So why she think you want to go to prom with her?

That's what I'm saying, I said, throwing my hands up and my head back. Des gripped my head again.

Be still, he said.

My fault, I said. So we was in the hallway and she asks what I'm going to wear to prom. Said she was wearing pink. So I say, I'm not going and she says, You got to go. I say I got to go to

States, but she ain't having none of that. Says I'm ruining prom
for her. I say I ain't know she wanted to go together and she
goes, Don't play me, Daniel. You knew I wanted to go.

Did you know? Des asks.

Hell yeah I knew, I said. But I wasn't going to tell her that.
Then she gets mad and starts crying and says I'm ruining every-
thing for her. I try to talk her down but ain't nothing working.
So I walk away.

Left her crying in the hallway, Des said. That's cold, Brown.

I shake my head. He grips the back of my neck.

Be still.

In time, friends asked about what they heard from Des and
I told the same story, inventing details to answer new questions. Eventually, I told the lie so much that it came to feel
like a part of my history. After I moved to California, Aubrey
became my high school girlfriend, someone whom I dated on
and off until I left, at which point we fell out of touch. That
was the way with high school girlfriends, people said, even for
queer folk.

I wonder if Aubrey told Des the truth, if she talked about
me much at all. Maybe if she did, I would know that our impact
on each other lasted, that I hadn't made it up.

I bob my leg up and down like a child waiting for class to
end. I look over both shoulders, though no one has come in
and nothing has moved. Des shoots me a look and I sit still.

You good?

I'm good, I say. When the next time you seen her?

A couple years ago. Must've been just before she moved. We

was down at the Lion, doing some drinking. Trying to smell the sea, get into a little bit of trouble, maybe go home with some girls.

Never been to the Lion, I say. Seemed mad cool when we was in high school.

The rain slows to a steady fall and the wind calms. The sky lightens. The tree trunks turn brown and the leaves green again.

Normal beach bar. Sand on the ground. Red-faced white dudes with short hair behind the bar.

All of them wearing flip-flops, I say.

All of us wearing sliders and our girls wearing Chinese slippers. I was pretty buzzed when it happened. Not drunk because I was driving, but I was feeling it. All I remember is Egypt—I tell you I been talking to Egypt? Nothing serious, you know. Got to get my money straight before I settle down. But anyway, she comes running up and she's yelling something to Tati about something happening by the bar when crazy Brandon rolls up.

Never knew why Aubrey went out with him. Said he was funny but that redneck ain't never made me laugh.

Man, after his mom died, he wasn't funny no more.

Mrs. Jacobs died?

Yeah, man. Cancer. Everyone saw it coming. She lived in a pack of Marlboro's.

Des pulls on his cigarette again, though it's little more than a tobacco stub burning the yellow filter.

So Brandon's looking bug-eyed and tweaked out. He's wearing a Confederate-flag tank and a camo hat and walks up looking like he's ready to thump. You know Tati, she don't take shit from nobody and she been hated Brandon. Plus she been getting bougie and acting like she live up north so she seen him wearing the flag and popped off. I was clowning with Earl and J-Boogie so I ain't notice what was going down. She starts something, but she's older now so she thinks she's too good for the shit she starts.

Tell me she ain't walk away.

She walked away, Des says. Screams in this man's face and walks away.

Screams? I thought Egypt was the hot-headed one.

Man, who you telling? he says. Why you think I ain't serious about her?

'Cause you don't like girls your age.

'Cause she can't stop yelling at a nigga in public, he says.

The rain lightens to a drizzle and the birds begin to chirp again.

So Egypt jumps in on Tati's beef and starts getting in Brandon's ear about how he needs to take the shirt off and how her cousins'll fuck him up. She takes her earrings off and talks about how she ain't got no nails on today like she's about to do something. Gets in his face and calls him a racist cracker. Now, Brandon, Brandon's crazy and he don't give a fuck about nothing no more, so he shoves her.

He hit a girl?

I'm saying, Brown, Des says. Brandon don't give a fuck about nothing no more. So Egypt runs back to us and tells us what Brandon just did when Brandon rolls up. Me, Earl, and J-Boogie step to him, but in the back of my mind I'm thinking, Every last one of these camo-wearing rednecks is about to jump in. Either that or I'm going to have to catch Brandon outside. And I know that crazy motherfucker's packing because them rednecks got more guns than teeth. So my mind's running and Egypt's yelling about how she's calling her cousins and Brandon says to me, You going to let your girl finish your shit?

Your shit? What'd you do?

I'm saying though, Des says. I ain't start shit. But I wasn't about to back down neither. So I look him dead in the eye and I say, We got beef?

The rain stops but water still falls from the leaves. A shower falls from the lone large tree in Des's backyard, though I can't see what stirred the branches.

Before anything happens, bouncer rolls up. Says take it outside. Brandon says I ain't going nowhere. I say we can squash this right here. Brandon squares up like the white boys do. You know, mad slow, looking like he's in the Matrix. Me, I been doing my UFC thing, hitting the gym hard, and Brandon looking like he ain't worked out in a minute, so I ain't worried. Plus I got J-Boogie and Earl with me. J-Boogie ain't worth shit if we scrapping, but Earl just got out the pen so we was straight. So I start to square up and the bouncer's trying to get between us and Egypt is yelling and Brandon's pressing me like he's about to do something and then that motherfucker calls me a no-good nigger. Now I'm about ready to stomp his ass out when Aubrey comes running out of nowhere.

Where she come from?

Bro, I got no clue. Deadass she pops up out of nowhere. Jess standing off in the corner not doing nothing, but Aubrey, she just slips right between the bouncer and me and Brandon and gets in his face. She's small and he's tall so she's looking up at him when she's yelling. Goes off like, Who the fuck are you calling a nigger? You know Desmond. He's better than that.

Man, I remember walking with Aubrey in high school one day, I say. You know, back before we dated. We walking and a fight breaks out between two Black kids younger than us. They're pushing each other and one of them stumbles into her and hits her Coke out her hand. First thing she says is god-damn niggers. I cut my eye at her and I'm about to say some-thing but before I can, she goes, Not you. Them.

Des turns to look at me and asks, She ever call you a nigger?

No.

All right then.

Des leans back in his chair and I shake my head. He always acts like he knows this world better than me. As the old frus-tration rushes to my head in the way it does when Mom chas-tises me for something that happened years ago, I exhale deep and survey the yard. The sun is out now, and the leftover rain-drops shine as they fall into murky brown puddles at the base of a lone tree in Des's backyard.

So Aubrey's getting in his face, talking about, Act like you got some manners. Can't nobody take you nowhere. At this point, me, Earl, and J-Boogie are just cracking up, watching this small girl run up on this big dude and dress him down in front of everybody. And then, to top it all off, she made him apologize.

He do it?

Yeah. Said he ain't been right since his mom died. I ain't say nothing because I still wanted to beat his ass. Aubrey sent him back to his seat. Then she just started talking to us like no one else was there. Asks how we're doing. We said we were straight and she said she was sorry. Said we shouldn't have to deal with him. Said I was better than this small-minded town and that I was going places and that she couldn't wait to see the cars I was going to design. Couldn't wait to buy one. Couldn't wait till I got out and didn't have to deal with this ever again. Then, get this, she fixed Egypt's hair.

Ain't no way Egypt let her touch her hair, I say. Ain't no way Aubrey know what she doing with Black hair.

Deadass, bro, Des says. Ain't never seen a white girl do Black hair before but she done it like she been doing it her whole life.

I roll my eyes. Then the familiar silence—the one that comes when talking about the dead sends friends deep into their thoughts—settles on the afternoon. Des keeps smoking. We don't make eye contact.

Even now, all these years after I lied to Des, I don't know how to tell him the truth. I still worry that I'll lose whatever little trust of his I have left. Perhaps today is not the day, I think to myself as I crack my knuckles. Then the sun's light makes me squint. It shines onto the back porch and the mesh screen casts a checkerboard shadow onto Des's face. He is shaking his head and grinding out his cigarette in the ashtray when he says, Normally, when stuff like that goes down, the whole ride home I'm checking my rearview. Looking for some redneck in a pickup with rebel flags waiting to run up and gun me down. Doesn't matter how many people are in the car, how much we smoked, I keep looking for that truck. Keep looking for the person who's going to come out the dark. I keep my hand on my piece the whole way. But this time, I drove home looking ahead. One hand on the wheel, the other out the window, just feeling the night.

Aubrey was special, I say.

You ain't got to tell me, man, says Des. I thought she was so special you'd drop what you was doing and fly home for the funeral.

Families

A *spiny curved back moves* through the brush, knocking rain off the leaves. An armadillo. They eat everything. No matter how much metal mesh Mom put up, the armadillos made sure her garden never grew past buds and shoots, strands of green clutching to what little soil they could. Mom screamed the first time she saw one scamper away from her plants, looking so much like this one, which walks to the edge of the wilderness, exposing its long snout and mouse-like ears. It peers out at the puddles in Des's yard then turns its head up to us, as if wondering what we are doing, before ambling back to the woods. Except for its occasional rustle, the day is quiet.

Always forget how quick them storms roll in, I say.

Here one second.

Gone the next.

Des opens his pack of cigarettes and counts them.

You trying to get active? I ask.

What you got in mind?

Fixing to go see Brandon.

In my peripherals, I see Des lean onto his knees and look

at me. I keep watching the backyard, where the reedy grass shifts. I cannot see what moves it. It could be a snake. Around here, most are harmless. In high school, I often saw their guts, pink and pulpy like smashed grapefruit, scattered on the road by some tire. Older folks said watch out for the brighter ones but never taught the difference between the poisonous snakes and the fakers. They just said enough carry poison around here that we ought to be careful.

You finally ready to stomp Brandon out? Des asks.

That's not entirely right, I think to myself. Brandon is one of the few people I know who was as close to Aubrey as I was and he was the last person to see her alive. I suspect he can tell me more about her than anyone else. But if I'm being honest with myself, Des isn't entirely wrong either.

Finally, I say, Just got some questions. Want to figure out why she was in his car. Maybe hear what she was like when he saw her. What I missed out on.

Whatever you say, bro. I been had a bone to pick with him.

Des walks into the house and I follow. We enter the garage, where cardboard boxes line the wall, framing a silver 240SX from the late 1980s. Two black racing stripes run the length of the doors. In the back, a small spoiler peeks out.

Old-school, I say. Always talked about building one of these together.

Then you went and left on me.

My fault.

Don't trip, he says. Once a brother.

Always a brother.

�֍

When we were in high school, though Des and I looked nothing alike, teachers often asked if we were related. Neither Des nor I argued with them. In fact, Des misled them, often referring to me as a cousin, and when people asked me if we were related, I said it was a small island. When we were alone, we joked they couldn't tell the difference between Jamaicans. We didn't mind. We took care of each other like family.

As Mom gets older, when she tells stories about our family, I often have to ask how we are related, and she often reveals that we don't share blood with many of the people we call Uncle or Auntie. We're not related to Auntie Selena; she grew up in the same village as Grandma and, years later, showed Grandma around Brooklyn, so when Auntie Selena returned to Jamaica, we visited her for dinner frequently. Uncle Eugene dated Auntie B when the two were in high school in New York; he had two boys with another woman shortly thereafter, and when Auntie B had her own children, he gave her all their hand-me-downs, at which point Auntie B's husband began inviting him to their dominoes games. Auntie Q worked with Mom at the university and the two became good friends before I was born; I was so used to seeing her around that, when I started speaking, I called her Auntie without prompting.

Though I have long thought of Uncle Rodney as a grandfather—he is the same generation as my grandmother—we're not related to him either. He was the brother of Mom's stepfather. When Uncle Rodney was ten, his mother died, and he went to live with Mom's stepfather and Grandma. Grandma helped him dress for his mother's funeral, at which he wore a tie that Grandma tied and a blazer, the sleeves of which hung to his knuckles. That evening, Grandma helped him get ready for sleep and sat with him in the bed in their front room until he dozed off.

On Monday, Grandma walked him to school and went to the white woman's house to clean. When Grandma returned home, she saw him sitting on his bed, crying. She asked what happened. He said the kids at school chased him and called him Red Man. That day, as on many others, Grandma ran her fingers through his hair and sat with him until he calmed down. Because she raised him as though he were her child, Grandma remained close with him after the end of her marriage to his older brother.

Like Grandma, Mom helped raise another's child when she was young. In the mid-1970s, after Mom and Auntie B bounced from house to house, Grandma finally sent them plane tickets to America. Mom was fourteen and Auntie B was sixteen when they arrived at JFK. Grandma met them in baggage claim. She was shorter than Mom remembered, mounds of wrinkles collecting beneath her eyes. She held hands with a light-skinned boy wearing overalls who stood to about her waist. His shoes were still soft. She told them he was their brother. (Mom never met his father, who had disappeared before she arrived in the States.) His name was Fitzroy Junior. Grandma said it meant son of kings. Mom later heard it meant illegitimate son.

That summer, Mom and Auntie B took care of Uncle Junior while Grandma cleaned homes. When Grandma returned from work, she watched him while Mom cooked dinner. They continued that routine until school started. Then Grandma left Uncle Junior with an auntie who lived upstairs. After school, Auntie B and Mom picked him up from the auntie, who left to work the night shift. Whenever I ask Mom about him, she says she raised her brother as if he were her son.

><

Though Mom and Auntie B reared a sibling they were too young to parent, they continued to beat each other. I assume they hit Uncle Junior too. I've never known a Henriquez to spare the rod. Even so, whenever he comes up, Mom says she should have disciplined him more. Maybe then he wouldn't have fallen in with a bad crowd. Maybe then he wouldn't have died alone in an abandoned warehouse in the '80s, when she was in her twenties and raising a child of her own.

Des slams the car door, knocking me out of thought. I get in. The seat feels firm against my body. I spread my legs wide and rest one arm between them. Des's Arctic Breeze air freshener is the same scent that was in Uncle Winston's car when he picked us up from the airport when we moved to the States. Cool to the nose, an earthy undertone. The passenger seat looks untouched, but the driver's is warped and wrinkled.

These bucket seats? I ask.

Just mine, Des says. Saving up for the other.

The engine roars awake and then purrs steadily.

New engine? I ask.

How much money you think I make? I got a new engine, but I'm working at the car wash? Nigga, that's the muffler.

My fault, I say.

Des clicks the garage opener and the chain rattles behind us. It lurches forward, stops, and repeats until open.

You been running around on them subways too long, bro, Des says. Made a jit out a grown man.

Who you calling a jit? I'm the one that put you on to souping up your car.

Des turns on his stereo. The console lights up and he plugs his phone in. Bass kicks from the trunk, the car seat shakes, and my back rumbles. I nod without realizing it. Pimp C raps about the hydraulics on his '64 Chevy, though I'm not moving to him so much as to the beat filling the car.

Man, they don't build speakers like this up north, I say.

Round every corner down here.

Folks ain't got money to eat but their subs still knock, I say as Des reverses out of his driveway and I lean my arm out the window, hoping the air will settle the nausea that a hangover or McDonald's or my nerves have brought.

Riding around in the car like this feels just like high school.

I ain't have a car in high school, Des says. You was catching rides with them white boys.

You right. More like we on the back of the yellow bus, on the way to school, sharing headphones.

We drive through the F section, passing lines of identical one-floor white houses. Their lawns extend from the homes through a divot where rain collects to the road. Where the two meet, grass leans over the crumbling asphalt, not yet piercing through.

Let me play something, I say.

Des gives me the cord and I plug my phone in. As the song begins, repeating high piano notes sound like a slowed-down theme from a horror movie. Des nods to the beat. A small smile creeps in when the bass hits. The chorus starts, but my ears are tuned to the yells looped into percussion, conjuring images of grown men circled around a fight, of fists beating against cheekbones, of drawn blood. Des and I rap along with Lil Scrappy about weak men afraid of dying in the streets, blood collecting in their mouths, heat filling their souls.

This song was the shit back in the day, Des says, clapping.

Man, tell me this ain't sound like the future back then.

Thought for sure Lil Scrappy was going to get huge, bro.

I can't believe he ain't blow up.

Turning onto Old Kings, Des's turn signal sounding like a metronome, he says, Now he just sounds old-school.

�֍

So much of the future became the past so quickly. When I was younger, I thought my brother would be there forever. Mom named my brother Junior after her own brother. In the late '80s, after Fitzroy Junior died and when Junior was still young, he and Mom moved back to Jamaica. When my brother was about six, Mom got pregnant with me and moved in with my father. After I was born, my father constantly reminded Junior that he was not my father's son. Sometimes, after Mom left him alone with my father, she saw bruises on his face. She always asked what happened. They never said anything.

When my father wasn't around, Junior hit me. Most of the time, he just slapped me upside the head. Once, he told me to climb into his sleeping bag. Then he zipped it up and held the exit shut. It was darker than when I closed my eyes at night. I clawed at the soft fabric. My breath rebounded hot in my face. I screamed and he laughed. Then I heard Mom yell. Her palm hitting his body sounded like the crack of the belt she hit me with. Junior's hold loosened. I crawled out of the sleeping bag. Mom slapped Junior across the face. I ran between them and hugged Junior until she stopped.

In the States, after Mom found a job, she made Junior pick me up from school. Sometimes, when the other kids picked on me in the schoolyard for my accent, for my mixed features and for being a sissy, he threatened to beat them up. When the men on our block talked to us, some of whom I now realize were homeless or slanging, Junior spoke so I didn't have to.

When I bothered Junior, when I embarrassed him, and when I was acting like a girl, he beat me. Once, when I was nine, I threatened to tell on him for hitting me and he ran away from me. I couldn't catch him. I had to find my own way home. When I got there, he stood on our stoop and asked what took me so long. He opened the door, took me inside, and made me something to eat.

When we got home, we usually watched reruns on TV. After an episode or two, Junior tried to sketch, from memory, the cars from James Bond movies. After Mom bought him a subscription to *Hot Import Nights*, he drew as many cars in the magazine as he could before the next issue came, when he started over and gave me the old issue. Every time I accidentally bent the pages, he hit me.

When Junior left for college, he called to talk to my mother but not to me. Sometime after we moved to Florida, he failed a class and lost his financial aid. He dropped out and moved in with us. His student loans defaulted. After a month, he started working part-time at a garage in the Publix strip mall to help Mom with his student-loan payments.

In time, Junior befriended the other mechanics. Because he

was too young to go to bars, they invited him to their houses to drink. After a few months, they asked him to join them on a side-job. He agreed. He drove them to Daytona and they told him to pull into a gas station. They hopped out and told him to keep the car running. He listened to the radio while they were inside. Then they came out wearing ski masks and holding a black duffel bag. The cops pulled them over before they made it to the highway.

�֎

For a long time, Aubrey was one of the only people I spoke to about Junior. Because her father was also in prison, she understood our relationship, which was too hard to describe to anyone else: Junior and I were never close, but once he was locked up, I was one of the only people on the outside that he talked to. That made Junior and me closer in a way, but it also kept us at a distance. And it certainly didn't make up for the beatings.

These days, I pick up when he calls, which is rare. I don't talk to him or Mom or any of the people who cared for me as often as I should. When I do, I never really listen; I mess around on my computer or do my dishes. They speak and I respond occasionally, mostly yeses and nos, and the occasional question to keep them speaking until it's been long enough that I don't feel rude ending our conversation.

There's always a distance between us, one I opened every night I lost to dancing and drinking at after-hours queer parties and awakened to a missed call. I feel that distance with Des too. Though we were there for each other when we were broke, I don't know how to make up for all the texts I didn't respond to.

Des rolls the window down. The wind coming in chills my face.

Where Egypt at? I ask.

Working.

On a Saturday?

You know how nurses are, he says. People dying every day of the week.

What she think about you spending your day off with the boys?

Told her we'd see her later on, Des says as we turn onto Palm Coast Parkway. What about you? You got anyone wondering what you're doing down here?

Was seeing someone. Over now though.

Got on your nerves?

Got busy. Started to get in the way of my job. Resented having to spend time with them when I was behind on grading and lesson planning. Sooner or later, I realized it wasn't that important to me. So I let it go.

Classic Daniel. Always working.

As we drive over I-95, cars racing below us, I hear Virgil's numbed voice after I told him I wanted to break up. That night, he called me and asked questions in quick succession at a high pitch. He tried to convince me that I was being rash. His voice sounds loud to me still, sitting in Des's car, until the silence of the song having ended stirs me from my thoughts. I put on Lil Wayne. The high, repeating piano keys move faster than the last song. Des looks at me, I look back at him, and he nods. He raps along to the best song from the year he was the best rapper alive.

This shit right here, Des says.

Thought he was going to rap like this forever.

You remember that day at practice, Des says, when we was talking about how Lil Wayne was the best rapper ever and your quiet ass got real loud and said we was dead wrong. Said it was Tupac.

I was in deep, boy, I say. Remember Junior always used to say Biggie was the best rapper, so you know me, I had to rebel. After he got locked up and I got his Walkman and his CDs, I listened to *Until the End of Time* on repeat because it was the only one he had.

Next day you caught me before practice and made me listen. Had me rewinding tracks in the locker room to hear what Tupac was saying. Then you just started shooting the shit with us at practice. You still hung with the white boys on the weekends because we ain't have no cars so couldn't nobody come pick you up, but we was the ones you was trying to make laugh at practice.

It all started with him.

We coast down the hill and Des turns the music down. Then he asks, You remember where Brandon stay?

Went out there with Aubrey once, I say. Should be able to figure it out. Off the same road Twig and me and his friends used to fishtail on.

Dirt road?

They got anything else out in Espanola?

We stop at the first stoplight on the other side of the bridge.

Just over the retention pond to our left is a Golden Corral that wasn't here when I lived in Palm Coast. A road built after I moved continues past it out of view. I wonder what new businesses and buildings have arrived after they stopped building when the crash hit.

You talk to Twig much? I ask.

Not really.

Sure he'd be happy to see you. Only white boy on our side in the Brawl.

Most of the distance runners didn't talk to the sprinters. I was the exception because I tracked into AP classes with some of them and because Twig befriended me. But they didn't talk much to Desmond.

While they were off doing distance runs, we ran the track. Coach Howard called us the Fam. They hired him my senior year to replace the previous sprinting coach, whose Army Reserve unit was called to Iraq. He was a short, jet-black man with small eyes and close-cropped hair on the side with waves on top. At our first practice, Coach Howard wore a black shirt, which clung to his chest. He spoke to us the way I imagined his drill sergeant spoke to him. Things were going to be different now, he said. Under him, we were going to sweat and bleed together. That would make us a family.

Behind me, Des whispered, That mean I can't fuck on Egypt no more?

Everyone laughed.

You, Coach Howard said. Come up here.

Damn, man, Des said under his breath, looking down at the ground as he walked.

Every family has nicknames, Coach Howard said. We just got our first one. Turn around, Junior. Your new name is Loudmouth. Now, Junior, what's your name?

Desmond, Coach.

You must not have heard me, he said. What's your name?

Loudmouth, sir.

After that, he gave the long sprinters our workout: four 350s at 80 percent. As we waited for him to start us, I tried to steer my thoughts away from the pain to come. He said go. I burst forward and accelerated almost to top speed. The adrenaline numbed me so that I forgot that I was running through the first curve. Midway through the first straightaway, I inhaled deep again. This time, my lungs burned. As I entered the second curve, my legs weighed me down. I tried to ignore them, but I couldn't block out the burning in my lungs. I was out of shape.

I didn't want to die again. Midway through the second curve, shoulder leaning over my left hip, I was running toward death. I wanted to slow down to let it pass me by. I tried to focus on my breathing. I couldn't give up. I had survived much worse: The time I vomited after my first practice, the time Junior beat me for embarrassing him in front of his friends, the time my father backhanded me until my nose bled. I couldn't let this break me. As I exhaled, I burned what little gas was left to accelerate and switched my hips faster. This was my ticket out of here. I wasn't going to end up like Junior. I couldn't lose, not even at practice. I slungshot out of the curve and onto the straightaway as my body went upright. I pulled my knees up and kicked down. The end neared. I was in front, but I wasn't running to win any-more; the race was over. I was running to rest.

When I crossed the finish line, my momentum carried me a few paces, until I slowed into a jog and then a walk. Hands on my head, I went to the infield, inhaling through my nose and exhaling through my mouth. I tried to pull in enough air to calm my lungs. Long before I could, Loudmouth was cracking on the freshmen rounding the second curve.

Loudmouth cracked on everyone, even me. He made fun of me for being too skinny, for being uncoordinated, for hav-ing ashy knees, for having curly hair, for having no common sense, for talking too proper, for not talking proper enough. The insults smarted at first, but when he busted out a big laugh at the end of his punch line, I couldn't help but join him, so I never took it too seriously.

The one exception occurred on our way to the Bob Hayes Invitational, the largest track meet we would attend that year. We boarded the bus at five a.m. because the meet started at eight. As I sat quietly, pretending to be unfazed by the meet, I was nervous. I didn't want to make a fool of myself in front of scouts. If I did well, I might earn my ticket out of here.

As usual, when stressed, I tried to sleep, but the bus was too noisy. Loudmouth was screaming from the back of the bus about how fast he was going to run and all the girls he was going to spit game to. In retrospect, he probably felt the same way I did. But at the time, he was keeping me up. After several minutes, I walked back there and told him to shut his mouth.

This skinny-ass Coolie talking real reckless like he run shit, Loudmouth said, like I won't beat his ass.

Don't make me tell you twice.

Last I checked, I ain't had no pops, so who you trying to son? Who the fuck you think you talking to?

You, nigga. Who the fuck you think?

Loudmouth raised his voice and told me to turn around and walk away. I told him I wasn't leaving until he shut his bitch ass up. He stood up and pressed his face close to mine. I pushed him. He pushed me back. Our teammates jumped in and separated us. The coaches yelled at us. I stewed in anger for the rest of the ride.

By the time our team warmed up on the practice field, about an hour and a half later, I cooled off. As I led our stretches, Loudmouth listened. At the end of the day, just before the last event, Loudmouth and I practiced our handoffs. On the infield before the race started, he talked shit about all the other runners, keeping our relay team cracking up as I did my drills quietly. During the 4x400 after he handed me the baton and I started our anchor leg, I heard him cheering me on, somehow screaming loud enough for me to hear, even though I knew he was out of breath from the race.

❖

All the Florida boys I knew were like that. We scrapped in the cafeteria and by fourth period we were friends again. It was proof that we always would be.

The light turns green and a long queue of cars turns left, heading to Walmart. On summer nights, when Loudmouth had his mom's car, the sprinters met there. We walked the aisles, cracking on each other and looking for something to buy. Then we gathered around someone's car and blasted music from the speakers. Eventually, the cops broke us up and we rode around town, looking for something to do. When we tired of that, we went home. I wonder if the new sprinters at our old school still wander that Walmart.

Loudmouth drives straight. On our right, a road winds through parking lots and around businesses in standalone buildings. There's a Chick-fil-A where there was once a Perkins, and there's the Advance Auto Parts that wouldn't hire Junior, and finally the Taco Bell.

You ever hear about Tits for Tacos? I ask Loudmouth, who shakes his head. Twig's friend Jason used to work the night shift. Whenever he was running the drive-through alone and some girl from school came by, he told them he'd give them free tacos if they showed him their tits.

That ever work?

He said it worked all the time.

Yeah, but that don't mean nothing.

Right, I say, but Aubrey told me she did it once. Got drunk with Jess and they wanted Taco Bell. But Aubrey was so drunk that, after she got there, she had to use the bathroom. Asked Jason if she could but he said he couldn't let anyone in. So she grabs her food, parks, and runs to the corner of the parking lot and just pops a squat.

She pissed in the Taco Bell parking lot? Loudmouth says, grimacing.

I made that same face when she told me, I say. And she just said don't be one of those guys. Said she would've done it sober too.

That girl was crazy, Loudmouth says.

We're on one of the only well-traveled roads in town, so we inch along in traffic. To our left, the median thins and the trees clear so we can see the cars driving in the opposite direction. Beyond them is a Publix where there was once an Albertsons. Are there any grocery stores in town that are not a Publix or a Walmart anymore?

I'm enjoying the trip back in time and all, Loudmouth says, but you got to play something more recent.

You heard that boy from Mississippi? I ask.

Loudmouth shakes his head and I change the song. A sped-up high-pitched voice sings from the speakers over a chorus sounding like a snippet of a soul song looped to make a rhythm. Then the bass kicks in and Loudmouth bobs his head to the beat. At the end of the first verse, the Mississippi rapper introduces the song's subject: muddy water, candied yams, lean, the Third Coast.

He real Southern, Loudmouth says.

He more Southern than us.

We from the suburban South, beach-town South, I guess.

Remember listening to UGK in high school, I say, wishing we was from the South like they was from the South.

Instead we got Palm Coast Parkway and school buses.

We pass Belle Terre. To my right, the four-lane road curves past the library. Before we got the Internet at home, which was long after many classmates did, I used the computers there on weekends. While I did my homework on boxy monitors, old folks played chess or flipped through the paper and parents read picture books to their kids. Sometimes the old folks or the kids asked what I was doing. I showed them. Then they returned to their part of the library and I to mine.

You heard from J-Boogie? I ask.

He's working today, Loudmouth says. Told him to take the

day off because you was in town but he couldn't. Working at the car wash and then at the bar. Trying to save money for studio time.

We drive past the dollar store and the old two-screen movie theater. In high school, boys took girls there to make out. From what I heard, every seat in the theater was stained with something. Today, the doors are shuttered and the lights are off. The dirt staining the board where they announced movies is visible even from across the street.

What about Fast Life? I ask.

He with the baby, Loudmouth says. Anna's working today so he's watching her.

They still dating?

They broke up, but he ain't want to be no deadbeat.

On our right, we pass the strip mall where the Jamaican restaurant used to be. On our left, we pass Palm Coast Data. Mom worked there in order fulfillment, making sure subscribers received their magazines. Loudmouth's mom and Aubrey worked there in customer service. Most people started in that department.

And Tati?

You ain't hear? She joined the army.

Why she do that?

Sick of it down here. Been sick of it. Then her mom died and wasn't nothing keeping her here no more.

How I miss all that? I ask. Ain't nobody call me or nothing?

Ain't know if you'd pick up.

We're quiet as we turn right onto US-1. A wide road for this part of Florida, two lanes run on both sides. Tall pine trees line the road. Loudmouth steps on the gas and my seat cradles me.

The engine roars through the open window until we roll them up. Then it's quiet, even with the music. Loudmouth turns his head in every direction, looking for something.

I'm feeling this country boy and all, he says, but you got to play something with some danger.

I got you.

As the beat begins, we hear a slowed-down, distorted voice. The words are inaudible, but the voice sounds like a memory. A slow, steady high-hat keeps the pace. Then Isaiah Rashad raps in a nasally voice about dragging on squares to calm his nerves. He continues, but I don't hear his words so much as the sound of numbness in his smoke-torn voice.

If we keep driving, we'll reach where Aubrey died. We turn off before then onto a small two-lane street. On our left is an empty parking lot and a warehouse. I don't see any movement inside. I don't know what it stores or who it employs. I've never known anyone who works there or seen anyone in its parking lot. We drive about a hundred feet to the railroad tracks. Beyond us is a dirt road. To its left stand more pine trees, untamed brush clawing at their feet. To its right is a clear field, patches of green shoots trying to reclaim the dirt plowed by some farmer months prior. Seeing all three at once, it looks like one of those Southern roads built in the nineteenth century, the sort enslaved people would have avoided for fear of night-riding paddy rollers. In front of the railroad tracks, the warning blinkers flash and the barriers lower. Loudmouth stops.

When we cross these tracks, he says, we're in Espanola.

Bad out there.

In the distance, I hear the train. It must be a locomotive carrying supplies. Passenger trains don't travel this route anymore. The tracks rattle in anticipation of the coming weight. The sound of metal pounding metal fills the car. The tracks screech a high-pitched noise, as if worried they cannot keep the train in line. If it derails, it will hammer into our car. I wonder if we'll feel the shattered windshield cut us before we die.

Loudmouth turns off the stereo and says, Check under your seat.

Before I reach down, I suspect I know what it is, and I am scared.

✳

I have forgotten how often I felt fear when I was with our team. Coach Howard claimed that sharing that feeling would make us a family. We would not be kin, he said, until we took a hit for each other.

Maybe that's why we were all so willing to jump in at the county fair on the fields off US-1. I went with Twig. After we parked in the muddy dirt patch, as we headed toward the well-lit rides and booths, we walked by the fair animals, where pink-eared hogs sniffed the ground. At this hour, the animal show had long been over, the lights were dim, and no one was around. I reached over the fence to try to pet one. Twig shoved me, told me to keep it moving. We entered the fair proper, where crowds of people walked, though there weren't many places to go. In the distance, a Ferris wheel jolted erratically. Twig had chipped a tooth on it a year earlier.

Before we could peruse the games I couldn't afford to play and make fun of the people losing their money on them, Twig pointed to Jalen. He was a brown-skinned hurdler with waves who ran the 4x400 with me and Loudmouth. He whipped his trail leg over the hurdles so smoothly that Coach said it looked like he was dancing. Then he started calling him J-Boogie.

Between the ring toss and the water shoot, J-Boogie stood almost chest to chest with Ronny. Ronny was yelling at J-Boogie, but I couldn't hear what Ronny said over the crowd. I assumed it was about Brandy, a white girl who was Ronny's current girlfriend and J-Boogie's ex-girlfriend. She was the first girl J-Boogie had dated. Before they started, J-Boogie assumed her parents forbid her from seeing Black guys. When he told her he liked her and she said she liked him too, he bragged about how amazing it was that they were going to date, even though her mom said she couldn't. They broke up a year later. A few weeks after that, she was with Ronny. But J-Boogie told the whole track team they were still fucking.

In the distance, I saw Earl run to J-Boogie's side. He was on the 4x400 with us too. He was the color of a pale grained wood and he always wore a fake diamond stud in each ear. Coach said that every time he saw him in the hallway, he was wearing a different pair of sneakers, so he started calling him Fast Life.

Fast Life stepped between the skinny J-Boogie and the broad-shouldered, much-taller Ronny. We cracked on Fast Life for being light-skinned (he often responded by making fun of my curly hair), but he was shades darker than the six-three self-avowed redneck he looked up at. Fast Life bumped Ronny with his chest. Ronny took a step back and looked behind him. None of his friends were there. Then he stepped to Fast Life and started yelling again. Fast Life yelled back. I started to walk toward them, but Twig told me to keep out of it.

A group of Ronny's friends ran over wearing camo hats or hoodies or pants. Brandon was with them. I heard that Ronny and Brandon once camped in the woods hunting wild boars for days. I imagined them covered in blood from skinning a boar as they yelled at Fast Life and J-Boogie. J-Boogie tugged on Fast Life's arm and tried to pull him away, but Fast Life didn't budge.

In the distance, I saw Tati weaving through the crowd. She was the girls' team captain and the anchor on their 4x400. Aside from me, she had the best start on the team. When Coach asked how she popped out like that, she said she took out her anger on the blocks. After that day, he called her Hothead. I didn't think the nickname fit until I saw her flip on her ex-boyfriend. He bought her flowers on Valentine's Day. She took the bouquet and beat him with it until we pulled her off. I thought of that beating as she neared Fast Life and J-Boogie. She tugged her green bandanna down and unhooked her hoop earrings. I got nervous. Twig and I started to approach. When Hothead reached the crowd, I heard her yell, The fuck you saying to my brothers?

Earrings in hand, Hothead stepped toward Ronny. J-Boogie grabbed her arm. She surged forward and J-Boogie pulled her back. Then Ronny said, Better call your girl off before she get herself in trouble. Never hit a girl before, but I'll beat the shit out a nigger.

My heart raced as I jogged toward them. Before I got there, Egypt arrived. She was a jumper whose approach was so graceful Coach Howard called her Doe. She also ran the 4x400 with Hothead. They did everything together. When Hothead was hitting her ex-boyfriend with flowers, Doe tried to jump in, but Loudmouth held her back. If Hothead swung on Ronny, Doe was going to join too. When I saw her take off her earrings, I sped up.

I collided with Aubrey. She stumbled back. I apologized and stepped toward my friends. A hand held my wrist. I looked down and saw her fingers digging into my skin.

Don't go over there, Aubrey said. I'm keeping out of it. You better do the same.

I yanked my wrist out of Aubrey's hand, her nails scratching as I pulled and ran to my friends. Aubrey returned to Jess and their friends. Behind Fast Life's shoulder, I saw Brandon, Ronny, and five other rednecks. Then Ronny said to Doe, What're you going to do about it, Fish Lips?

Y'all getting in girls' faces now? I said, stepping to the front.

J-Boogie tried to pull Fast Life and Tati back. He said it wasn't worth it.

Call the bitches off, Ronny said.

And the sand nigger too, Brandon said.

I pushed Brandon. He stumbled back. His crowd held him up. He leapt at me and grabbed my neck. Before I could pry him free, a dark-skinned fist connected with Brandon's cheek. He stumbled to the side and Loudmouth rushed him.

Bitch, he's Coolie, yelled Loudmouth.

Fast Life jumped at one of the other white boys. I swung on Brandon. He ducked and grabbed me. His arms wrapped around my waist and he tried to tackle me. Barely keeping my balance, I punched at his back. Over his head, I saw a bunch of white kids running toward us. I craned my neck and saw the rest of the sprinters joining in. In the middle of them, Twig sprinted toward us. He pulled Brandon off me and told me to get out of there. Loudmouth punched Brandon and Twig pushed me out of the crowd. I stumbled back and fell. Twig yelled to Aubrey and told her to get me out of there. Aubrey shook her head angrily, grabbed my arm, and led me away. I turned around and saw police officers running in. One held his Taser out toward my friends. Another held his hand by his waist holster.

The fuck I got to take care of you for? Aubrey said.

Let me go then, I said.

I tried to pull my hand from Aubrey's, but her grip was stronger this time. Her nails dug in, drawing blood. As she tugged me toward the parking lot, I gave in. I knew she was berating me about my scholarship and how I would lose it if I got arrested, but I wasn't listening. The sight of the officers rushing the crowd and the teenagers fleeing muted her as she pushed me into her car. Aubrey drove away before I saw how it ended.

Just after we turned onto US-1, Aubrey rolled down the window and lit a cigarette.

Over something someone said, she muttered, Can't believe I'm babysitting a grown-ass man.

Back off, Aubrey.

You trying to end up like your brother?

This ain't none of your business.

The hell it ain't. I ain't going to no more trials and I ain't visiting nobody else in jail, Daniel.

I can handle myself. Let me out, I said, unbuckling my seat belt.

You think I'm about to slow down? she said. You better tuck and roll.

I re-buckled my seat belt. Aubrey exhaled smoke and repeated, Can't believe I'm babysitting.

We drove in silence. Aubrey watched the windshield as she

smoked, the cold of early spring rushing through her window. The anger hot in my stomach cooled. Aubrey turned onto Palm Coast Parkway and we headed back into town. When the car stopped at Belle Terre, I turned to look at her. She looked back at me. Her thin, dark-brown eyebrows bore down, wrinkling the base of her forehead and the top of her nose. I chuckled.

The fuck are you laughing about? she said.

The laugh grew louder and my stomach lighter.

What you laughing at? she asked, biting her lower lip, trying to keep a straight face.

You got so mad.

Ain't shit funny out here, she said, stifling a chuckle. I'm serious, Daniel.

I'm saying though. I ain't never seen you this mad before. I ain't know your face got like that.

Like what?

I don't know, I say. You was kind of cross-eyed. Ain't never seen someone get cross-eyed mad before.

Aubrey slapped my arm.

Stop, she said. Stop it. This isn't fair.

I kept laughing.

Man, your eye was damn near kissing your nose.

Stop it, she said, laughing now. A car honked behind us. She raised her middle finger to her rear window and we both cracked up.

I'm still mad at you, she said, driving down Palm Coast Parkway.

My fault.

Aubrey and Twig and Loudmouth and so many others made sure I got home safe that night, as they did on many others. Once I started getting good grades and posting fast times, my teammates sped me out of bad situations and started fights to protect me. They made sure I could get the scholarship to make it out. At first, I thought they did so because they wanted me to succeed. Then I thought they guarded me because they weren't sure if they were going to get out of Palm Coast themselves. But if I escaped, we all did.

Remembering the nights my friends kept me safe, I worry that their loan was all for nothing, that I never repaid the debt I owed them, that I never got famous or rich. It's debt that I feel as I finally reach down and feel something hard and cold under the seat. I pull it out by the peeled leather handle with both hands. The barrel is long and metal, pockmarked and tarnished. A Magnum. I let one hand go and its weight, heavier than I expect and distributed differently than I remember, turns my wrist. It's been a long time since I've held a gun, since Twig stole his father's handgun and we shot glass bottles in the woods. I pop open the cylinder. The bullets inside shine. Then I close it and look around. There's no one else here. In the distance, police sirens flash blue and red atop a Dodge Charger. I duck and try to place the gun quickly but carefully, as though the slightest mistake will make it go off, back under the seat. Peeking just above the dashboard through the windshield, I see the cop swing around the curve on US-1 and disappear around the bend.

The fuck I need this for? I ask, turning to look at Loudmouth, who watches the passing train.

In case we get into any trouble.

What trouble you looking for?

Don't act dumb.

I ain't trying to shoot nobody and I ain't trying to get shot.

And what you going to do if he flips on us and we all the way out here in Espanola? Loudmouth says. You going to let me get shot?

The boxy train covered in graffiti proceeds as we sit still. Its sound follows its weight. The last car leaves our sight. For a moment, the barrier sits still and its warning lights continue blinking. Beyond its thin post, a wind shuffles loose pebbles. Then the railroad barrier raises. The ringing of its alarm stops. It's quiet. It will only get more so once Loudmouth presses on the gas and we head down that dirt road into Espanola, the town that arose years ago around Old Dixie Highway and then turned ghost when the interstate came in. After the people and the hotel left, it became a long unpaved stretch marked by the occasional farm, known now for the annual Cracker Day celebrations.

Shit done changed, Daniel. Ain't no more fistfights. Everybody's carrying now. So I need to know: You backing out?

His jaw shifts where he chews his cheek. His shoulders are raised and his arms are stiff. One hand holds the wheel tight. He is ready to keep going if I say the word. Knowing that Loudmouth will have my back again, years after my last fight, makes me nod slowly.

No, I say. I ain't backing out.

Then we cross the tracks. If I'm going to find more answers about what happened to Aubrey, this is the road they're on.

The Dead

Des turns off the music. On the pale dirt road, rocks kicked up by the tires sound like loose sand scuttling across a shore. We reach a slightly paved stretch, and the gravel clinks against the undercarriage. The car slides as we round a curve. In our rearview, a dust cloud hangs in the distance and then disappears.

Been a while since I been on a dirt road, I say.

Dirt roads and Confederate flags.

The thick forest to our right gives way to a clearing. Another field whose bright brown soil bears the marks of last season's tilling. Strands of pale straw are scattered across this one, but the patches of bright-green weeds resemble those on the last. I don't know how many fields we've crossed now. It feels like Palm Coast is miles behind us.

What's the play? Des asks.

Knock on the front door.

Find out if he was fucking your girl.

I begin to say Aubrey wasn't mine and she could sleep with whomever she wanted, but I refrain. Des might be right, but I don't want to think about that. In our quiet, I estimate how long we've been driving. With the music off, there's no record of time passing. We haven't missed a turn. There are no turns to take. But I don't remember the drive feeling this long. Did we take the wrong road in?

My mind slips to the picture of us. Viewed from the car window, we're two dark boys. Stubble and whiskers collect on our faces, sullying our lineups. The forest beyond Des blurs into nondescript wilderness. Then, seen from above, our car drives alone down this unpaved road. The field on our right comes to an end. Thickly settled trees replace it. The car disappears beneath their canopy.

You sure this the right road? Des asks.

Pretty sure, but it's been years since I been on it.

So long you forgot how to get there?

No, I say. Last time I came out here was senior year. Aubrey had to return something to Brandon. Fishing poles, I think. Came along for the ride. To tell the truth though, it's hard to remember.

If you lost, just let me know.

Ain't nobody lost, I say. It's just what happened with me and her done happened so long ago I can't tell if what I think happened is what happened.

Des rolls down the window and leans his arm out.

I keep remembering these jokes we told, he says, cracking on the bald-headed dude when we was out there picking up trash. But I don't know if I said it or if she said it. Tell the truth, I can't tell if anyone said it.

If you been thinking you said something for so long, you think that's what happened. Maybe if she was here, she'd tell you something different.

You been telling the same story for so long, it start to feel true.

�֍

What Aubrey knew is gone. I can't ask her about our memories or make up for any of the mistakes I made. Though I live my life by the belief that if I do wrong on Friday, I will repair it on Monday, next week will never come for Aubrey.

I think Mom and Grandma speak about the dead so much to keep the weeks going. They talk far more about Uncle Junior than his living sisters. They tell different stories about how Junior died.

According to Grandma, Uncle Junior befriended all the Jamaicans in high school. Teachers treated him and his friends poorly because they didn't understand islanders. Frustrated, Uncle Junior and his friends dropped out. His friends needed money, so they started selling, but Uncle Junior never did. Jobless, he struggled to make ends meet. He started gambling. Hoping to settle his debts, he met his friends in an abandoned warehouse. They played Russian roulette. He lost. They ran. The police ruled it a suicide.

According to Mom, Uncle Junior ignored the law-abiding Jamaicans and ran with a bad crowd in high school. They all dropped out to deal. A few years after that, in the late '80s, Mom got pregnant, moved out of Flatbush, and had my brother. Late one night, when my brother was still a baby, Uncle Junior banged on her door. Mom opened it a crack. Junior was covered in blood. Stab wounds pockmarked his shirt. He asked her to let him in. Mom said she couldn't endanger her child.

Two days later, Uncle Junior was found in an abandoned warehouse with a bullet in his head.

✳

I don't think Mom ever told Grandma that Junior came to her that night. The pain of grieving and the fear that Grandma would blame her silenced Mom. When they do talk about him, they mostly catalogue what they don't know about his passing: what the police found out in their investigation, who was there when he died, and why he didn't reach out before things got bad.

Since Aubrey passed, I've thought a lot about all the things I can't know about her because she was so secretive, in part because she broke laws and skipped school and in part because people talked about her too much. Rumors circulated about her temper, her home life, who she slept with. The lies I told about us made that worse. Now that she's gone, I don't know how to atone.

My brow tenses and my lips purse. The road curves and we slide with it. Around the bend, a large F-150 approaches, a rebel flag on its front plate. A brown cloud hangs behind it. Its headlights aren't on, but they point at us. As we near, I see brown streaks scattered across its body. They've just been mudding.

Des pulls over, reaches under the seat, and places the gun on his lap. Then he rests his chin on the other hand and perches a finger on his upper lip. I consider reaching for the Magnum under my seat. Anxiety floods my stomach. I don't know that I'll be able to hold the gun still.

Des looks ahead, and I stare out the window. In my peripherals, I keep track of the slowly moving truck. There's barely enough room to pass. Its mirrors near the car. They're less than a foot away. I resist the urge to look at them. They drive by. I lean forward, place my elbows on my knees, and run my hands over my face. Des eases us forward. I turn on the radio. Static. I turn it off.

After an exhale, I say, You hear she moved up north?

Who'd you hear that from?

Jess.

Blond girl with the glasses? The one who sat with you and Aubrey at lunch?

Yeah. Called her after Aubrey died. Jess said Aubrey was getting her life together. Moved in with her grandma. Became a bartender or a waitress or something like that. Met a dude who worked construction. Got engaged. Quit drinking. Was trying to quit smoking. Wanted to buy a house.

Who'd have thought? Des says.

Not me. Definitely don't sound like the Aubrey I know.

A dull pain begins throbbing in my right hip. I stretch my leg out, pull my knee back to me, and then repeat. An old track injury acting up, as it always does whenever I sit for too long. My leg bobs. I try to calm down, but I'm riled up. I picture myself throwing the door open and running out when Des slides to a stop at a paved, T-shaped intersection. Ahead lies the Espanola Fire Department. A single, shirtless man washes a fire truck. His hairless head shines in the sun. Black-ink tattoos cover his back. A faded bald eagle, stars dropping from its wings, words I can't read. He turns around as we stop and looks at us. His eyes are cold blue.

Turn right, I say.

A thicket of trees and bushes lines the road. They rustle with unseen deer or armadillos or boar. As we drive, branches extend over the road. Spanish moss colored golden by the late daylight sways in a breeze, frays like rope. To our left, squat houses sit twenty feet back from the road on permanent foundations, though they look like trailers. Grass driveways extend from them. Underwear hangs from a clothesline at the last one. At its edge is an uncleared lot where a dog trots, stops, and turns to us. As we pass, it runs with us until we outpace it.

Pretty close now, I say.

Can't believe you came out here to his house, Des says.

Ain't know how far out it was at the time. This was before the brawl, so I ain't really know him. He was just this dude who came through lunch sometimes when I was eating with Jess and Aubrey.

We leave the gathering of buildings and head into the woods again. The gravel road forks and we turn onto another dirt road. We pass an old, burned-down building, marked only by an exposed foundation, on top of which sit some cages. They look like they've been there for years, but I don't know what for. I shudder. On our left lies another field of scattered dead straw. A lone tree stands in its center. I think I see a silhouette of a man sitting at its base, back against its bark, but I might be seeing things, mistaking windmills for dragons. Above, pink gathers in thick ruffled clouds, rolling in with the night. Soon we'll be on this unlit dirt road in the dark.

✳

Being this far out on a dirt road makes me wonder why I'm here at all. Mom says we came to Palm Coast because of my great-grandmother. I never met her—she died when I was still living in Jamaica—but after we moved to the States, Grandma told me what she remembered. She was a caramel-skinned, strong-jawed woman who left Jamaica and Grandma just after World War II to find work.

Most of Grandma's stories were about their time together in Flatbush, where they reunited when Grandma moved to the States. Her mother helped her find work watching other people's children. They shared an apartment, but, according to Grandma, they were so tired when they returned home that they said little and fell asleep early. They spoke most while they drank their coffee in the morning before work, when it was still dark. Sometimes, Grandma said she was too tired to go to work, to which her mother always responded, No wait till drum beat before you grind ax. Other times, Grandma complained about the way her employers treated her, and her mother always responded, Every day devil helps thief; one day God will help watchman. Whenever Grandma told me about their mornings, her eyes lit up and she seemed like a child again, passing on her parents' explanations for the world like elementary-school kids at recess. She made me wish I had met my great-grandmother.

But Mom's stories make it seem like I was better off not having known her. According to Mom, she was a mean, stubborn old woman who disliked her children and her grandchildren. She made Grandma pay most of the rent on their one-bedroom apartment in Flatbush. After Grandma's mom retired in the '80s, she spent all day watching soap operas and every evening berating Grandma. Then, one afternoon, when Grandma's mom was watching *Days of Our Lives*, she saw an advertisement starring Erik Estrada. He stood on the deck of a boat bobbing in the Intracoastal. His unbuttoned shirt billowed in the wind. Water gleamed on his hairy chest. He spoke about the weather and the real-estate prices in Palm Coast. That night, Grandma's mom told Grandma she had to move there. Grandma borrowed money from her daughters to put a down payment on a house. Grandma's mom moved to Florida alone.

According to Mom, Grandma's mom fell ill in the early '90s, so Grandma moved down to take care of her. There was only one bed; Grandma slept on the sofa. After some months, Mom flew from Jamaica to visit them, leaving me and Junior with my father. That Sunday, at church, she overheard Grandma's mom tell the dark-skinned Jamaican women that Grandma was her Coolie helper.

✳

I have overheard my family argue about the kind of woman my great-grandmother was—nice or mean, racist or a product of her circumstances—so much that I learned not to trust anyone's remembrances of the dead. I certainly don't trust my memories of Aubrey or my motivations for being here.

I squint to see what lies in the distance and then look over both shoulders to see what's behind us. The road is clear on all fronts and the woods are beginning to look familiar, but who can tell the difference between one patch of forest and the next? Then, just ahead, on the clay-colored road, there is a small opening in the woods. Clay-colored dirt in the shape of two wheels marks a path. Pale-green grass shoots up from the driveway made by tires.

That's it on the left, I say.

You sure?

Positive.

Des slows at what looks like a snake. The wind stirs and it floats.

Just the skin, I say, wondering if it's from a rattlesnake. Des continues driving as trees crowd the road. The open fields feel long gone. The sky is hard to see through the canopy.

Nigga, where are you taking me?

Des stops. He looks around. Then he turns left. The woods continue on both sides. The bark shines golden, and the leaves and the grass a bright green. They look untouched, as if they have shone this color for many sunsets before, as if the animals live in homes long settled. Brandon has walked through these woods with a gun, I am sure, hunting them.

After a half a minute, the driveway branches out and we approach a square wood house, raised from the ground by a wood foundation. It's small, maybe three rooms. I wonder if it was built by hand or if they somehow got a truck down these roads.

The building is paler than it was when I came out here with Aubrey, just after Jess and Brandon had broken up. She asked me to stay in the car and met Brandon on his porch. She said something and tried to hand him the poles, but he didn't take them. Then she dropped them on the ground. He yelled. She yelled back. While his voice was still raised, Aubrey turned around, rushed back into the car, and slammed the door behind her. Tears collected small dots of mascara at the corners of her eyes as she turned the engine on. Her hair was slipping out of her ponytail and into her face as she drove out. I asked if she wanted to talk. She didn't say anything. We were silent until we reached US-1, and I spent the whole drive wondering what she said to Brandon, the boy who became the man sitting there today on the porch in the shadow of the sunset.

That's him, I say.

Des parks the car on the side of the yard and gets out. His shorts sag on the left, his gun weighing him down. I leave mine under the seat, feeling a little foolish for coming out here and even more so for letting Des almost talk me into carrying his Magnum. Nothing's going to happen; Des's just being paranoid. Then again, we are out here on a dirt road in what might be a sundown town. Maybe we should turn around, leave well enough alone.

Before I can make a decision either way, Des starts walking toward the house. I get out of the car. Brush rustles all around us, some unseen animal stirring it. Maybe it's just the wind picked up by ears perked for something dangerous. Aside from the rustles, it's quiet. The day is cool but the air is thick with the scent of soil. Somehow, I feel much farther from home, though we have only driven thirty feet off the main road.

I follow Desmond to the house, which seems like it sprang from nowhere. Brandon's beard is longer than I remember. Red patches obscure his lips. His eyes are glass, liquid brimming at the surface. He's staring at the unmarked bottle of brown liquor in his hands. My stomach feels uneasy with nausea. Brandon looks up and I say, It's Daniel.

He leans his head against the wall behind him and pulls his brim low.

Me and Des, I say.

Well, I'll be damned, he says.

Heard about Aubrey, bro, I say. Tore me up real bad.

Shit. How you think I feel?

Worse, I figure. But I ain't been able to talk to nobody up north who knew her like I knew her.

Brandon waves us up to the porch and holds out the bottle.

Ain't much left, he says, but it helps.

The bottle is warm in my hands and the alcohol even more so in my mouth. It stings my gums enough that I don't taste it. I swallow and it leaves a hot trail down my throat and in my core. I pass the bottle to Des. He shakes his head and I shove it in his arms.

Who posted bail? Des asks.

My dad.

How long you out for?

Next court date's next month.

What're your chances? I ask.

Whole world knows I was driving drunk, he says. Ain't no way in hell I'm going to win the case. Just trying to get less time.

I shake my head and the silence lingers. Then I ask, Brandon, man. I got to know. What happened? Why was she down here?

Came down to see her grandma, Brandon says. She was diagnosed with cancer a few months ago. After Aubrey heard the news, she decided to get hitched. Wanted her grandma to be there. Then her grandma got worse so she came down to see her. Said it was in case she didn't make it to the wedding.

I grab the bottle from Des and take another swig. My breathing slows and my face warms. I look around for something to lean against. I walk to the post at the porch's corner and perch my back against its rough wood. I swig again. My throat and chest burn.

Easy on the drink, Baby D, Des says.

I'm good, I say. Go on, Brandon.

So Aubrey comes down, he says. She's mostly with her grandma so we don't see her till the last night. Me, Jess, Ronny, and her meet up at the Roadhouse. Jess ain't drinking because she said she'd drive Aubrey home. I drove up there, but I'd driven US-1 drunk a million times so I figure I'm fine.

Brandon stops talking and I pass the bottle back to him. He pulls from it and then starts to roll a cigarette, staring down at the loose brown strands in the paper.

So we're drinking and having a good time when Jess says her and Aubrey got to go. She's got to work in the morning. We try to convince them to stay out but she ain't having it. Says she's going home. I say I can drive Aubrey. Jess asks if I'm sure. I say yeah. Jess says it's up to her. And Aubrey, I guess Aubrey wanted to stay out for a bit. Ain't been home in a long while.

Brandon strikes a match and lights his cigarette. The paper burns unevenly so the ember forms a red shard at its end.

You drove? Des asks.

We all done it, Brandon says. I'm just the one who crashed.

Des, chill, I say.

Brandon pulls from his cigarette. Smoke comes out when he says, Aubrey's looking different. Cheeks filled out. Must've been eating right. Smiling the whole night. So it's getting late and Ronny gets in his truck and we get in mine. We're driving and talking and I can't believe I ain't tell her I loved her. She's about to get married to some Northern chump I ain't never met and I ain't never told her.

I drink again and it burns less. My eyes droop a little and my body loosens. But my hands are clenched tight, uncut nails digging into my palms.

So we're speeding down US-1 and I figure this is my last chance. I tell her it's me she should be marrying. And I'm trying to look her in the eyes, but it's hard because I'm driving and we been drinking. So I'm looking at her and then the road. I'm bouncing back and forth and I say it. But Aubrey, she just starts shaking her head. Asks why I'm telling her this. Says I know she's getting married. Says she didn't fly down here for this bullshit. Says she left for a reason. So she rolls down the window and puts a smoke in her mouth. Gets real quiet. And me, I'm freaking out. Talk to me, Aubrey. But she's looking through her bag because she can't find her lighter. I say it again. Talk to me. She says she ain't got nothing to say. Turns the light on in the car. Keeps digging for her lighter. Aubrey, look at me. Say something. Don't ice me out.

Brandon takes a long drag on his cigarette.

Next thing I know, I'm on the side of the road. Windshield's broke. Glass all over the dash. Aubrey ain't in the car. I try to move but I'm stuck. Then I wake up in the hospital handcuffed.

❖

Normally, my brother calls once or twice a month. Around the time of Aubrey's death, I hadn't heard from him in almost a season. Then, a few days after I got the news, he called and said he'd been in and out of solitary. Some white folk tried him on the yard. His boys had his back, but they all ended up in the hole. He was there the longest. When he got out, they tried him again and he ended up in solitary again.

Junior asked what I was up to. Time was running out on the call. Not knowing what to say, I told him I was staying near where Uncle Junior used to live.

Sometimes, he said, his name feels like a death sentence.

We were quiet for a moment. Then I told him Aubrey died. Junior didn't know who she was. I told him she was my ex-girlfriend.

White girl?

Yeah, I said. Went to high school with her.

The little dark-haired redneck? The one you started dating after I got locked up? The bitch who ain't like niggas?

Yeah, I said. She was racist and I was sexist. But I loved her.

I don't know, baby bro. Folks she hung out with probably the same folks jumping me on the yard.

✳

If Brandon is convicted, he might be sent to the same prison, become one of those men jumping my brother. My stomach boils. I walk to the end of the porch, and it feels like they are miles away. Water begins to collect in my eyes, aching with what's coming, but I blink it back.

The light coming through the woods is gray now. The sun must almost be down. I lean off the porch and look around the house. In the distance, the sky above the trees is pink, but behind me, it's a dark blue, approaching black. A sunset ending in one direction and night coming in strong in the other, I must look less like a man than a shadow on his porch.

That's the whole story, Brandon says.

I'm shaking my head and trying to inhale deep to calm myself but can't. My breath moves fast and out of control. So many of my people have died young. I don't want to be another Henriquez led to an early grave or to prison, but I feel the heat rushing to my head, the fear of death fading, and the dead possessing me. I am near yelling when I say, Jess's going to drive, but you take Aubrey home anyway. Then you tell her you love her while you're driving. Not when you drop her off. Not in Palm Coast. Not at the bar. You tell her when you're driving at eighty miles an hour.

My body is hot and I don't know if it's the day, the alcohol, or the anger. I breathe faster. I step toward Brandon. Des shifts on his feet.

You ain't think this shit could wait? I ask.

It was dumb, he says. It was wrong.

I approach Brandon. He stands up quickly and his chair falls over with a thump.

Lord knows it was dumb, he says, backing away and stepping down from the porch.

You killed her, I say, following after him.

Brandon starts to walk faster and I do too. He hops over the steps into the ankle-length grass and I follow. He backpedals toward the woods and I chase. He turns to run when I close the distance at the edge of the first gathering of trees. He's half facing away when I grab his shirt cuff with one hand. I swing with the other. He tumbles backward into the long grass and I fall with him.

Crouched over him, I say, That's it?

I punch at his face, but he moves to the side. My fist hits the ground. Pain shoots up my knuckles and through my forearm.

Daniel, he says, grabbing my arms and trying to push me off.

You fucking killed her, I say.

Leaning over him, I'm pulling on my arms to get free, but he won't let go. His grip is tight. The pressure shoots pain up the bone.

Daniel, someone's coming, Des says.

You killed her.

We got to go.

Lord knows I ain't scared of you.

You fucking killed her.

Time's up, Baby D, Des says as he grabs me by the collar and tries to pull me off. Brandon's hands drag along my forearm, burning them with friction. He pushes me away and swings but misses. I lunge at him and swing wildly.

We got to get the fuck out of here.

I hear a truck approach and pull to a stop. Des turns around and puts his hand on his waist. I jump back on Brandon. I start swinging but he grabs me. He won't give me any room. He knees at me and I do the same, but there's not enough distance to connect with any real force.

Get off my boy, I hear.

I knee Brandon in his side and hear the air leave his body in a wheeze.

This ain't none of your business, old-timer, Des says. Get back in the car.

I said get off my son before I shoot.

I turn around and see the old man's pistol pointed at me. Des draws his and aims at the old man.

I ain't going to tell you boys again.

I'm getting up, I say. I'm getting up slowly.

I roll off Brandon and onto my knees. I put my hands in the air.

I'm getting up slowly.

I struggle to raise myself without my hands. I stumble and then catch myself. Finally, I stand up, hands parallel to my face, palms facing the old man.

That's right boy, says the old man.

Fuck are you calling a boy? Des says.

Better do like your friend there and put your hands up, says the old man, before I blow a hole in his face.

Better put your gun down, old man.

The old man stands in front of the truck, which blocks the road out. The barrel points at my face. I can see the shadow it casts over the path the bullet will travel. In my peripherals, I see Des opposite him, feet planted in the middle of their barely mowed yard. His hands clench his pistol's handle. His arms bulge. They are no more than ten paces from each other. At this distance, they won't miss.

Des, it ain't worth it, I say.

Put the gun down, Des says.

You first, the old man says.

Behind the old man, I see another truck approaching, rising and falling with the terrain of the woods. Branches snap as it slows. The windshield is tinted black. I don't know who or how many people sit behind it.

Des, if we're going to get out of here, we got to go now.

I ain't letting him blast you, Brown.

The second truck's door opens. I look at the old man. My hands are up. Our car is too far to run for. I hear the car door slam.

Des, put the gun down, I say.

Listen to your friend, boy.

I ain't putting shit down till you put yours down.

Then I hear a roar loud enough to shatter an eardrum and I drop to the ground.

Returns

My ears ring. I only hear a high pitch. I don't feel any pain. Am I in shock? My hands rush to my body, searching for a wound. Nothing. The ringing quiets and is replaced by a sound that resembles hearing a wave passing overhead. Then comes the slight pitter-patter of feet. And, finally, a voice: All right, boys. Guns down.

My stomach is flat against the rocky ground, which itches my arms and scratches my chin. A woman stands in front of the truck wearing jeans and a tank top. The long rifle points up as she looks at us. Her hair is shoulder-length and blond, but a shadow cast over her face hides her features. She's a silhouette framed by the truck and the sky's dying light.

Mr. Jacobs, Desmond, guns away.

The old man crouches. His head darts from side to side, scanning the area. To his right, Desmond lies flat on the ground. I can't see his gun. He's not moving. Did they hit him? His head turns. He's safe too.

Come on, now, says the familiar voice. Get your asses off the floor.

Bright-blue eyes peer beneath the shaded brow.

Jessica Ann? the old man calls. Though its end points down, he still clutches the gun tight as he searches his periphery. Now raised to one knee, Desmond does the same.

That's right, Mr. Jacobs, Jess says. It's me. Just a warning shot.

That's one hell of a warning, Mr. Jacobs says, shaking his head.

Go on and get up off the ground, she says. Ain't nobody going to shoot you. They're friends of mine.

They're on my property.

They ain't mean nothing by it, she says, and they wasn't going to hurt no one. You know them Palm Coast boys, they all bark.

The old man stands up and dusts himself off, but still holds on to his gun.

Palm Coast's a long way off, he says.

They're friends of Aubrey's.

Wish I'd known, the old man says as he points his weapon down.

Desmond, put your gun down and get up. Otherwise I'm going to tell your mama about how you damn near got yourself killed out in Espanola.

Damn, Jess, Desmond says. You ain't got to worry my mom like that.

Desmond stands up and tucks his gun in his waistband. Then he runs his hand over his forehead.

Daniel, Brandon, she says, ain't no use rolling around in the dirt all day.

When I stand up, Brandon's still on the ground. His arms wobble when he plants them on the ground. He is close enough for me to help him up, but I watch him come to his feet. He pulls a can of dip out of his cargo shorts and his hands grow still.

Now, I know y'all ain't out here scrapping over a dead girl, she says.

My cheeks burn and I inhale deep. The dirt we turned up rushes in, smelling of iron, of blood.

Should've let y'all finish the job, Mr. Jacobs says. Least I wouldn't have to worry about him no more.

Come on, Pops, Brandon says. I done said sorry a million times.

Mr. Jacobs, Jess says, we talked about this.

Old dogs, Mr. Jacobs says. Then he walks to his truck, places his gun inside, and says, Reckon I owe y'all an apology.

Mr. Jacobs gets in and pulls into the yard. After he parks, he tells Jess to say hello to her folks and walks into his home. Brandon follows, spitting brown liquid, and I watch him as he goes. My lungs still heave, my head's still hot. I want to rush him, tackle him as he ascends the steps, slam his body into the porch and my fists into his ribs. But I bite my lower lip, the sharp pain erasing the image as he disappears inside the house. After the door closes, Mr. Jacobs, muffled by the house, yells. Metal clanks and something heavy thumps.

Desmond, Daniel, y'all ain't got to say sorry, Jess says.

I ain't saying sorry to nobody, Desmond says.

Shaking her head, Jess puts her rifle in the car and walks across the yard toward Desmond. She forms a fist close to her chest and swings at him. She doesn't lean her shoulder into it. Her arm isn't quite straight.

Goddammit, Desmond, Jess says.

What you mad at me for? Desmond says. I ain't do shit wrong.

That ain't entirely true, I say, chuckling.

Jess turns around and her hair sweeps with her.

Don't you go acting all high and mighty neither.

This nigga, he says.

Y'all both should've known better, she says. You seen what he looked like when y'all rolled up.

As something clangs and voices scream in the house, the wind stirs. It picks up as night falls and the air grows cooler. It's thick, comforting in a way. But soon it'll be cold.

Sorry, I say. I just lost it.

Jess walks back to her truck.

Can't believe I got to babysit y'all two, she says. And you. You ain't even tell me you was coming back.

I'm here now, I say. You can get mad at me and we can go another ten years without talking, or we could hang tonight.

Jess gets in the truck and says through the open door, My house. Dinner. Hour and a half. If you're lucky, I won't be so goddamn mad.

Jess slams the door and drives away. Desmond and I walk back to the car. The wind rustles in the woods and the thumps inside the house continue. My mind is running. Jess knows what happened between Aubrey and me, what I've hidden from everyone else. There's no way I'll be able to keep up the act when we see her again. And when the truth comes out, I don't know what Desmond will do.

I thought coming home would feel different. We would have some drinks, sit around a back porch, and talk about Aubrey. When the alcohol hit me, my shoulders would drop. If I stood, I might stumble. And when the liquor was warm in my stomach, I'd tell everyone how much Aubrey's death wrecked me and how, even though I haven't spoken to her in a long time, I fell in love with her again. I felt it in my chest every time I thought about her. Everyone would get real quiet until someone would pat me on the back and say I wasn't crazy; they felt it too.

Instead, I dragged Desmond all the way out to Espanola. If it wasn't for Jess, I might have gotten shot. I might have died. Desmond might have too. Or he might have caught a case, ended up with my brother.

�֍

Maybe the memories of Jamaicans returning to danger are why Mom told me not to come back here. Home wasn't safe for her or her stepfather. When she lived with him in New Monklands in the '60s, every Friday, he stuffed his week's earnings in cash into his rucksack and hopped in the back of his boss's truck with the other workers. They drove down the hills until the road became gravel and houses began to appear. In town, Mom's stepfather deposited his earnings at the bank. If he had extra time, he drank rum at a nearby bar and listened to cricket or football on the radio until it was time to return.

One Friday, after he hopped out of his boss's truck and walked back to his home, he saw his front door open. He called to Grandma. No response. He called to Mom. Nothing. He entered the house with his handgun out. No one was in the front room, though the furniture was turned on its side and books were spread across the ground. In the second room, rope bound his wife and daughter to their chairs.

Mom's stepfather unbound Grandma and Mom, who cried immediately. When he untied her arms, she latched onto him, digging her head into his side so his pants dried her tears. Grandma said they used her name. It was someone they knew. Mom's stepfather asked if she saw who it was. Grandma said no. He rolled a cigarette and asked Grandma what they took. The guns.

�֎

From then on, every Friday that Mom's stepfather returned from the bank, he entered the home with his gun drawn. He taught Grandma how to shoot in case the robbers ever returned, though they never did. He didn't know how else to protect his family.

I reach under the driver's seat, pull the Magnum out, and run my hand along the cold barrel, careful to point it at the door, though my fingers are nowhere near the trigger. I place it back under the seat.

We've already passed countless fields, the ruins of the old building, and the fire station. We've exited the paved road and are back on Hargrove. The sky is a dark blue now, a hint of light keeping its color. Spanish moss hangs above us like long fingers reaching for the car roof.

What're you going to tell Egypt? I ask.

About what?

Scrapping with Brandon. Almost getting shot.

Ain't telling Egypt a damn thing, Desmond says. Least, I ain't got to tell her nothing long as you keep your mouth shut. Now, you already know how I'm fixing to tell J-Boogie and Earl. I was brawling with about ten or fifteen rednecks. Kicking them in the chest. Fucking them up Bruce Leeroy style when you lost your shit.

Oh, so this my fault?

Nigga, you the reason Brandon's pops pulled over to begin with.

You the dumbass that brought the gun.

What you think would've happened if I ain't bring my piece? Desmond says. Shit, if I wasn't carrying, I'd be calling your mom right about now. Telling her how you bleeding out in a no-name town.

Man if you wasn't packing, I would've stepped off Brandon and we'd be straight.

You keep telling yourself that.

I shake my head, roll my eyes, and lower the window. The air is just about the temperature of early morning in late spring, when I walked from my house to the school bus stop and the night's chill lingered. I hang my arm out the window and the wind buoys my hand up. After some time, the cool stings.

Jess looked bad with that rifle though, Desmond says. Never looked at her twice before. But today, bro? My God.

You serious right now? I'm about to get shot and you over there trying to beat?

Ain't nobody trying to smash, he says. Don't go spreading that rumor neither. I was just, you know, looking.

Desmond turns to look at me. The light of the console shines on his teeth when he smiles. Then he laughs until I do too. My stomach bubbling with the fading adrenaline, I lean my head out the window and laugh more, feeling as invulnerable as I always do after a close call with death. The wind in my ears roars as loud as the rush after the gunshot, but I keep laughing, as if I want everyone in Espanola to hear. When the fit subsides, I look up. Through the tree branches hanging over the car, every few seconds, the night peeks out. Even this early in the evening, the stars are out. There are more of them than I have seen in a while.

When outside is too cold, I pull my head back in and roll my window up. After a few moments of silence, Desmond turns to me and says, I ain't playing about telling Egypt. We been fussing recently. Last thing I need is for her to hear I'm out in Espanola chasing down some white girl.

Don't trip, bro.

Mind if we go get her? Told her she'd see you tonight.

I'm only here for another half day, I think. If I don't see Egypt now, I don't know when I will.

Let's go get her then, I say.

There's nowhere to turn on this thin one-lane road. There isn't even enough room to turn around. We're on this path until we reach its end. I picture myself throwing the door open, tucking and rolling, disappearing into the night. Then I run my hands over my face and shake my head.

You good? Desmond asks.

I'm good.

At the dirt road's end, we stop in front of the railroad tracks. On the other side is Palm Coast. Once we cross, we'll be heading to Egypt's and, eventually, Jess's. I heard that she runs a restaurant out of her home. I can't imagine it's legal, but it doesn't seem like much of a secret either.

Des looks both ways and makes sure a train isn't coming. We cross the tracks and then he stops on the first patch of paved road.

Tell the truth, Baby D, Desmond says, I ain't know you had it in you.

What you mean?

Thought you were going to chicken out way before we got there. Thought maybe you'd listen to Brandon and walk away. Never thought you were going to swing on him.

Ain't think I was going to neither, I say. But I just heard him talking and felt like I was in high school again. It just took hold of me and I rushed him. Tell the truth, felt kind of good, but it kind of ain't.

Desmond opens the window. A mosquito flies in. He swats at it and misses. Then he guides it out of the car and rolls the window up.

Ain't you had no other girls in your life? Desmond asks.

Had other folks, I say.

Way you lost it back there, wouldn't have thought you had no other girls.

A sedan approaches. Its headlights make me squint. Desmond stares ahead without moving. As we wait to see what the car is doing, I wonder if it's time to tell the truth. I don't know how Desmond will react. I can't imagine he's as homophobic as he was in high school, but it's been so long since I've been home that I don't know where anyone stands. Without warning, the car ahead drives toward us. Des pulls over and they pull alongside us and lower their window. A family fills its seats. Des lowers his window too.

Y'all know where the nearest gas station is? the driver asks.

Des gives directions, and they turn around and drive back onto US-1. In the renewed quiet, I figure now is as good a time as any.

Truth is, I say, I ain't had no other girls.

Nigga, ain't you just say you had other girls?

Had other folks.

Oh, he says. Then he doesn't say anything. After a few moments, Desmond turns to look at me. Then he turns back. He pulls his hand from the wheel and rests it in his lap.

Should've figured, he says. Fruity way you stretched.

Way I stretched?

Ain't no straight man that flexible.

You just mad I was faster than you.

I chuckle and Desmond does too. A deeper quiet than the one before settles. Ahead of us, headlights race left and right. They appear for a moment and then disappear around the bend. I chew on the inside of my lip. Desmond has not said anything for quite some time. I wrinkle my nose to scratch the itch on my nostril's inside, where a hair grows too long and tickles me. Still quiet.

How long you known? he asks.

You asking if I was checking you out in the locker room? I joke. Desmond remains quiet. I continue, College.

What happened?

Wasn't any one thing, I say. Ain't know right away. But when I got to college, people was calling me out for saying shit's gay. For calling people fags. Started to talk different. Wasn't nobody concerned with who I was fucking. Started to think different. It was like, for the first time, it seemed possible. Started to look at dudes differently. Realized when they were hitting on me. I got to wondering if they knew something about me I ain't know about myself. Sooner or later, took a guy up on it. Then I started thinking differently about all the folks I kicked it with in high school.

So you was crushing on me, he says.

Not you, I say, and then pause, cheeks warming as though I'm still a teenager when I say, Twig.

Twig? Damn, this nigga always chasing after white folk, Desmond says, laughing and shaking his head. He looks at me and then laughs louder. I join in.

Then, in the quiet, I ask, You going to be weird about this? Weird how?

I don't know, bro. I know folks down here ain't always that nice about this.

Nigga, Desmond says, turning to look at me. It's 2015.

I'm saying though.

We got a nigga in the White House. He's cool with y'all. Y'all getting married and shit. On TV and shit. And you think I'm tripping over who you date? You think we ass-backwards down here? Keep on talking like that and I'm going to have to go upside your head.

Desmond chuckles and eases the car forward. The ride is smooth and the seat beneath me feels solid as we wait for the traffic to let up so we can merge onto US-1.

So we cool? I ask.

Yeah, we cool, Desmond says. Long as you don't hit on me.

Man, why y'all always think we coming for you.

Cause a nigga know a nigga's cute, Desmond says. Shit, I get bitches. I get mad bitches. If I wasn't talking to Egypt, bro, there'd be about ten or twenty bitches blowing up my phone all day.

Whatever, bro, I say. Way you talking, I don't even know if Egypt want you that bad.

Desmond punches me in the arm. I shrink away into the car door.

Oh, you scared? he says.

Ain't nobody scared of nothing.

We turn onto US-1. The road is dark but filled with cars. Twig's friends and I used to take US-1 south on Saturday nights to go to Ormond for the Movies or north to go to Saint Augustine to walk around Saint George's and look for rules to break. These cars are probably doing the same, racing past Flagler County. But I don't know where they're going anymore.

You been with other people though? Desmond asks.

Yeah, I been with other people.

No one serious?

Since college, one.

White? Spanish? Asian?

Black.

When?

Up till a few weeks ago.

Caribbean? I know you been fucking on some islanders up in New York.

More like they been fucking on me, I think to myself. Then I say, Yeah man, he's Jamaican.

Must be funny, he says. Two Jamaican men fucking. I bet y'all be like, Come here battyboy.

You really think we call each other battyman?

What else y'all call each other?

When our chuckling subsides, even though cars surround us, US-1 is quiet without the radio on. We ride the curve approaching the L section and stop at a red light. Desmond rolls his window down and I follow suit. The air here is lighter and cooler than in Espanola.

So what? he asks. You heard about Aubrey and you just broke it off?

Something like that.

�֍

Now that we're heading back into Palm Coast proper, now that I have come out to Des and nothing has happened, I want to let my guard down, but I still don't feel safe. Maybe, like Mom, I never will. She never got over the robbery that happened when she was a child or that night in the late '90s, when she came back to Jamaica from visiting Grandma's mom and picked us up from my father's house. It was dark when we returned home. The car's headlights lit a yellow square of our driveway as we parked. Mom opened the front door. Books lay strewn across the ground. Nearby, a vase was broken into thick green shards the color of a frozen sea, dark soil and a flower sitting on their ice.

Mom cursed. Then she told Junior and me to wait by the door while she checked the house. When she returned, she told us to go through our things. I went to my room. My sheets were tucked in, the drawers unopened, the clothes in them still folded. I returned to the living room and sat on the couch, knees close to my chest. Minutes later, Junior returned and said they took his Super Nintendo and the allowance in his underwear drawer. Mom said they took the money in her nightstand. Then she called the cops.

After what felt like an hour, they arrived. Two tall men wearing freshly starched uniforms stepped out of the car. One examined the perimeter with a flashlight as the other spoke to my mother. He asked where her husband was. She said she didn't have one. When the other cop returned, he said the grills on the kitchen window were cut. They probably used a blow torch.

You have a gun? the cop asked.

Mom shook her head.

No man and no gun? he asked. Miss, you from here?

Where me look like me from? she said. Me favor boar-faced Coolie to you?

I just asking, miss.

Clarendon.

Your daddy have a gun when you grow up? She nodded. Him teach you how to shoot? She nodded again. Must get a gun. Woman can't live alone without one.

No one ever broke into our house again, but every time I returned home, I was afraid that someone was inside. As a child, I worried about monsters; as I got older, I feared armed robbers. When I opened the door and people didn't appear, I checked closets and under my bed in case a burglar hid there, not that I would have been able to protect myself if I did find someone.

I feel those old worries returning, shortening my breath, as we enter Palm Coast. Hoping to stamp them out, I ask Des, When did you and Egypt start? Last I checked, you was chasing her but she wasn't paying you no mind.

Desmond looks at me in the corner of his eye and says, That ain't how I see it.

How you see it then?

Don't know, bro. After you left, after we graduated, after folks started going off to college, wasn't too many of us around.

Mom lost her job. Money got tight, even tighter than before. I got real introverted. Not sad, you know. I wasn't depressed or nothing. Just working a lot. Had to. Making up for Mom not making nothing. Car wash during the day and Ruby Tuesday's at night. Cutting hair whenever I could. Was too busy to kick it with the folks who stayed behind because they was all taking classes at DBCC. They was all on that college-student schedule and I wasn't free till about ten or eleven. Even if I did have the time, I always rushed home when I got off from Ruby Tuesday's. Brought leftovers. It was usually the only thing my mom ate for dinner. She probably could've made food or taken a little bit of what we had to buy something, but she wouldn't eat without me.

Wish I'd known.

What was you going to do? Desmond says. You was a student.

Could've sent you whatever I had.

You ain't had nothing.

Desmond rolls down the window and lights a cigarette. Though it's dark, the bones in his face are more pronounced now, his eyes more sunken in.

After about nine months, he continues, got tired of working so much. When Mom got a job at Publix, I quit Ruby Tuesday's. Started thinking about going back to school. You know, my grades wasn't never good so I couldn't go away. Started taking classes at DBCC. Figured I'd get my associate's, maybe transfer somewhere else. At the very least, get me a job that ain't have me on my feet all day. Walk into that first class—college writing—and there she is. Girl I used to spit game to in high school grown up a little, put some weight in places she ain't used to have it, lost some in places only kids have it. I sit next to her and start jawing. She rolling her eyes and chuckling. When she finally opens her mouth, she talking about how she ain't seen me in a minute. Figured I done forgot about her. You know the kid's slick so I let her know I ain't without seeming too thirsty. Then the professor walks in and starts class. But you know me, I got to keep cracking jokes. So I'm trying to whisper to her and Egypt cuts her eyes at me. I figure it's about something else, so I whisper again. She tells me to shut up.

Egypt? That girl hated school.

I'm saying though, Desmond says, turning left into the L section. Through the window, the air blowing in smells of fresh cut grass. The scent is so strong I can almost feel it, soft but prickly beneath my feet. There were so many days after practice that Desmond and I took off our spikes and walked barefoot across the field. Now grass turns my skin itchy, red.

I don't know, bro, he continues. Maybe she took them classes seriously because she paid for them. Maybe it was because there wasn't much else to do, especially after everyone left. Or maybe she thought classes would get her somewhere. Either way, seeing how serious she took school made me think different. She busy writing all these notes in lecture and I can't have her thinking I'm dumb. Pull out my paper and start writing too. End of class, I said we should kick it. She said she was busy. Knew she wasn't because there ain't shit to do round here, but I let it slide. Said maybe next time. Think she seen the change in me though after a couple weeks of me being quiet in class and taking notes all the way to the margins and shit. Sooner or later she made time.

Feel like y'all learned some shit I'm still trying to learn, I say.

Desmond turns to me and smiles as if surprised. The

moment passes quickly. He looks back at the road and flicks the butt out the window, blows smoke after it.

Egypt smart though. Let me in a little but kept her distance. Wouldn't kick it with me alone, so I was always meeting her and Tati out somewhere. Starbucks. The beach. The barbecue joint. Ain't too many places to go, so we hit the same spots a few times. I ain't mind though. Figured I had plenty of time now that my future looking long, way longer than it looked when we was running laps and I ain't think I was going to make it past high school. And I liked Tati. She ain't take no shit.

Bet she got you into trouble.

No question, Desmond says. She almost got my ass beat a few times for talking sideways to some redneck. I always got real mad at her in the moment, but everything always worked out, so sooner or later I got proud of her. She wasn't letting nothing around here stop her.

At a stop sign, Desmond leans back. He looks to his left. Over a one-floor house's roof and a cluster of overlapping tree shadows, which look like an army amassed in the distance, the stars peek out.

Sooner or later, he continues, I must've gotten Tati's seal of approval because Egypt invited me back to hers one night. We coasted like that for a while. Everything was real cool. Then Tati and Egypt got close to finishing their degrees. Started talking about transferring to UNF or UCF. I said I'd join them. My grades weren't great, but they was better than they was in high school. Future started looking real big, like I might live in Orlando or Jacksonville. Never thought I'd live anywhere else before.

You living in Central Florida? I say. Two hours from the beach?

I'm saying though, Desmond says, we was dreaming real big. You don't even know. Then Tati's mom died. Her and Egypt was spending lots of time together. Sometimes I was there too, but not much. It's too hard to talk about feeling sad and shit with niggas you ain't that close with.

Someone honks. Desmond jumps, then eases forward and drives along.

Forgot we was on the road, I say.

Ain't forget, he says. Just ain't care.

We drive in silence for a little. Desmond rolls down the window, then rolls it back up, as though he were considering smoking again and then decided against it.

Then Tati joined the military, I say.

Right, he says. Fucked Egypt up real bad. Decide she ain't want to transfer till Tati left. So she got a job working the front desk for some realtor. I was still working at the car wash. We was just filling our time with work and kicking it and feeding ourselves I guess. But when Tati left, I think she got scared. Her mom fell and had to get knee surgery and go to rehab and Egypt was helping her through it. Figure she got worried about what'd happen to her parents if she left.

Or maybe the cost scared her off, Des continues. Her pops ain't never recover from 2008, so she'd have to pay for college all on her own. The day she seen what tuition cost at UCF, all of a sudden she talking about how she could take classes at DBCC and become a nurse or a dental assistant, about how she could make good money and live cheap in Palm Coast. Sooner or later, she stopped talking about leaving. I finished my classes and did the same. We just been living that way since. Wake up, work, eat, maybe see each other, go to bed, do the same thing the next day. Maybe go to a bar or put something in the air on Fridays and Saturdays. Start the week over again.

After a row of near identical homes in the L section, Desmond pulls into a redbrick driveway and parks behind a black SUV and a small silver coupe. The lawn here is perfectly kept, as are the hedges in front of the house, the small line of flowers in front of them, and the carefully laid stones at their base.

Let me talk to Egypt real quick, Desmond says, stepping out of the car.

The summer after we graduated, when Desmond got his car, she used to run out of the house and slam the grille on the front door behind her. Its clang sounded like the high pitch of a hammer striking steel. Her father always yelled about the noise, but she kept running, rolling her eyes as she did. Today, Egypt stands on the step in front of the grille, leans into the house to kiss her mother on the cheek, and closes the door softly. Desmond meets her in the driveway. She stands an arm's distance from him. Egypt's mouth moves quickly, but I can't hear what they're saying. He shrugs. She shakes her head. Desmond gestures to the car. She rolls her eyes. He kisses her on the cheek and then waves me out.

Outside, the night is brighter than I expected. Stars cover the sky from one end to the other. I walk over to Egypt and Desmond. She smiles. At the edge of her lips, a soft pink cloud sits just beneath where her cheekbones jut out and I can see the one-half Ethiopian she would never let me forget. I wish I looked like her, I think to myself as she walks toward me, her smile growing and her steps awkwardly long like that of a child forbidden from running in the school hallways. She throws her arms around my neck, clutches tight, and then pulls away.

Look at you, looking all grown, Egypt says. But why y'all covered in dirt?

Ask Des, I say.

He told me to ask you.

He got the story.

What'd that fool get you into?

Egypt lets go, her hands slide to her hips, and she looks at Desmond.

Nothing, Egypt. Damn, he says. He just kidding.

Egypt crosses her arms. Lips pouting, she stands about a half foot beneath Desmond, letting him hold her.

You better watch yourself, she says.

See what I'm talking about? he says.

I don't want no part of this, I say.

What you were saying about what? she says.

Let's get in the car, I say.

I walk to the passenger seat and open the door.

Out my throne, clown, she says. The Queen sits there.

I look at Desmond and he shrugs.

Don't you go looking at him, she says. He knows who runs this town.

I slide the seat forward, climb into the back, and slouch against the worn cushions. As I shift to get comfortable, my legs feel heavy with fatigue. It would be nice to close my eyes for a minute. The adrenaline has long since worn off. But my stomach is still fluttering and my worries about dinner prop my eyes open.

✣

One night when I was in middle school, in the early 2000s, Mom was cooking dinner and Junior was drawing when we heard a knock at the door. Mom told me to see who it was. When I opened the door, a brown-skinned man shorter than me shifted on his feet. He wore slacks and a white button-down shirt. Laugh lines creased his cheeks and wrinkles folded his forehead. His hair was white. His deep-set eyes lit up. He reached out to touch me.

Daniel, he said.

Mom yelled from the kitchen, asking who was at the door. I was still shocked, so I didn't respond as he pulled me into a hug. Moments later, Mom walked over to the door holding a glass bowl. She saw my father and cursed under her breath. She dropped the bowl and it shattered. Mom cursed again. I pulled away from my father to help her.

She's got it, he said.

My father came inside and said he wanted to take us out to dinner. Mom asked me what I wanted to do. I said I wanted to go. We went to a Caribbean restaurant in Flatbush. The dinner passed in such a blur that I don't remember what anyone said. When we left him and returned home, Mom asked Junior and me if we had given our information out. We said no. She had long since told us never to give out our address. She had our number taken off the phone books. He must have hired a private eye. We were never going to get rid of him.

✣

Shortly thereafter, we moved to Florida, and my father never appeared on my doorstep again. But I have spent a lot of time thinking about what I would do if he did. Sometimes I fantasize about hitting him. When I do, I eventually picture the cops pulling a young man off of a frail old-timer, removing him from the scene in handcuffs. Then I remember that I could have hit him when he showed up on our doorstep and I didn't. I can't believe I hugged him. Even now, sitting in Desmond's car, I'm disappointed with myself.

Y'all been riding around in quiet? Egypt asks.

Tell the truth, Desmond says, I ain't even notice.

Pass the cord back here then, I say.

Nigga, Egypt says, where you think you at?

Egypt plugs in her phone. Over mid-range piano chords, a voice pitched impossibly high by autotune sings about crying. It continues at a slow pace, elongating the syllables. The processed voice sounds robotic as it sings that it cannot be there, and a human one responds that he can still dream of the other's return.

You got to cut the R&B, I say.

Thought you were an R&B type of nigga, Desmond says.

Fuck's that supposed to mean? I ask.

You know, now that you be fucking men and shit.

Egypt slaps his arm and the car swerves left for a moment. Then Desmond corrects its course.

What'd I tell you about hitting me while I'm driving?

Just because you driving don't mean you holding me hostage, Egypt says, and then kisses her teeth. Sorry about him, Daniel. You know how he's insensitive and shit.

What I'm being insensitive about?

You know what you did.

Sorry I don't speak proper, Miss Brown Skin, Desmond says.

Egypt stifles her laughter. After a moment, Desmond laughs too, like a kid who didn't think he would get away with his trespass. In the silence, the singer recalls a conversation with his friends about his father, whom he has never known, but whom he misses all the same.

You don't like Frank Ocean? Egypt asks.

That nigga like Frank Ocean, Desmond says. He just fronting because I'm here.

He's your people, Egypt says.

We crack up as we drive over the bridge connecting the L section and the F section. In high school, we spent one practice a week sprinting to the top, turning around, and jogging down. Back then, when I crested the bridge, I couldn't feel my legs. My lungs heaved so heavily I thought they would never slow down.

You think he's ever going to release more music? I ask.

Heard he's working on some new shit now, Egypt says.

That ain't what I heard, Desmond says. I heard he was making a fashion line.

I heard he was in South Korea writing a novel, I say.

A book? Desmond says. That nigga crazy.

As we descend the bridge, to our left, opposite the school, is a field of low-lying brush that looks like it belongs in the desert. The soil here is too sandy for anything with deep roots to grow. On our right, we pass the metal bleachers and the football field and the track. It looks unnaturally empty, as though someone should be out there, popping out of the blocks late into the night, chasing a faster time, a brighter future.

You ain't tripping though, Egypt? I ask.

About what?

Me being gay.

You think I ain't know?

Desmond turns to her and asks, You knew?

Seen that coming from a mile away, she says. Way back in high school.

But I dated girls back then, I say.

You wasn't never really feeling them though, Egypt says.

Desmond rolls his eyes and says, You ain't know.

I stay knowing a lot of things you ain't never even thought about, Desmond Robinson, she says. I done forgot things you wish you knew.

She called you stupid, Des, I say. You going to take that?

You better shut your mouth back there, Baby D, Desmond says. I'm about five seconds away from pulling over, taking you out that car seat, and beating your ass.

We keep talking as we pass our old school. A chain-link fence surrounds it. The building is a long stack of bricks that sits two floors high. Thick metal grates cover evenly spaced windows. The school was built to function as a hurricane shelter, though no one I know ever went there during one. Since I left, I read that they've installed metal detectors. The school security officers carry Tasers now.

The boy in your pictures, Egypt says, the one with the Clark boots. That your boyfriend?

He was, I say. We broke up.

After the school, a ditch runs on our right, where one of our classmates rolled his car and died our senior year. After that, a reflective barrier went up where the road curves to announce the turn. People still crashed, but fewer died there.

Know it ain't my business and all, Egypt says, and I'm happy to see you and whatnot, but you look like you ain't had a haircut in months.

He ain't right, Desmond says. Lost his cool about Aubrey today.

You stop him?

Desmond says nothing.

Don't even know why I'm tripping, I say. I don't even date white folk no more.

※

One Friday during the spring of my senior year, Aubrey drove us both to Saint Augustine, playing country as she sped. As we neared the city, she said she knew a secret parking lot and rerouted to A1A. At a red light, the ocean on our right and the shadowy fort looming over it in the distance, we stopped to turn into the city. I asked her to turn off the country. She turned on the radio. Over a timely snap, a high-pitched electronic harpsichord, and autotuned humming, T-Pain sang of a night at a club when he took a girl home. I joined him in falsetto.

You're ruining the song, she said.

You like T-Pain?

Aubrey shrugged. After a few moments, she hummed along. I nudged her with my elbow and she rolled her eyes. I did so again and she started singing. As I grew louder, she did too. The light went green and she turned left. We heard a honk and then the loud sound of metal crunching against metal. Aubrey screamed. A moment later, we were sitting still, the overhead light now on. Smoke or dust filled the car and glowed yellow. The airbags hung out of the dash like inflated pillows.

Get out, Aubrey said.

She shook me and I opened the door. When I stepped outside, the front of her sedan was crunched inward. One head-light was gone. The metal innards under the hood fell out of a hole where the bumper used to be. The car that hit us looked equally bad. Aubrey asked if I was okay. I was fine. She was too. The couple that hit us was shaken up, but no one was hurt.

After the cops arrived and Aubrey gave them her informa-tion, we waited for a tow truck. I sat on the curb nearby. My body felt numb and my mind was blank. Aubrey walked over to me and asked how we were getting home. She tried to call Jess and I tried to call Twig, but neither picked up.

I can't tell my mom, I said. She'd kill me.

Don't worry. I'll call my dad.

She called him. He was on his way. After the call, Aubrey said, Glad you're okay. They hit your side. Could've been bad.

Real bad.

But you're still here, she said. She put her palm flat on my chest as if to feel for an injury I wasn't aware of. I looked down at her hand and then up at her. When we made eye contact, she pulled her hand away and made a joke about her driving. I told her it wasn't her fault. She rolled her eyes, said we both knew that wasn't true. I shrugged. She prodded my side with her elbow. I tried to scooch away but fell off the curb. As she chuckled, I shook my head and sat next to her. She put her head on my shoulder. I was as still as possible so as not to dis-turb her. We were quiet.

About a half hour later, Aubrey stood up. She figured her dad would come soon. He arrived a few minutes later. He was polite to the officers and the couple that hit us. When the car was towed and the debris cleared, he told me to get in the back of his car. Inside, his face contorted.

Fuck were you thinking? he said.

I'm sorry, Daddy.

You totaled my car, he said, riding around with this piece of shit?

The whole drive back, he yelled at her for wrecking the car and for driving with me alone. She said nothing was going on between us. He didn't believe her. He couldn't believe his daughter was a whore. He didn't raise her like this. Her mom didn't raise her like this. He ought to make her walk home. Then Aubrey yelled she wished he would. She wished he never came back. I was silent as they went back and forth until we got back to Palm Coast. Just past the exit, I told him to let me out. Aubrey said he could drop me at my home, but I didn't want him to know where I lived.

When I saw Aubrey next, at school, she apologized about her father at length. I acted like it wasn't a big deal. I didn't want to talk about it. Then she said her father was an asshole. I worried he was abusing her and implied as much. She said everything was fine. I tried to tell her that I understood—my brother was locked up too; he hurt me too—but she changed the subject.

❊

I let out a deep exhale and shake my head. A few minutes later, we arrive at Twig's house. Desmond honks. A new song fills the silence, the music a score for the night. Desmond bobs his head to the up-tempo, happier beat. Over the song, the rapper speaks in a nasally voice, somehow deep and high at the same time, about a night cut short by the sun, when he goes to see a girl instead of returning home. He has not seen her in a long time. He assumes she has written him off.

What you put on this light-skinned man for? I ask.

Nigga, you a few shades away from Steph Curry, Desmond says. And you stayed at a white boy's house last night, so who you fronting on?

Just because you brown-skinned don't mean you tough, Egypt says.

Oh, so you like them light-skinned? You think he tough and shit.

Don't listen to him, Des, Egypt says. I'm sitting in your car.

Until Drake calls, I say.

Twig walks out wearing a white T-shirt and cargo shorts. No camo hat. Egypt steps outside and Twig gets in the back next to me. He shakes Desmond's hand and nods at me.

Ain't Jess running the restaurant tonight? Twig asks.

Ain't open tonight, Egypt says.

You been? I ask.

Yeah, I been, she says. Food's good. Looks nice in there.

Who you go with? Desmond asks.

Don't get jealous, she says. Went with Tati before she left.

We pass our high school again. An electronic screen sits out front. Red letters scroll across a black background, advertising upcoming events: a play, a basketball game, and FCAT tests. We turn left onto Matanzas Woods, past the route where Coach Howard made the sprinters do long-distance runs as he rode along on his bicycle. Once, a white sprinter we called Ghost twisted her ankle on the run. Coach had her sit on the seat and he rode his bicycle standing up all the way back. I know he lost his job for sleeping with Tati, getting her pregnant, and paying for her abortion, but I wonder if anything happened with Ghost.

How's Ms. Henriquez? Twig asks.

She's all right, I say. Tell the truth, she ain't want me to come. When I left for college, she said there wasn't nothing here for me and never would be.

What you think now? Desmond asks, watching me in the rearview.

Think I know some things she don't, I say.

After a pause, Twig says, Thought your mom liked us.

I did too, I say.

Ain't about her liking us, Egypt says. Already got one son locked up down here. Probably ain't trying to lose another.

I shrug and run my finger along the window's cool glass as I say, She might lose me anyway. Now that I'm here, I want to move back.

Could live with me, Twig says. Extra room at my spot since my brother moved out. Mom would love to have you.

Ain't no jobs down here, Desmond says.

Could get my old job at Mezzaluna's back.

You trying to bus tables again? Twig asks.

Just till I figure it out. Maybe work at PCD. Maybe teach.

You ain't serious, Egypt says.

Deadass.

No, you ain't serious. You just sad.

I have forgotten how hard it is to be around people who know me so well that I cannot hide. That intimacy is one of the things that made me flee Virgil after Aubrey passed. I never could lie to him. He always knew what I was thinking, even the night that I met him at a Halloween party hosted by one of my Teach for America colleagues in Crown Heights. When I entered the apartment, I saw him immediately. At six-five, he stood well above everyone else in the room. Hair shaved to the skin on the sides, he wore a high-top. A dark-maroon lipstick coated his mouth, and that color smudged the cigarette dangling from the corner of his lips. He wore a black blazer with no shirt underneath. When someone introduced me to him, I asked if he was Grace Jones. He was.

"Tempted to Touch" came on and we danced opposite each other. When it ended, we joked about how old the song was. I told him that I remembered hearing the song growing up on the island. Years later, after we moved to the States, Hot 97 played it as though it were new. He said they always did that with Jamaican imports.

As the night continued, he and I talked in the corner. He placed one hand on the wall, just above my shoulder, and looked down at me. I asked where his people were from. He said Yallahs. Mine were from Clarendon and Saint Thomas. He called me country and I said he looked like country come to city. Then he talked about places I had never been and used phrases I had never heard, and I pretended to know them.

After a few more drinks, Virgil invited me back to his apartment. On the walk deeper into Crown Heights, he asked if I was a Gold Star. I said no. He asked who I slept with and I told him about a skinny white girl I dated in high school who I ate lunch with most days. Then he changed the subject to New York. As we walked south on Franklin at around three in the morning, we talked about how freeing it was to be gay here. We crossed Eastern Parkway, which cars still raced down, even at that late hour, and Virgil put his hand in mine.

Heading toward Flatbush, we turned off Franklin and onto an empty side street when a car slowed down. Someone leaned out the window and screamed, Chi-chi man fi dead. I heard a loud pop and pulled Virgil to the ground. After a minute, when no noise followed, we stood up. The car was gone.

They must have run over a bottle or something, Virgil said as he put his hand back in mine. His fingers trembled and my heart raced, but we didn't say anything.

✶

Though Virgil and I thought it easier to be out in New York than in Jamaica, that wasn't the last time someone would harass us. Each time it happened, we didn't talk much about it, in part because Virgil already knew how I was feeling. In time, that frustrated me; I wanted to be able to hide, and that wasn't possible with him. I worry it won't be possible at dinner, either.

As I watch the road pass by, the images of Virgil keep coming until I put my hand against the cold window. At the first B section entrance, we take a left. Occasionally, a man only visible as a white T-shirt and a red glowing ring smokes on the front step or standing in their driveway. Otherwise the houses are indistinguishable.

As we drive, I remember that J-Boogie used to live back here. His family moved to Palm Coast in the '90s, when the first housing developments started appearing. Shortly after they settled, Hurricane Andrew hit, knocking out the power and flooding roads. Not long after that, a wildfire spread across the region. It was so large that ash rained gray snowflakes from the sky. The image lingers as the car stops and the liquid in my stomach rocks. I breathe deep, hoping to calm myself, but I'm still nervous when I exhale.

Meals

Anyone bring wine? I ask as we exit the car.

Goddamn you got bougie, Egypt says.

Got something else, Desmond says.

Desmond opens the trunk and pulls out a mostly full bottle of Jack Daniel's. He holds it by the neck as we walk to the front door. I knock. Jess yells that the door is open. We enter. The hardwood floors shine streaks of white in the fluorescent light. No carpet and no tile. There aren't many houses in Palm Coast without one or the other. In the front of the room sit two round wood tables shades darker than the floors. Behind them is a long, rectangular glass table surrounded by eight chairs. They lie five feet away from the sliding-glass door that leads out onto the back porch. The room looks half like a restaurant and half like a regular Palm Coast home.

Framed photographs line the eggshell walls. Closest to us is a picture of a man and his son wading into the Intracoastal. Then a woman walking up the first hill in Graham Swamp. A man bicycling down Linear Park. Bucket-hat-wearing old men lining the pier. A long-haired white teen skim boarding. A man sitting on his back porch, arm drooped over the neck of a border collie. Two camo-hat-wearing teenage boys sitting in the bed of a red pickup on a dirt road. And finally, above the head of the table, is a picture of Aubrey in black and white, hair pulled back into a ponytail, strands falling over her forehead. Her skin is textured with lines and pock-marks where she presumably popped zits. Her eyes are closed as she pulls on a cigarette. A wisp of smoke rises from a glowing ring. Beyond it, a half inch or so of ash crumbles, ready to fall.

I'm in the kitchen, Jess says.

I follow the voice and see her slicing scallions on a champagne-colored wood cutting board. She refuses to look up. I hope that's because she's still mad about Espanola.

Place looks nice, I say. Where'd the pictures come from?

I took them, she says.

Check you out, being all artsy.

Well, you know, after I got my first job and got some money I decided to buy myself a camera like everybody else.

One of them big ones with the long lenses?

You know it, she says, chuckling. Me and half the other twentysomethings. Taking pictures like it gives us a personality.

You still shoot?

Boy you know that camera's in the garage.

After a pause, I say, Seems like you cooled off.

A little, she says.

I walk to her side and try to hug her. She continues looking down at her work. Her shoulders are stiff and her hands move quickly. My arms settle awkwardly around her body.

Don't get yourself cut, she says.

Don't cut me.

In Mom's food stories, violence shadows each meal. Our cuisine, she says, comes from slavery: unwanted bony cuts of meat mixed with produce and starches from other lands. Our recipes abound with heavy meals meant to be eaten in the morning to sustain through fieldwork, even after Emancipation, as she suggested in stories about her Indian grandfather.

The first day Mom's grandfather joined his father in the fields, he awoke to loud sizzling and the scent of fried dough. While his younger siblings slept, he joined his older brother, father, and mother for dumplings and salt fish. His early-morning nausea kept him from eating much.

The sun was down when they got to the fields. By mid-morning, sweat soaked through his soiled clothes as he lagged behind his brother and father in the coffee rows. Around noon, he fell, surrounded by the not-yet-ripe fruit. Then he felt a pull. His father propped him up onto wobbly knees. He spent the day flanked by his father in front, his brother behind, and the coffee bushes on his side, hoping to go unseen.

After work, they walked home, where his mother served curry goat. He ate so quickly that he didn't realize he burned his tongue. Midway through his first plate, his brother berated him for not eating enough to last through the day. His father said he slowed them down. Who knows what would have happened if they got caught?

As they complained, he looked down at his meal until his mother intervened. She was tired of her husband getting on her children, of him ruining meals with his screaming. When the two started yelling, his brother took his father's side. The argument escalated until his father stormed out of the house, as he always did. They were never sure if he was going to return.

✳

This dinner that we are about to eat will be the only time I have ever spent with this group of friends: Twig, Egypt, Desmond, and Jess. I'm sure they never hung out when I was gone and won't after I leave.

Quit your fidgeting, Jess says, and I realize I'm tapping my feet. She places four thick pork chops on two cast-irons. They sizzle like static on the radio. Smoke rises. She turns on the stove fan and the gray gas shoots upward. She reaches for a wooden spoon and stirs a brown gravy in the pot behind the cast-irons.

You about ready? she asks.

I got you.

I pick up the bowl of transparent amber liquid. She flips the chops, I pass her the bowl and she pours it over the meat. The stove hisses and bubbles as Jess spoons the liquid deglazing the pan onto the pork. She ladles the gravy from the back pot on them and turns the heat up.

Smells great, I say.

Thank Mr. Jacobs. He raises the best pigs around.

They free-range?

Free-range? Jess asks. Where you think you at?

All right then, Miss Big-Time, I say. Just asking a question.

Ain't nothing fancy here, she says. Just trying to cook better than my momma.

Jess sprinkles a pinch of salt atop the smothered chops.

Then she takes the tongs, pulls out a limp green from the pot, puts it into her mouth, and smiles.

Think you staying in Palm Coast for the long haul?

Ain't nowhere to go, she says. Folks know me here.

Probably can't run a restaurant out a home in Jacksonville anyway.

You'd be surprised.

The red-brown gravy thickens and bubbles slowly like gas escaping a swamp. Jess turns the heat off. She pulls a pan of biscuits out of the oven and places them on the trivet. I put them in a bowl. They're crusty on the outside but give a little in my hands. I hold on to the last one too long and sear my finger. By the time I'm done, Jess has plated the greens and the chops. We bring everything to the table, where Twig, Egypt, and Desmond sit grinning from ear to ear, holding a glass of whiskey.

Watch out for the bones in the collards, Jess says. It's just pig tail, but I don't want none of y'all to chip your teeth or nothing.

She over there acting like we ain't eat pig tail, Desmond says. You hear that, Baby D?

Like Jamaicans ain't born eating pig tail.

You know this fool had the nerve to ask if my pigs was organic? she says. You better go on back to California with that.

I said one thing.

Boy, quit your yapping and sit down, Jess says. Food's about to get cold.

Got to say grace first, Egypt says. Desmond rolls his eyes, and Twig and I laugh. You got something to say, Desmond Robinson?

No ma'am.

That's what I thought.

Egypt, you know I'm just clowning.

When our laughter subsides, I put my hand in Jess's and Egypt's. The smell of the kitchen—salt and heat dug deep into the grooves of Jess's palms—floats up to my nose. Everyone bows their heads. Their chests rise slowly. Desmond grins as he shifts in his seat. Egypt sits still with pursed lips. This must be how they look when they sleep next to each other. I close my eyes.

Dear lord, Egypt says, thank you for bringing this warm food and this beautiful home into our life. Thank you for bringing us together to share this meal. Thank you for blessing Jess's hands and this kitchen and for bringing Daniel home and for everything that you've done for us. Amen.

Amen.

�֎

I can't recall the last time I prayed over a meal. Though most Jamaicans are Christian, Mom was an atheist by the time I was born. She says the last time she was in a church was at her stepfather's funeral. After the service, his family, Mom, and my six-year-old brother drove from the church high in the hills to a small home. One of Mom's stepfather's cousins prepared a meal of oxtail, cabbage, and rice and peas. When she finished cooking, everyone took their chipped plates outside because there wasn't enough space in the house for everyone to sit. They ate beneath the sun on an early spring day and surveyed the town in the lowlands.

According to Mom, Junior sat cross-legged atop a large rock

and balanced his plate on his lap. He and Mom shared a fork. As she ate, he tired of waiting for her, picked up a piece of oxtail, and gnawed the soft, fatty meat off the tough bone, its dark juices dripping onto his pale chin. The people around him laughed at the city boy. The American was more country than all of them combined.

They berated Mom for not raising her child with manners. She had been gone too long. She was basically an American. Mom said she knew where she was from. They said she missed birthdays and funerals, holidays and illnesses. She moved abroad to make money and forgot about all of them when they needed her. When Mom started screaming, asking where they were when her mother left and her father didn't know how to do their hair, or where they were when That Woman beat them, her sister dragged her to their car.

�֎

Mom always ends that story by saying that they never apologized. She wouldn't talk to them until they did. When she left, she ran away from them for good, in the same way I once thought I was escaping this place.

The memories of how much I hated Palm Coast and everyone here come rushing back: when Desmond called me bitchmade because I didn't want to run anchor, when Jess called me faggoty for not dating anyone, when Twig compared the difference between white people and white trash to the difference between Black people and niggers. Because there was nowhere to go, I hid in silence, dreamt about moving away to find a new home. Nearly a decade has passed, but I'm still pissed, especially now that they all act frustrated with me for falling out of touch. As much as I owe them apologies, they owe me too.

I pour a glass of whiskey and reach for Desmond's glass, but Egypt pulls it away.

He's driving, she says.

I'm good to drive, he says.

You already had one.

Let me put something in my liver, he says. Ain't going to be but two sips.

Egypt cocks her head and chews her bottom lip.

Four sips, tops.

You ain't drinking a lick more, she replies.

Come on, Egypt. I'm just playing.

When I put the bottle down, it's heavier than I expect so it clanks against the glass table. My body must be exhausted. I've barely eaten today. I sip from my own cup. It's cooler and less strong than what we drank at Brandon's earlier. My tongue is still numb from his moonshine. The whiskey doesn't sting as it goes down. When I swallow, its fumes spread in my mouth. I cough.

Can't handle your liquor all of a sudden? Desmond says.

All of a sudden? Egypt asks. Y'all been drinking?

What had happened was, I say.

We wasn't drinking, Desmond says.

Everyone laughs but Egypt, who leans back into her chair, crosses her arms, and shakes her head.

Y'all still covering for each other, Jess says.

Same as when we drove to Miami, Twig says.

I forgot about that, I say. Told everyone we was at each other's house.

And your mom called and asked to talk to my mom, Twig says.

And Twig jumps on the phone, I say, and he starts speaking in this high-pitched voice. Hello? Janet? Yes, this is Rose. How are you?

Can't believe we got away with that, Twig says.

Ain't no way in hell y'all got away with that, Egypt says. Ain't no way in hell you and your big old deep voice sound like a woman. Bet on my life your mom knew and just ain't say nothing.

Desmond chuckles a low-pitched, closemouthed rumble. Twig joins in at a higher pitch. I follow suit, my shoulders rising and falling with my breath. Then Jess lets out a laugh that shakes her body. Finally, Egypt joins with a sway.

When we quiet, Jess says, Funny thing is, I done cooked all this food and now I ain't hungry.

That's because you tired, I say.

And you been tasting, Egypt says. Every time I cook, I eat damn near two meals before it even comes off the stove.

I know that's right, Jess says.

Can't tell, Twig says. Small as you always was.

Still look good, Desmond says.

Oh, you been looking? Egypt says.

Who me? Desmond says. Shit, I ain't seen Jess once today. Close my eyes every time she walk in the way. Me personally, I'm just saying what Baby D said. He was the one what was talking about how she look good.

Daniel? Egypt says. That fruit?

Excuse me? I say.

You know I ain't mean nothing by it, Daniel.

Better watch yourself.

Nigga or what? Shit, I wish you would.

We laugh, and Twig laughs harder than the rest of us. I wonder if he knows I've slept with men. We settle down and look at our plates. I split a biscuit with my hands and push the butter-colored inside into the dark gravy on my plate and then into my mouth. The biscuit melts. I bite and the outside crunches. I tell Jess they're amazing. Everyone praises her cooking. She says thank you and that there's more if we want. Twig nods and reaches for the collards. His face is turning red from the whiskey and the heat, hiding the freckles on his cheeks.

So what y'all done today? Twig asks, food stuffed into his cheeks like a chipmunk. Been waiting on you for a minute.

My fault, I say. We just been running around.

Where y'all been though?

I look at Desmond and he shrugs as he turns away, scratching behind his ear. Egypt leans over her arms on the table, her eyes darting between us. Jess is still, watching me closely, though her face is expressionless. I don't know what she'll say if I tell a lie, but I hope she'll cover for us.

We was just driving around, I say, checking out the old haunts. Bumped into Jess.

Y'all used to hang in Espanola? Jess says.

Espanola? Egypt asks.

Desmond crosses his arms and leans back. His eyes widen as if to say, Do something. I turn to the picture of Aubrey smoking with her eyes closed. She looks deep in thought. I wish I knew what she was thinking about.

What'd you find them doing way out in Espanola? Egypt asks Jess.

They was rolling around in the dirt, playing grab-ass with Brandon, Jess says.

Man, I done told you to leave well enough alone, Twig says.

Ain't nothing happen, I say. Ain't that right, Jess?

They was fine, she says. I mean, they was arguing with Brandon, but they was fine. Ain't nothing get out of hand.

What you out here chasing Brandon down for? Twig says. You and Aubrey dated like seven, eight, damn near ten years ago now.

Date? Jess says. They ain't date.

I flinch, as if someone's going to hit me.

Even though Junior beat me when I was younger, he also kept me fed. After Junior started picking me up from school, when we got home, he always made us a snack. Sometimes he made boxed macaroni and cheese. If we had cold cuts, he made sandwiches. After Mom lost her job, he made the instant noodles that she bought by the dozen or bread and margarine. Even when it seemed like there was nothing in the house, he kept us full.

Sometimes Mom had to stay late at work, so Junior made dinner. She always called and gave brief instructions. When Mom was planning on making Jamaican food, her instructions were inscrutable because she had been cooking those meals for so long. Half of a palmful of flour and a little bit of water for dumplings. Enough allspice that you get the flavor but not so much that it's all you can taste for other dishes. The meals were usually disasters. But by the time they reached my plate, even if he had hit me hard enough in the day that I was still angry at and afraid of him, I made sure to eat as much as I could. He beat me, but he kept me alive.

�֎

Putting my elbow on the table and my hand on my chin, I look away. When I exhale, my body feels deflated. Sitting at the head of the table, Jess crosses her arms, thin lips squeezed tight. Twig leans forward, his eyebrows arched up. Opposite him, Desmond's body is still, but he strokes the stubble on his chin as he chews the inside of his lip. Egypt doesn't move, but she's watching for my response too. I breathe deep but the nerves stay. I open my mouth to speak and then close it.

Where do I start? I can tell them what happened, but I can't capture everything Aubrey and I said, everything I thought but didn't say. We spent so much time together that I'm not sure what the main scenes are or how to describe all the hours we talked about nothing at lunch. How can I tell them what she meant to me then and has meant to me since, in a way that they can hear?

What she mean y'all ain't date? Twig asks.

They continue to watch, waiting for their answer. Their stares cast my eyes down. I inspect the glass table. Someone has nicked the edges so thin white scratches run along the otherwise clear glass.

Daniel, Desmond says.

I hear you, I say, resting my heavy arms on the table. From cruising yesterday through seeing Grandma and the fight with

Brandon to now, I'm fatigued. I feel like a wet rag wrung out. In my exhaustion, the voices in my head quiet and I become aware of a weight that I'm carrying. I'm not sure what it is, but I hope I will let it go when I say, Truth is, ain't nothing ever happen between us.

Nothing? Twig says.

For a moment, the silence hovers in the air. Then I feel relief when I say, Nothing. As bad as I wanted it to, nothing ever happened.

This motherfucker, Desmond says, shaking his head and chuckling to himself. He isn't facing me, so I can't read his face for his response. Egypt rolls her eyes. Twig and Jess keep looking at me.

She wanted it too, Jess says.

She ain't never tell me, I say.

You ain't never tell her neither, Jess says, raising her voice.

But everybody knew, I say, leaning back into the chair so hard the legs rock beneath me. When they wobble, I grab the chair and my body seizes. Desmond laughs and Egypt slaps his arm lightly. The fear of falling passes, the chair feels solid, and I continue, Everyone could see it. Teachers teased me about it. Sometimes they teased me when I was with Aubrey. Talked about how I was always following her around.

How she supposed to know? Jess says. Mrs. Reynolds say so and she just supposed to believe it?

I tried to tell her, I say. Told her she was pretty. Shit, I even wrote her a poem.

Daniel, she wasn't nice to nobody in high school but you. Laughed at your corny jokes. Took you gigging. And the bass tattoo, Jess says, turning to everyone else. Check this out. The minute Aubrey turns sixteen, she gets a tattoo on her hip. First thing she does Monday is run go tell Daniel. But is telling him good enough? No. She pulls her shirt up and her pants down. Damn near flashes the whole hallway just to show this boy her tattoo. I had to grab this girl's jeans to keep her from showing her ass. Wasn't for me, I swear to God, Aubrey would've pulled her pants down to her knees.

Egypt laughs and runs her hand down her face, Desmond hasn't stopped chuckling, and the rest of us join in. Our shared sound grows and, for a moment, I can't tell the difference between my laughter and anyone else's. When we quiet, I say, Egypt, don't listen to her. Wasn't nothing like that.

Maybe not, Jess says, but she damn sure showed you enough that you should've known.

I ain't saying I shouldn't have known, I say. But I wasn't sure. I thought maybe, but I wasn't sure.

My eyes feel like smoke singes them. I feel the water coming, cold against the edges of my eyelids. I blink fast. My throat feels scratchy and sore as though swollen.

I didn't trust it, I say. Didn't think she dated Black folk.

She drove you back to her house, Jess says, and sat you on her bed. She told you. You just wasn't listening.

For a moment, we're quiet. I rest my forehead in the crook between my thumb and my index finger. I can't believe I was so worried that Aubrey wouldn't like me back that I overlooked the times she scowled at other people but smiled at me. The times she leaned in close enough that I caught her scent. The times she hugged me and her touch lingered. The memories come rushing all at once. I breathe deep, hoping to push them away, but they won't go. I can still see the fluorescent school lights catching her pale brown eyes, feel her soft shirts against her prodding collarbone when she hugged me, smell the sea salt on her.

I close my eyes to dam the tears. Aubrey spoke a lot, but I didn't know how to listen. When I open my eyes, I rub the moisture away. I knew her so little, even though we spent so much time together.

Desmond's knife scrapes against his plate. Twig chuckles first, then Egypt and Jess, and finally I join them. When I look up, we're smiling. Then the laughter ends.

Heard y'all made out in her bed that day, Twig says. Matter of fact, I heard that from you.

That ain't what I heard, Desmond says. I heard y'all ain't do nothing that day, but you beat like a week later.

So what happened? Egypt asks.

She sits back against her chair, one arm on the table and the other on her lap. Her brown eyes shine in the light as she gazes at me. Desmond still looks down as he works on a third pork chop. Twig leans forward, and Jess, arms over chest, leans back and watches me.

✖

I first saw her at lunchtime. On my first day of school, I sat alone at a table in the courtyard just outside our crowded cafeteria. When I returned the next day, Aubrey was sitting there. I asked if I could join her. She shrugged. I ate quietly and Aubrey did too, then popped her hairbands against her wrist and doodled in a notebook. As we waited for the period to end,

I noticed her big, dark eyes. I must have been staring because she looked up at me. For a moment, neither of us looked away. Then I took my Styrofoam tray of food to the trash can.

On the third day, as we ate, I asked her name and she told me. Then I introduced myself.

Why ain't you sitting with your friends? she asked.

Guess I don't got none, I say. Just moved here. You?

I'd tell you, Aubrey said, but if you told anyone, I'd have to kill you.

I look like a snitch to you?

Don't know what you look like.

Later, I learned that she fought Jess, who was her best friend at the time, for dating her ex, Brandon, on the first day of school, so she didn't want to sit with their friends anymore. At the time, though, I didn't wonder too much about why she was there. Instead, we spent the rest of the period sharing the occasional word, and I tried and failed to make her laugh. As the days went on and we got to know each other better, we talked more, mostly about the shows we watched, the fights we saw at school, and other happenings in the hallways. Aubrey often made fun of people walking by and the teachers she hated. When my hair started getting long, she made fun of me too.

You looking real homeless, she said.

Ain't got a barber, I replied.

I know a couple.

Probably can't cut hair like mine.

The next week, I came to school with a new, but bad, haircut.

Eventually, I joined the track team and made other friends that I could sit with, but I kept eating lunch with Aubrey. She had run out of people to make fun of and fights at school to discuss, so she started talking about skipping school to go to the beach and about going to parties with her sister where she drank and smoked. Even when she repeated the same story, I laughed at the punch lines and leaned in during moments of suspense. I envied her social life; I spent all my free time doing homework or at track meets. I never had any stories to share, so I always asked for more details, which made her stories wilder and her voice more animated, all of which now makes me wonder how often she lied. But at the time, I was content to listen and to sit with the feeling stirring my stomach as she spoke, even in winter, when the days dipped into the thirties and we wore our jackets as we ate.

The day after Junior got locked up, I met Aubrey at lunch. It was February, so the weather was in the forties; Aubrey was wearing a camo hoodie and I wore a Sherpa-lined XL hoodie. She talked like everything was normal, but sooner or later she got quiet. She must have noticed something was off. When she asked what was wrong, though I hadn't told anyone else, I explained.

Can't believe he was so stupid, I said. Swear he's the dumbest person on the face of the earth. Can't keep his grades up in college. Can't stay out of trouble. Calls my mom asking her to post bail with money we ain't got. Don't know what he good for.

You talking real mad, she said, but you look real sad.

I ain't about to cry, Aubrey. I'm pissed.

Aubrey nodded and put a hand on my shoulder. I turned away.

I get it, she said. You know my daddy's locked up.

Then Aubrey started talking about her father. He got arrested when she was ten. She kind of understood what was going on, but not entirely. When they talked on the phone, he never told her much about what it was like on the inside. She didn't hear about how hard it was until she got older and her mom shared more. When he got out, things looked okay for a while. Then he violated parole and now he was sitting in the county jail again.

When I was a kid, I used to love talking to him on the phone, she said. Now I hate when he calls. Every time we get off the phone, I get so mad. Can't tell if I'm mad at him or mad he ain't here.

Had no idea.

Ain't the most fun thing to talk about. Besides, folks hear that your dad's in prison and they get to thinking all kinds of stuff about you. Start whispering things they don't think you hear. Look at you different. They ain't get it. But I get it, Daniel.

I nodded. I wanted to say more, but the bell rang and people started filing out of the cafeteria. Lunch was over. Aubrey gathered her things and walked away.

We didn't talk much more about her father or Junior. When they called or when something important happened on the inside, we shared details, but other than that, we talked about all the normal things. Still, our conversations felt different from then on. She kept making fun of me, but she smiled at me more, too, and offered little compliments, sometimes about a haircut or a shirt I wore. I tried to repay the favor—to tell her she was pretty or that I liked her hair when it was up—but she always deflected.

Eventually, Brandon and Jess broke up. Jess reconciled with Aubrey and joined us for lunch. We talked about Junior and

Aubrey's father less, and in general I was quieter, but I liked Jess. When they recounted their adventures together, Jess made me laugh.

Aubrey made me feel something different. When I saw her, I wanted to smile; when we made eye contact, I wanted to stare. I tried to impress her and avoided saying things that I thought would annoy her. After school, I kept thinking about her. I thought about her so much that eventually I realized I had feelings for her.

Sooner or later, Aubrey and Jess invited me to hang out after school. I never could because I had practice and homework. Then, when I complained about lugging all my books and track gear around because I never paid to rent a locker, Aubrey gave me the combination to hers and I kept my stuff there. Each morning, after I deposited my books, I hung around, pretending to look for something until either Aubrey walked in or it got so late that I assumed she was skipping school. A few weeks later, Mom bought me a Virgin Mobile phone with limited minutes for emergencies. Aubrey and I texted until I ran out, at which point Mom yelled at me for wasting her money. I apologized and, in time, she added more minutes to my phone. The cycle repeated. Luckily, I had minutes when the hurricane hit.

The time she took me to her house after school was a few months after that. Based on what she said at school, I thought she was more experienced than me, so I assumed she would make a move if she wanted me. She didn't. When I went home, I thought she didn't like me.

Then she took me gigging. I thought something might happen when we were on the water. We watched each other without saying anything for a little, but she didn't kiss me. Maybe she never would, maybe she just thought of us as friends. When we got tired, we let the current carry us. I had never spent those hours of the night with a girl. As we faced away from each other, Aubrey started talking about how mad she was at her father. Then I told her about my father beating me when I was young. She said she was sorry and ran her hand through my hair as I cried. When I finished, we didn't say much. After a few minutes, we turned the boat around and returned to Bing's Landing. We disembarked the boat quietly as the river slapped against the cement. Something wet coated my forehead and hers, and I didn't know if it was sweat or the river's oily waters. While connecting the boat to the truck, our hands touched and she looked at me.

Feel so good and tired right now, I said as I pulled my hand back. If I lied down and never got up, I wouldn't be mad.

You talking about dying on me? Boy we just got off the river. Night's young. We young. Ain't no parents checking for us. Reckon we got some time to kill.

I agreed and got in the truck. We towed the boat, parked the car, and went to a bench overlooking the Intracoastal. In the quiet, Aubrey threw a rock into the river and lit a cigarette.

You sure talk about death a lot, she said.

You don't ever think about it?

I do, she said. How I'm going to go. What's going to happen after. But I don't tell nobody about it and I don't let myself keep thinking about it.

So what you think about instead?

All the life I'm going to live, she said.

Oh, you got big plans, huh?

You ain't the only one with dreams, Daniel.

What you dream then?

We sat on a bench at Bing's Landing and kept talking, but still nothing happened between us. I told stories I had not shared with anyone before and the stories she shared seemed to be the same, but I didn't know if that meant anything, if the way she comforted me earlier in the night was the action of a friend or a girlfriend.

The next time Jess and I were alone, I asked if Aubrey liked anyone. Jess said Aubrey was thinking about getting back with Brandon. That afternoon, at practice, I asked out Ghost, the white hurdler on the track team who I knew liked me.

When Ghost and I started dating, I stopped eating lunch with Aubrey. I spent my time between classes and at lunch flanked by the track team, hoping to avoid her. But my stomach still fluttered whenever I bumped into her, even when I pretended not to see her. I thought the feelings would go away, but after two months, I broke up with Ghost.

The next day, I returned to our table for lunch. Jess asked where I had been, but Aubrey didn't say anything. I changed the subject. That Friday, Aubrey drove me to Saint Augustine and crashed her car. On Monday, at our locker, I told her all I could think about was what would have happened if I died. What my funeral would have looked like. What my mom would look like. Who would miss me. She stared at me as I spoke, mascara clumped on her lashes, eyelids hanging low. I asked what she would have done if I died. She said she would've cried. Then the bell rang and I said I had to go to class. Aubrey hugged me and walked away.

The next day, I waited for her at our locker again. She walked in with her hair in a ponytail, clutching a textbook to her chest. When she got close, I joked about expecting her to skip school. She said she thought she might. When our chuckles stopped, I looked at her. Her eyeliner made her brown eyes even larger, but I couldn't read them. I chewed my bottom lip. Finally, Aubrey asked what was on my mind.

Aubrey, I broke up with Ghost because I still like you.

Figured as much, she said.

You like me? I asked.

I used to, she said.

What you mean, used to?

Aubrey shifted her mouth so that her left cheek plumped. Then she looked around. The hallway was empty. She leaned her back against the wall, half facing me and half facing away. She swayed from one side to the other, looking down at her feet. I repeated my question.

Used to, she said. In the past.

If you felt that way once, I said.

Things're different now.

How're things different? You're still you and I'm still me, right?

They just are, she said. I seen you with someone else. Don't know how else to explain it.

That's over now, I said. We can go back to the way things was.

Daniel, I don't like you like that no more.

Aubrey said something about wanting to stay friends and I sped away to my first-period class. After, I returned to her locker to move my things out. Aubrey came by as I shoved my books into my bag and pulled out my trainers and my spikes. She said I was being dramatic. I didn't respond. When I finally stuffed my drawstring and backpack as full as I could, and held a few things in my hands, I began to walk away. Before I made it out of the hallway, Aubrey tugged on my shirt.

Meant what I said, Aubrey said, about you dying in that crash.

When I looked into her eyes, liquid brimmed on the surface. My eyebrows bore down and my jaws clenched. But before I could say anything, Aubrey wrapped an arm around me and leaned her head against my chest. I smelled sand in her hair. When she pulled away, she took the books out of my hands and my drawstring from the crook of my elbow and pulled me back to her locker, where she helped me unload.

For a while, we continued as if everything was normal, but our conversations felt different. Sometimes she made jokes that I didn't hear because I was off in my thoughts; sometimes I asked questions she never answered. There were little silences where there didn't use to be, details left out of stories and pauses before responses. We interrupted each other more than before. We were two dancers listening to different songs, stepping on toes and bumping into each other.

Then, a few weeks before prom, as the gossip spread around the school about who was going with whom, Aubrey and Jess started talking about it too. Although both derided it and anyone who thought it important at first, their voices grew animated when imagining after-proms: Empty beer cans, clouds of smoke, an endless night. After a few days, they decided to go, only for the after-parties.

We're going to get little Daniel drunk for the first time, Jess said.

Can you imagine? Aubrey asked. That settles it. You're coming.

The next day, I met Aubrey at her locker. She was wearing one of her many Hollister shirts, ripped jeans, and a stack of hairbands on her wrist. As she put her backpack in her locker and rifled around, without looking at me, she asked, What color are we wearing to prom?

You going as my date?

As friends. You're like my best friend here, Daniel.

You mean aside from Jess.

I can't take Jess as my date, she said, now can I?

I'm going to stay late at States. See everyone run their last races.

I ain't ask you about States, Daniel. I'm telling you I want to go to prom with you.

Yeah, well, I wanted to date you, but that don't mean we dating.

You're such an asshole, Aubrey said, thumping my chest with a fist hard enough to push me back. You knew I wanted to go to prom with you and you ain't said nothing.

How I'm supposed to know? You ain't tell me.

Don't play me, Daniel, Aubrey said, her eyes beginning to water and her voice getting louder as she hit me again. Don't play me. You knew I wanted to go.

People were collecting in the hallways as the beginning of first period approached. Some were friends, many were people I didn't really know, and most of their eyes turned to us.

You heard me and Jess talking about what we was going to do, Aubrey said, and you ain't say nothing. I'm sick of you being spiteful because I won't fuck you.

My cheeks burned as I watched Aubrey, aware more people were entering the hallway. I had only ever been the person observing events at school; I had never been the event. I didn't want them to see this, to see me making Aubrey cry. I didn't want to make Aubrey cry. I even wanted to go to prom with her, but only because I hoped we would draw close during a slow dance and she would kiss me and change her mind and date me until college. And I knew that was never going to happen. Whatever you chase, Mom always said, will run.

I'm sorry, Aubrey, I said. I ain't going.

Aubrey slammed her locker shut and rushed off to the bathroom, and I walked away into the stairwell.

From then on, Aubrey and I avoided each other in the hallways. A few weeks later, Desmond and I skipped prom and stayed at States to watch the 4x400, for which our team didn't qualify. After the event, we went to an after-party in the Hammock Dunes. I checked all the rooms, hoping to see Aubrey, and turned my head every time the door opened, but she never came. We went home around three in the morning. I lay in bed awake long enough to see the sun come through my window.

For the rest of the year, I ate lunch in the cafeteria with my track teammates. I saw Aubrey a few times that summer in passing at the supermarket or the gas station, and we usually shot the shit until I made up an excuse to leave. Then I left for college. After a few months, she texted that she drove past the cross-country team running down Old Kings and thought of me. I said I was surprised to hear from her. She said it had been too long since we spoke and asked if I still hated her. I didn't hate her. I never hated her. I just had to remove myself from our situation. She said it would've been nice to know that I didn't hate her. I said I fucked up bad. She said she missed me, said I was one of her best friends, said she hated it down here now that I was gone and Jess was in Gainesville at Santa Fe and her parents were getting on her nerves. She wanted to move. I didn't know things had gotten so hard. I tried to call her but she didn't pick up. I texted her about a time to talk, and we set one, but she didn't pick up again, texted she was busy.

We kept texting, but our conversation fizzled out, in part because we couldn't connect on the phone and in part because we didn't have much spark in text. That and I was more preoccupied with getting drunk with my friends and trying to sleep with anyone who wanted to sleep with me. After we stopped texting, we never talked again. Then she died and all I could think was, I love her.

Hold up, Egypt says. She won't date you, so you ask her what she'd do if you died?

Oh, you won't date me? Jess says. Well, what if I was dead?

Like she wasn't in the same car, Egypt says.

It ain't my fault we crashed, I say.

Yeah, but you ain't have to say nothing like that neither, Egypt says.

You right, I say. Wasn't none of it right. Shouldn't have never stopped talking to her. Shouldn't have never dated Ghost. Shouldn't have never done any of it.

At this, Desmond laughs shallowly, a sound more performative than anything else. He moves more than he makes noise. My lips fixed tight, I glare at him, but he doesn't notice.

This nigga so dumb, Desmond says.

I know you ain't talking about me, I say, but he isn't listening. He's facing everyone else.

This nigga want Aubrey, Desmond says, but he start dating someone else. Comes back at her with, Either date me or I'll die. Then he ghosts her anyway. Desmond turns to face me. Come on, bro. You tripping off being dumb like ten years ago. You was seventeen.

It ain't just that.

Nigga, I heard what you said, but you ain't hear what I said. That's why you still running around here like you still a jit.

I done told you ain't nobody a jit, I say, leaning forward over the table, shoulders raised. I'm tired of you trying to son me.

Desmond turns to Egypt, who looks away when he says, This nigga fronting like he going to do something. Y'all believe this?

How I'm fronting? I say, anger and liquor raising me to my feet. You think I ain't fixing to scrap because I don't live here no more?

Nigga, sit your punk ass down. Ain't nobody afraid of you. This nigga talking reckless like he about to do something. He better go on back to New York with that shit.

Talk about me like I ain't here one more time.

This nigga think he tough. This battyboy? Desmond laughs and shakes his head. Twig swivels, keeping an eye on both of us. Egypt shakes her head. Jess gestures at Desmond and me, telling us to let it go, but her sign only reminds me that there's an audience. I can't let everyone watch me get punked like nothing has changed since high school. I lean over the table and reach for Desmond. He stands up, so my arms swat at him. Before I make contact, Twig is forcing me into my seat and Egypt is pushing Desmond into his.

I ain't having no fights in my house, Jess says.

You know better than that, Desmond, Egypt says.

You better sit your ass down, Daniel, Twig says.

If y'all can't talk like adults, Jess says, you're going to have to go elsewhere.

I ain't tried to swing on this nigga once tonight, Desmond says. I'm cool if he cool.

After a moment of staring at Desmond, I say, I'm cool.

I sit back down. For a moment, everyone is watching us, making sure we won't throw any more punches. When neither of us stirs, they know it was just a flash in the pan, one of many almost-fights that flare up and disappear around here.

Ain't you never lost nobody? Desmond says.

No one I was ever this close to.

Ain't you fucked up? I know when you teaching, you must lose your temper on them kids.

'Course I fuck up. I fuck up all the time. But it's different in the classroom. I lose my temper one day and I apologize the next. Ain't no next with Aubrey. Can't say sorry no more.

Desmond turns to Egypt, who shrugs. I don't know what they're thinking. Desmond faces me and says, Bro, I thought you wasn't never coming back. I used to get so mad about it, every time you came up, I'd tell everyone it was on-sight next time I seen you. Then one day Egypt talked some sense into me. Said you was living in the big city. You was busy school- ing them kids so they ain't make the same mistakes we did. You was trying to pay rent like me. And I got proud, bro. And

Egypt said I could be proud or mad, not both. So I had to make peace with all the wrong shit we done to each other. I just let it go because I didn't think you was ever coming back. Even if you did, it couldn't change nothing.

I get it, I say. I fucked up. My fault.

No, you don't get it. I'm saying ain't nobody sitting around waiting for you to say sorry. It's over man. She gone.

How come I see her everywhere I go then?

She with you, but you can't do nothing about it no more. What's in the past is dead. It's past. Ain't no second chances.

Desmond drops his cup to the table a little too hard, clanking a high-pitched noise that lingers like a bell. When the noise fades, I hear the frogs droning outside.

You two done? Jess says. We nod. Then Jess fills everyone but Desmond's glass halfway full of whiskey, which is still far more than I need. When she sits down, she raises her cup in the air and says, Suppose it's time for a toast.

Twig and Egypt join her. Desmond reaches for the whiskey bottle, but Egypt bats his hand away. He holds up his water glass. They all watch me, glasses raised, waiting for me to join the toast. And I shake my head.

That's it?

I'm with Des, Jess says. You can't bring her back. Even if you could, she still ain't want to date you. So you better quit holding us up and raise your goddamn glass.

Desmond lowers his cup and turns to me. His eyes are dark and unmoving. Through my rapid blinking, his gaze meets mine, and he nods. I nod too. I raise my glass and Desmond follows suit and we all drink to Aubrey. The liquor burns less this time going down. When its warmth has gone, Desmond looks at me and says, Always figured you were lying about some of it.

Didn't know it was all of it though, Twig says.

Desmond, you ain't got no room to talk, Egypt says. You was running around telling everyone you smashed when we were in high school.

I ain't never said that, Desmond says.

Please, Egypt says. J-Boogie told me that the other day.

See this is why I don't be telling J-Boogie my business no more, Desmond says. Nigga gets a little drunk and he can't keep his goddamn mouth shut.

Desmond shakes his head, but we all laugh. Our shoulders and heads moving in sync, I begin to feel that we're on the same page again. The light fixture is a soft yellow, and in its glow they look not like friends with whom I'm having dinner so much as a memory of them, a feeling our laughter taps into and amplifies. Before quiet can fall on the room and we return to our separate sounds and bodies, when our chuckling has settled to a low percussion, Twig, wanting to extend the moment, says, Remember how Egypt swore T-pain was her cousin?

Yeah, but I ain't never lie about fucking nobody.

Me neither, Jess says.

Ain't you say you fucked Joakim Noah when he was at UF? I ask.

Correction, Jess says. I lied about fucking one person.

Just a lie, Desmond says. It's in our blood.

They're right. There's no future for me in the past, nor did Aubrey and I want the same future. She never wanted to return here, not like I did when she died, not like I do now. And I don't think she wanted kids.

I never thought I would want kids either, but after Virgil and I started dating, I thought I might. We talked about it at the Jamaican restaurant where we went for our anniversary. That night, I wore a navy blazer that was a little too long for me and dark jeans. I arrived at the restaurant first. Two older Jamaican women stood behind a counter, switching between stirring pots and filling Styrofoam containers. I asked if there was anywhere to sit. The younger woman looked me up and down.

Where you from? she asked.

Kingston, I said, but my folks are from Clarendon and Saint Thomas.

Been here a while?

I said yes and she sent me upstairs. As I walked up, I heard her comment on me being a Coolie. Did I know this wasn't a Trinidadian restaurant? I rolled my eyes and sat at a round table covered in a floral-patterned, plastic-wrapped tablecloth. A few minutes later, Virgil came upstairs, apologized for being late, and hugged me. His arm around my back was bony as usual. His black sweater hung from him like a robe.

When the server came, we ordered curry goat and curry chicken. The meat was a brown yellow and came with plantains, cabbage, and rice and peas. The chicken fell off the soft bones, but when I bit in, something was off. The heat was there but the flavor was wrong.

Not perfect, he said, but it's good, right?

It's good, I say. But I wish they had scotch bonnets.

They're hard to find around here. Everywhere's missing something.

If they got scotch bonnets, I said, they didn't add enough allspice.

Or coconut milk.

Or gungo peas.

Then we talked about our favorite Jamaican meals and the closest approximations that we found in the States. We suspected that we misremembered those meals or that our parents cooked in idiosyncratic ways that didn't represent the dish, but the memories still became the standard.

After, Virgil took me back to his place and we kept drinking. Tongue loosened by alcohol, I told Virgil I wanted to have kids one day. Did he? He said no. I opened my mouth to respond, and my father came to mind and my throat caught. It felt swollen and sore. Tears welled up in my eyes. When I tried to speak, they ran down my cheeks. When I finished crying, Virgil got up to make rice and peas, he said, the right way.

❊

Since then, Virgil and I avoided talking about children, but we both knew that conversation put an expiration date on our relationship. It was too hard to watch the end as it approached. It still is. Even tonight, with all these friends whom I know won't spend time together after I leave, I am trying to ignore that my flight is tomorrow. But as the fatigue settles in, the night's approaching deadline comes into view.

I'm going to step out for a smoke, Desmond says.

He slides open the screen door and walks to the back porch. Jess and I follow. Two more tables sit out here and beyond them is the screen, its rough mesh meant to keep mosquitoes out. Christmas lights wind around the ceiling.

We exit into the backyard where the dirt is soft, thin, and sandy between my toes. As in most Palm Coast backyards that aren't covered in imported grass and manicured by landscapers once a week, little grows by the house. Farther away, shrubs and reedy grass surround the base of a tall tree whose branches reach toward Jess's home. Beyond it, a small forest is a layer of shadows.

Jess and Desmond light their smokes.

Can I bum one? I ask.

You smoke now?

I ain't say all that.

Desmond passes me a Newport and I light it. Its aftertaste is a dried chemical, overpowering whatever food was left between my teeth.

Look at Mr. Goody Two Shoes over here, Jess says. Smoking with the bad kids.

It's quiet, aside from Twig and Egypt's muffled voices inside the house, where they're cleaning up, and Desmond and Jess's exhales. In the dark, the cigarette's red glow casts a soft light on Desmond's face. I drag again and this time the singeing in my throat is too strong and I cough. Then Desmond says, Can't handle the smoke?

You must be talking about someone else, I say.

I still feel the burn and consider smoking until I can't talk. Then I run my toes into the soft, cool soil. A wind ambles by.

Since y'all are still here, I say, figure I owe y'all an apology. Dragged y'all into that mess with Brandon over nothing.

You still over here saying sorry? Desmond asks with a raised eyebrow.

Y'all not mad? I ask.

Oh, I'm mad, Jess says with a tone that makes my cheeks burn. But you only here for a little bit, so what I'm supposed to do?

I'll make it up to you.

Boy, you don't never learn, Jess says.

Sorry. Habit.

Just like Aubrey, Jess says, making promises you can't keep because someone's mad. She did the same damn thing when she moved up north and wasn't picking up my calls. Every once in a while, she'd text and promise she'd call me back soon. But she never did. So one day I see this picture on Facebook. Her hand. There's a silver ring and a little tiny diamond. I mean real tiny. Hard-to-see tiny.

Probably cubic zirconium, Desmond says.

Like what you got in your ear? I say.

Nigga, this a diamond.

You ain't got no diamond, Jess says, laughing, and neither did Aubrey. Anyway, I see the picture and I call her. She picks up and before I can say anything, she's saying Jess, I'm so sorry. I been meaning to call. I let her apologize for a little bit and then I tell her I know life's busy. She ain't the only one what's busy. So how come I got to find out she getting married on Facebook? She apologizes again. She was going to call. Then I say congratulations, tell her I'm excited for her. Better not hear about that wedding on Facebook though. And she goes, You kidding? You know you're my maid of honor. You know we're throwing the wildest bachelorette party. Beer. Four-wheelers. Mudding. Boats. Fishing. Dirt bikes. More beer. Strippers. Maybe back on the bikes.

Y'all going to be sober enough to ride? I ask.

We chuckle and Jess drags on her cigarette. The frogs keep

buzzing. Above, the dark, fleecy clouds that rolled in while we were at dinner begin to part. Patches of the sky reveal clusters of stars, small alone but numerous together.

We was just talking, Jess says. We wouldn't ride drunk. Well, we wouldn't ride too drunk. So she's telling me about the bachelorette party and we start laughing and planning. Then I got to go. She says she's going to make it up to me. Going to call more. This was back when I was working at Sonny's. I was on my break and stepped out to smoke when I looked on my phone and seen the news and called her. Break was about ending now. So we hang up. But if I'm being honest, I'm still pissed. I mean, we been best friends since middle school. Our moms are best friends. Only picture my mom got in her wallet is me and Aubrey at the beach. So I'm crying and I'm mad and when I'm done crying I tell myself, You're not calling that girl till she calls you. Sure enough, weeks go by and she don't call. So I pick up the phone.

You just let it go? I ask.

Hell no, I ain't let it go, she says. I was pissed. I'm still pissed. But I wanted to talk. So we talked and then I called her again and she picked up and we talked again. Pretty soon we was talking every week. Then she came down. Picked her up from the airport. Drove her to the Publix to get some things. Stopped by the CVS for a toothbrush. That girl forgot a toothbrush.

She never was much good at remembering things, I say.

Or taking care of herself, Desmond says.

I know that's right, she says.

The low-lying weight of the clouds moves fast across the sky, leaving wisps in their wake, some of which are thin enough to see through. Elsewhere, the star-covered night grows and a half-moon comes into sight.

So then I drop her off at her mom's. Couple hours later, she calls me. Says she's at Flagler Hospital visiting her grandma. Her whole family's there and her pops is being a dickhead and she needs me to pick her up. So I go. Then we go to a bar. Whole week's like that. She's with her family until she can't stand them no more and then we drink. I drove her about five, six hundred miles that week. Drove her everywhere except the night I didn't.

Jess looks down and shakes her head. I put a hand on her back. Her shoulders tremble; maybe she's about to cry. We are quiet for a while, until Jess's body grows still. Then she drags for a long time. The burning end glows a bright pink. The length of the inhale seems inhuman. Time stretches. Then she finally exhales a long plume of smoke, and her breath is the loudest sound around.

Nobody I chill with really knew Aubrey like y'all, Desmond says. Everybody I talk to always be like, That sucks.

As if I ain't know it sucks, Jess says.

Or they say I'm sorry, I say.

As if I don't know they sorry, Jess says. Whole damn town's sorry.

I'm saying though, Desmond says. It fucks me up that ain't nobody get it.

The night is not clear yet, but the clouds are moving quickly enough that I know it will come soon. For the moment, we are somewhere between an unlit night and one with too many lights.

Well, we here now, Jess says, chuckling as she drops her smoke into a pot.

We do the same. I hear the water running and dishes clanging behind us. The mess we made, like the food we ate, will soon disappear as though nothing happened. As we walk back in to join the cleanup crew, my eyes no longer droop. Jess puts her arm around my mid-section and says, Glad you're home.

Her eyes are red. She has cooked, eaten, listened to me bullshit, told the truth, and she is still here. Beyond her, Desmond drags his feet, his body struggling to keep up with the night. When we step onto the back porch, we see Egypt and Twig through the kitchen window. Egypt leans against the counter as she washes and Twig sways from side to side as he dries. They are as tired as the rest of us.

Then, in the dark, I see her. Aubrey's standing in front of her locker facing me, her dark eyes wide and her lips half-pursed, half-grinning. She looks like she might say something and I want to say something too and to hold her, but I know that's not where this memory leads. I'm grateful to have seen her so vividly and to have felt and to feel so strongly about her that I want to change the laws of time. Jess tightens her grip on my waist and I know I'm not dreaming alone.

Afterlives

As we leave Jess's, my limbs feel elastic, the way they did after warming up at track practice. Tonight, their lightness stems from a little to eat and a lot to drink. To my left and right, Des and Twig grin wide from some joke Des made about my lineup, and I let the liquor carry me away.

Des, Twig, and I circle each other on Jess's lawn. We swing and back away without breaking our smiles. Des talks a lot of shit about how lucky we are that we aren't actually scrapping. Twig manages a few words in response. I am breathing too heavy to say anything. Soon enough, this light jogging strains my lungs and I stop to spit phlegm. While I wipe what remains from my lip with my fist, I feel a hit and fall. Twig has tackled me.

Dogpile, Des screams. He taps his elbow, mimicking a professional wrestler, and leaps at us. When he lands on his side, Twig's arm lingers for a second around my midsection and the three of us are a tangle of limbs in the night. Twig and Des stand up. I stay staring at the starry night. They pull me to my feet and usher me into the car.

We leave Jess's and joyride. With each turn, liquid sloshes

in my stomach. We plan for the remaining hours. Twig says he knows a place nobody knows; he has something to show us.

How we get there? Desmond asks.

Ninety-five or Old Kings, Twig says.

Let's take Old Kings, I say.

Desmond shakes his head and says, Man comes home and thinks he's in charge.

Bro, tell me why Baby D always thinks he runs shit, says Twig.

Thinks this his car and shit, Egypt says.

Like he bought this shit, Desmond says.

Like he owns this town, Twig says.

Like we a bunch of no-good niggas without him, Egypt says.

All right, fuck y'all then, I say. Just won't say nothing at all.

They ain't teach you how to laugh at that big fancy school? Egypt says. Ain't they teach you about cracking?

Oh, so now I'm dumb, I say.

Nigga, you been dumb, Egypt says.

We keep joking as we ride down Old Kings. I look for the town's changes: The ABC liquor that used to be an abandoned lot, the Moe's that used to be parking, the paved-over grooves in the McDonald's lot where the Greyhound used to stop. Everyone keeps talking, but my buzz makes it harder to follow the conversation. The ride, the streets, and the twinkles in the night blur.

Before I realize it, we're far south on Old Kings, and I say, Y'all think Coach Howard still lives down here?

Egypt kisses her teeth and says, Don't remind me.

Des shoots me an angry glance in the rearview. I suppose Egypt finally told Des about Coach Howard and Tati. Des turns the music up.

Twig directs us into one of the housing developments they abandoned after the 2008 crash. There are no streetlights. The moon tints everything blue. We follow a winding road, grass encroaching on both sides. As we make our way in, the trees recede and the lots flatten, leveled a decade ago by some ambitious contractor. Greenery sprouts in their midst.

Everyone gets out. Twig pulls fireworks from his bag. We shoot them at the sky and they streak yellow, orange, and pink. We aim roman candles at and run from one another. We laugh in the high pitches of prepubescent children. My stomach swells with glee and my heart pounds from the gasps for air. I call a time-out to bend over and catch my breath. My head spins. The ground tilts one way and then the other. The ecstasy in my gut turns into nausea. I burp and smell whiskey. I wrinkle my nose, stand up, and walk to Egypt, who sits on the hood of Des's car.

Scared? Egypt asks.

Who? Me?

I don't know who you fronting for.

Her regal cheekbones and large eyes shine in the moonlight. She watches me with caution as though she knows what's on my mind.

Thanks for coming with us, I say.

We friends, ain't we? she says.

Still. Can't help but feel like I been dragging y'all around.

Boy, you don't never learn. Ain't nobody come who ain't want to come.

My cheeks burn. I turn away from her and watch Des and Twig weave around the lot, shooting roman candles at each other. Out of the corner of my eye, I watch Egypt smoke one of Des's cigarettes. My thoughts blur and my memory of the time since Jess's comes in patches, as does the shame of risking Des's life and lying to everyone for so long. The heft of keeping secrets presses down once more, and I imagine telling her everything about my father, about my brother, about Aubrey and see myself bent over crying in her arms. When I turn to her, before I can say anything, she speaks up.

You ain't got to apologize to me, Daniel.

But I want to.

Well, I ain't a priest and this ain't a confessional.

Almost wish it was.

If wishes were horses, beggars would ride. Egypt takes a long drag of the cigarette and keeps watching the boys. Then she turns to me and continues, It ain't my job to tell you if you a bad person. You want to swap stories or pour one out, I'm here. But you got to go somewhere else with all that other shit.

Figure you're right, I say, stroking my chin's stubble. Don't know how I survived so long without you giving it to me straight.

The weight you put on, looks like you figured it out all right.

Watch it now.

No, it look good, Egypt says. In high school you was just bones in a skin bag. Looking like you might fall through your jeans one day if your legs wasn't so damn big. You the only one whose speed suit ain't fit.

You remember that one meet when I wore boxers and they was too big for me so the plaid was just sticking out the bottom?

Your knees all ashy like you been rolling around in dirt and your boxers falling out your speed suit. Remember me and Tati was screaming, Let's go, Ashy Larry! the whole damn race. Had everybody in the stands rolling.

As we talk, the ground feels unsteady beneath my legs. I sit on the hood and think Aubrey would be happy that we are all together. Egypt hands me a bottle of water and makes me drink. Its cool distracts for a moment, but the feeling of being on a dinghy tossed by a ship's wake returns. My mouth sweats. I wander away to one of the undeveloped lots. I spit. Liquid keeps pooling in my mouth. I exhale, feeling fine for a moment, and in the silence, I remember the day Aubrey and I rode the flood. Something gathers in my eyes. I close them. In the dark, my head spins. My body seizes as I drop to my knees and vomit. Between the pain of my sore throat and clutching stomach, I barely feel the liquid pouring out of my mouth, the mucous from my nose, or the tears on my face. Everyone gathers around me as I spew my insides onto the grass. When I finish, Egypt hands me the tissues from her purse, and I wipe the vomit and the tears.

✖

My face still cold from the liquid, as I fade out of consciousness in the front seat of Des's car, I recall the story Mom told about her ancestor, a tale she heard from her grandfather, who heard it from his wife. My ancestor followed the enslaved preacher Archer Sharpe in Montego Bay in the 1820s. Sharpe traveled the island, teaching the enslaved in huts on the outskirts of farms after long days of harvesting. In one of those homes, Archer told my ancestor's congregation that, to be reborn, they must be baptized in a river, where the spirits of protection lived. They must clear the land of European witchcraft. Only then would Jesus return to deliver them from the whip.

In the early 1830s, he changed his name to Samuel. Shortly thereafter, he and his brothers stole a British newspaper and read about Parliament's debate on abolition. They claimed it granted them freedom. They spread the word in late December. Close to the anniversary of the birth of the Lord's son, they went on strike. The enslavers alerted the Colonial armed forces, who attacked the enslaved people to strike fear into their property. The survivors assaulted their aggressors and burned their crops. The sweet sugarcane fumes blanketed the air like gaseous molasses, the smoke visible from miles away.

Over the next two weeks, the enslaved people killed fourteen enslavers, and the enslavers killed over two hundred of the enslaved. After, the enslavers imprisoned and executed three hundred more, including the preacher, Sam Sharpe. When they held him at gunpoint on the gallows, a noose around his neck, he repeated the words he said not long before: I would rather die among yonder gallows than live in slavery.

The rope snapped Daddy Sharpe's neck. His head hung in some inhuman direction. But as his jaw rotated behind his shoulders, it opened. Through the gap between his yellowed teeth, his spirit rushed upward like the smoke of the sweet burning sugarcane sent heavenward on the back of the wind.

�֎

A grin stretching my cheeks, I look at Des, who asks, You feeling better?

Crackers helped.

Think you're going to vomit again?

Nothing left in my stomach.

Good, he says. They asleep back there?

Des tilts the rearview mirror to get a better look. I turn around. Twig slouches against the door, his legs stretched along the floor. Egypt lies still, curled in on herself, her head leaning against the window and her feet on the seat. Soft purple eyeshadow, a shade I suddenly wish I was wearing, covers her closed eyes, which flutter whenever we hit a bump.

They asleep, I say.

I take the cord from Egypt's phone and plug in my own. Because I have heard this song so many times, it sounds like a memory. I stare out the window and watch Flagler passing by until I hear Des rap along with Tupac, the two addressing some young gun, trying to hide from all attention, who has forgotten that he is one of the hopeless. Lines collect on his forehead. Brown streaks of dirt cake the thin straps of his white tank. The moonlight reaches through the trees and catches his face, which shines. I've been watching him for a while, but he doesn't look back at me. I want to tell Des what's on my mind now that Egypt and Twig are asleep, but my gut remains shaky.

That girl falls asleep so easy, boy. I'm telling you, Des says. She be falling asleep head bobbing in the car or in her chair. Swear to God, we was at this club in Daytona and she fell asleep standing up.

You lying.

How I'm lying?

She ain't never fall asleep standing up in no club.

Swear to God, bro. On my mom.

Out the window, Spanish moss hangs low from branches

overhead. The bases of the trees beside the road are obscured by muck. In late summer, when the thunderstorms roll in daily, this is all swamp. After a heavy rain, its waters lap against the road like the ocean storming A1A in a hurricane. The water beneath our wheels would carry us away.

This my favorite drive in all Florida, I say.

Who you telling? Des asks. Been known this was your favorite.

We turn left on Old Dixie. Down here, it's a small patch of road connecting US-1, I-95, John Anderson, and A1A. It's a short detour connecting better-traveled highways for those racing north or south, hoping to escape Flagler County, a scenic route between scenic routes in this suburb of a suburb. We ease to a stop behind a line of cars whose taillights blare red. The Intracoastal's waters splash against the dirt-sand shore in the distance.

Always got to wait for this goddamn drawbridge, Des says. He rolls down his window, lights a cigarette. I exhale and my nervousness is still there. I look out the window, inhale the swamp. Finally, I turn to Des and say, You believe in an afterlife?

✕

Before he responds, the image returns, a newly freed ancestor, older now, taking her daughter to Myal rituals in the town center. The Myal men proclaimed that British witchcraft was killing their crops. At dusk, they began dancing and chanting. Near the night's midpoint, I imagine my ancestor's daughter stole away to nod off under a tree. When my ancestor found her, she carried her home and put her to bed.

Months later, the Myal men's rituals spread. In their wake, the freed Jamaicans assaulted their former enslavers and burned their property. Fearing another Christmas Rebellion, the constables raided the huts on the edge of the farms where the newly free worked for their former masters. They killed all my ancestors except the one who had slept through the Myal ritual months before.

When the bloodshed ended, the survivors cleared the debris and scrubbed blood out of what they could repurpose. Then they rearranged the remaining furniture and flipped over their mattresses so the newly arisen duppy wouldn't recognize their homes. By the time their hands ached, they had to leave. My ancestor's daughter followed them to her first day of fieldwork.

In the evening, everyone prepared food, gathered what little alcohol they had stashed away, and carried both to the clearing in the middle of their huts. They ate and drank and shared stories about their families. As the night darkened, at a moment of silence between tales, my ancestor's daughter sang. Everyone joined in a ritual they continued for eight nights.

On the ninth night, they piled food on a table for the rootless, hungry duppy. Some of the living beat their drums to the rhythm of a horse running, which moved them to dance until the oldest turned away from the festivities. The elder stared openmouthed at the horizon and said she recognized a duppy, her husband. She greeted him. The word spread through the party, the dance ended, and everyone joined in. My ancestor's daughter said goodbye to her father and her mother as she watched them drift skyward to join the billowing cloud of the others, who were catching the wind that would carry them to Africa.

In time, when people died, the community continued those nine-nights celebrations, reminding one another that death began a homeward journey, an occasion for celebration.

�֍

Des adjusts the rearview mirror, which creeks. I say, She's asleep. You ain't got to censor yourself.

You think I speak different when she's around? Des says. You must not know me.

The cars ahead lurch forward. Des flicks his butt out the window.

Do I believe in an afterlife? Des asks. I go to church with Egypt now and then.

The metal-grate bridge rattles beneath us. The Intracoastal smells like a river approximating a swamp. Its steady-churning brackish waters shine gray.

But do you believe in life after death? I ask.

I don't believe in heaven, he says. Don't get me wrong. It'd be cool with me if I opened my eyes and was draped in some soft-ass white robes, but there ain't never no niggas in them pictures. You telling me you can't get into heaven if you got melanin?

I'm saying though.

Matter of fact, he says, I don't want to go to no heaven with white folks anyway. I know all them racist rednecks ain't supposed to get in, but how I'm supposed to know they ain't make a mistake? I spend my whole damn life in Florida worrying every cracker's a racist redneck and what? All a sudden

I'm supposed to see the clouds and the wings and just forget all that?

�֎

When my surviving ancestor became an elder, she and her descendants moved to August Town. There, she saw the preacher Alexander Bedward on the bank of the Hope with hundreds of other Jamaicans. Standing on a makeshift stage, he looked down on the crowd and told them their salvation had come. A new life awaited them in Africa.

How would they get there? They would fly, he said. And how would they fly? They would drape a bedsheet around their shoulders like a cape and climb the breadfruit tree. They would pull themselves up by its branches, never stopping to pick its fruits because there were plenty where they were going. At the top, they would leap and when they did, God's winds would carry them away from this island, across the ocean, and back home.

A lone voice yelled out, You first. Others joined in. The crowd urged him on. Bedward, in turn, tied the corners of the starched-white bedsheet around his neck. Its ends settled by his calves. He turned to face his followers. The wind flared and caught his cape. The crowd cheered. Then Bedward grabbed hold of the lowest branch, jammed his foot against the bark and climbed. He disappeared into the tree's green leaves. The followers in the back couldn't see him. They screamed because they thought he had already left. Then, finally, he emerged atop the tree. The clamoring voices grew louder. Bedward watched the excitement stir them. He leapt. When he hit the ground, he broke his legs.

✳

Though she never tried to fly from a tree, my ancestor continued to believe in Bedward, according to Mom. Her story
always ends there. I can't picture Mom worshipping anything.

We turn down John Anderson. On our right, the river flows
until it disappears around the bend. On our left, trees shade
the road from moonlight, hiding a long expanse of lawn running back to a house designed to look like a plantation.

I think once you get to heaven, I say, you don't worry about
that stuff no more.

Fuck that, Des says. I ain't trying to forget all that. I'm trying
to go to the all-Black heaven.

The segregated heaven?

Not segregated, he says. We just, you know, doing our own
thing. My parents, their parents.

All the way back to the slaves, I say.

They started the joint. They died, went up, looked around,
and was like, We ain't having none of this shit.

So they just grabbed the other Africans and said, Let's dip?

I lean as the car glides around a curve. The shrubbery grows
tall and a breeze wafts through the window. I smell salt. When
the last car in front of us turns onto the road, I see the ocean,
lines of white foam rippling across its surface. A long slice of it
glows silver in the moonlight.

Exactly, he says. They grab their uncles and aunties and say,
Let's go somewhere we can dance.

And they just Cupid Shuffle they asses out of there?

Nigga, they Electric Slide, they Jook, they Twist, they Soulja

Boy, they Nae Nae, they Jive, they Two-Step, they do it all. And they busting they guts while doing it.

And the white folks watching like, What's gotten into those niggers?

Some cracker goes, Too much to drink.

That crazy voodoo shit again.

Howard, I done told you to stay away from the niggers when they got their chicken feet, Des says, laughing as we turn onto A1A. Beyond the railing lies a long stretch of sand. The angle of descent is shallow. Low tide. In the distance, I spot a sandbar.

And then what? I ask.

Well, you know we always late, Des says. So the young impatient dudes, they start dancing they asses out of there, drinking out of brown paper bags and laughing the whole way. Behind them, you know some of the girls is doing their hair. Other folks is gathering their belongings. Some of the uncles and aunties grabbing pots and flour and eggs like, You never know when we're going to need these.

Others grabbing drawings of their relatives like, You can't leave these behind. Sonny looks so good in this picture. Got his kufi on straight and everything.

And the little ones, you know, the ones big enough to walk alone but still little, they help the old ones. Hold they hands while they leaning on their walking sticks. Help them adjust the chains on they ankles so they don't trip on the way out.

✴

My ancestor's children moved to New Monklands. In the 1930s, a member of a new religion arrived and gathered a crowd in a house that the Myal men had visited. Surrounded by the men and women of Saint Thomas, he told them their savior had arrived. He was a descendant of the lost tribe of Israelites. Haile Selassie I, the Lion of Judah, was here to lead them to the Kingdom of God.

When his sermon ended, Mom's grandmother and the rest of the crowd left. Though she never joined the Rastas, she talked about those early days when the Bobo Dreads began appearing. She claimed they were crazy. Her husband, Mom's grandfather, wasn't so sure. Even though their beliefs said nothing about a Coolie like him, he defended the Rastas well into old age, long after Mom's grandmother left for the States.

Mom learned her grandfather believed in a different afterlife when the diabetes reached his foot and they cut it off. For weeks, Grandma stayed by his bedside in New Monklands until he healed enough to be alone. Then she returned to work. That day, my great-grandfather asked Mom to sit by his side. As she approached, she stared at the depression in the blanket where his foot used to be. My great-grandfather asked her to tell him what it looked like outside. She described the river, the guinea grass, and the goats. He asked about the lime tree. It looked the same.

My great-grandfather asked Mom the same question every day until a month later, when he asked her to help him up. She grabbed his large hand and tried to tug him out of bed, but she couldn't move him. He laughed and said, Not like that.

He rolled onto his side, pulled his legs off the bed, and pushed himself upright. He motioned for his crutch and Mom passed it to him. He hunched over the wooden pole and hobbled to the doorway. The sun silhouetted his tall, broad figure when he turned around to say, You coming?

Mom rushed to the door. He grabbed her shoulder to stop her, then held out his hand. Mom put hers in his palm. They walked along the thin dirt trail carved by decades of passersby, Mom's feet landing where the pale grass encroached on the light-brown dust to make space for her grandfather. His crutch left an imprint the shape of a dog's paw. At the lime tree, Mom held her grandfather's hand as he lowered himself. Then he leaned against the rough bark in the shade of the lime tree.

They repeated that routine every day for a long time. Mom sat with him through the afternoons as he told her about life on the plantation where he grew up and about the stories his parents told of India. After weeks of their ritual, Mom asked if he wanted to go anywhere else. They could go to the river. He could put his foot in the water. He inhaled deeply and looked up at the tiny green pods beginning to blossom. He told her he liked it there. When he died, he wanted to come back as the lime tree.

❋

Mom's grandfather held on for a few years longer. After he passed, Mom spent afternoons in the shade of that lime tree and thought of him. She was sad to leave it behind when they had to move, not because she thought he became the tree but because she worried she would forget him. She and he both wanted to stay close after death.

You really think they'd stay up in the clouds? I ask Des. If it was me up there, I wouldn't want nothing to do with none of that.

Matter of fact, Des says, you right. They'd find them a patch of sky closer to the action. When the rain clouds roll in, they'd be all up in it, feeling the cool water, riding the wind. And when it's clear, they can watch their kids and their kids' kids.

And their kids' kids' kids.

And their kids too, Des says. Watching all the cane folk.

To our right, the Flagler Beach pier extends out over the ocean. If this were a summer day, old men in bucket hats and their grandchildren would line the pier's far reaches. Thin black fishing lines would extend down to the white froth beneath, bobbing in the waves. Tonight, less than a day after I hid in the bathroom with a man whose hands were callused with sand from the shore, it's empty, only the moon looking down on it and us as we pass by.

Over the music, Tupac asks if gangsters get to go to heaven, and if they do, will he finally, after his short life that sounds so long when he speaks, find peace? The light turns green. We pass the Lion, where Aubrey saved Des from a fight some time ago, and then the buildings stop. For a while, there's only the beach, unoccupied lifeguard highchairs every hundred feet or so, watching the ocean battle the shore. Then the houses reappear, two floors in a county where most have one. Mercedes SUVs clutter the driveways, the new money that flooded the region before the housing crash, now blocks our view of the sea.

And it goes on, Des says. It goes on. Heaven gets more packed. A big Black city with all your cousins and aunties.

And all their cousins and aunties, I say.

All their friends from when they was young.

And every time someone dies, it gets bigger.

It's just like one big-ass wedding, man, Des says. First time you leave your body and you float up there, it's like you stepping off the floor from your first dance. First thing you see is your parents. And they smiling and crying.

Your drunk uncle's cracking some mad inappropriate jokes.

And he's wilding out because he's hitting on everything that moves, Des says. And then him and your folks is busy running around introducing you to your folks. And their folks.

And their friends.

And people you damn sure should've met a long time ago.

And you blinking real fast because you know you ain't supposed to cry but damn if your eyes ain't burning.

Damn if your nose ain't running.

And finally they introduce you to the slaves.

You looking at these skinny, ribs showing, hollow cheekbone, chain around the ankle,

Scraggly nappy gray-haired, ain't had a haircut in about a hundred years,

Grown folk. And you just looking at them shocked.

You like, How you cut cane looking like that?

How you carry cane on your back with them chicken legs?

And you so shocked you don't notice they smiling and laughing at you.

But it's all love.

It's all good.

And they take you by the hand and show you all the brothers and sisters they made on the ship.

The folks who ain't make it.

The ones they threw overboard.

And they're looking at you like you're theirs.

And, truth be told, you as much them as anybody else.

Music starts again.

Some shit everyone gets down to.

Something like "September."

People start busting out moves you ain't never seen.

Same shit they used to dance they asses out of white heaven.

And somehow, just from seeing them bounce, you got it too.

They passed you the juice.

And you moving like them, and y'all dance and laugh

And drink and smoke

And sing till everybody turns in. But you, you're still buzzing. Electric running all up and down your skin.

And you burning up so even the sweat on your forehead feels hot, I say. You need to chill. So you go to the nearest lookout and watch your kids leaving your funeral.

Des lights a cigarette.

That's the kind of heaven I can get down with, he says. Don't talk to me about that other shit.

※

Des's family is as Christian as my own. Grandma inherited her Christianity from her mother. When she moved to the States, she attended the same Baptist church in Flatbush that her mother did. Every Sunday, she saw Jamaicans that she thought she would never see again. What a blessing, they always said, to start new lives and rediscover each other.

According to Mom, the same church hosted Uncle Junior's funeral service. Grandma gave the eulogy. Before she reached the front, she was in tears. It was hard to bury anyone, she said, let alone a child. In his time on Earth, he lived to please the people around him. He made his siblings laugh, so they spoiled him. He did the same for his classmates, so they flocked to him. Whenever she saw him, people always surrounded him.

As she spoke, her tears dried. At the end of her eulogy, she said that the Lord knew Junior made mistakes. But He sent His only son to live among the sinners and save them from themselves. He called Junior back to save him. This was not their loss, she finished, but heaven's gain.

Shortly thereafter, they laid Junior to rest. After the pallbearers carried him and the casket was lowered, people approached to say their last goodbyes. Grandma was the last to go. She laid a single flower down, but Mom says she didn't cry. She knew her son was with the Lord.

A green sign announces the distance to Saint Augustine and to Jacksonville.

You ever hear the joke about Jacksonville? I ask Des. The one from back in segregation days? Where they put colored orphans in Jacksonville?

Where? he asks.

Jail.

White folks crazy, man.

Driving this stretch of A1A in the daytime, I always look for the sand-and-soil mixture at our sides. Strands of green, barely rooted down, flare when the wind passes by. They grow thicker the farther they get from the road as the land slopes downward to the Intracoastal. In the night, it's so dark that I can't see past A1A's end, but I know they're there, clinging to the patch between pavement and water.

This my favorite part, I say. Could live my whole life out here.

On our right, the houses begin to cluster together. In the distance, I see the bridge. Beneath is the inlet where the man-made river roils against the ocean. We curl around the gas station and onto a road that runs diagonal to A1A. We park on this empty road. On our right sits a row of glass-fronted houses whose porches overlook the water. Thin films of skim glisten even at night.

Why you ask me about the afterlife? Des asks. You been dreaming about her?

Des's cheeks pull back to reveal his teeth in a sly grin.

How you know? I ask.

When Tati's mom died, Des says, Egypt told me she kept dreaming about her. Had her wondering if there was ghosts in town. Figure that's why she moved away.

Des looks at the ocean in front of him. I do the same.

What'd you dream? he asks.

Man, you already know. Dreamt about Aubrey the night she died.

Des rolls his window down and lights another cigarette.

Felt so real, I thought she was there. Woke up clutching the sheets like I was holding her. And I'm half-asleep so I think it's real for a moment. Then I come to and she's gone. Fall back asleep and dream about her again. And I wake up in the morning and stare at my ceiling and wonder for the first time in a long time if maybe there's an afterlife.

Mr. hardcore atheist? Des says. Mr. I'm going to shit on anybody who even mentions God?

For a minute or two, I say, I wasn't sure.

Des exhales the smoke slowly. His breath is soft against the steady sound of waves clapping against the shore.

This where I tell you some shit like she'll live forever in your heart? Des asks. No, you a smart nigga. I'm supposed to tell you she'll live forever in your brain? Just another wrinkle in that big old gray ball in your head?

Don't think I'd believe you if you did, I say, and then pause. You dream much?

Do I dream? Des asks. Me? Nigga, I can't sleep for the dreams.

✴

I have long hated dreaming, its interruption of rest. When I was younger, Mom, an atheist, said death was dreamless sleep. One night, after she put me to bed, I tried to picture it and saw a black screen. Nothing. But if I was picturing it, then it was something. Death had to be more nothing than that. As I tried to imagine a nothing that I was not imagining, my heart raced. I threw the covers off and ran to Mom's room. She pulled me under her blanket and rocked me to dreamless sleep. After all the anxiety about what would happen to me after I died, sleeping that night provided a relief, a vision of death as uninterrupted rest.

✴

Want to go down? Des asks and then yawns.

Des walks to the back, pops the trunk, and pulls out a bottle of whiskey.

Egypt gone to sleep and you figure you can drink as much as you want?

This for you, he says.

Des holds the bottle by the neck and we walk to where a fence breaks in the middle. We step through it onto the bluff of rocks and hop down the large boulders, avoiding the loose ones and the broken glass. At the bottom, I take off my shoes and Des kicks off his sliders. The sand is grainy and thick with moisture. On our left, the inlet normally flows into the ocean, but tonight there's a long stretch of sand covered by skim and pockmarked by tide pools left behind when the salt waves fled back out to sea. We walk toward the ocean along this flat stretch of beach. At high tide, this shore is the ocean's floor.

Bro, what're you so afraid of? Des asks.

Me?

You doing all this talking about dying, sure don't sound like you ready for it. Got me wondering if this the same nigga I walked back with from J-Boogie's house.

The night you were mad high?

Paranoid as hell. Walking through the F section, looking into every patch of woods. Worried lights rounding the corner was a car coming to kill us. Every time I seen a truck I thought some redneck was about to hop out with a shotgun and spray us. And finally one more car rounded the corner and I flinched and you flipped. You remember what you said? You quit laughing and your face turned to stone. You just looked me dead in the eye and you said, It's been open season on niggas for a minute now. If some redneck's going to blast you, ain't nothing you can do about that. So what you scared for? And what you said had me shook. You ever heard of a Florida nigga shivering in the summer?

Quit lying, bro.

Deadass. Looked at you and ain't know who I was walking with. Then the chill went away and I felt it.

Des lights a cigarette. A thin line of smoke curls around his face and he blows out a plume that catches the wind. It rushes left and dissipates into the air.

Felt what?

Numb. Straight numb. And it ain't scare me or nothing. Sometimes when I get scared, I remember that. Remember how calm it felt knowing that if I was going to die, there wasn't a damn thing I could do about it.

Des pulls on his smoke. I look at the ocean. My eyes haven't yet adjusted to the night. The Atlantic's a far-off dark mass, seething and roiling like bodies trapped beneath a black blanket.

You remember what happened next? Des asks.

I started cracking on you.

Your stone face busted open the biggest fucking smile, man. Turned from killer to comedian on a dime bro. Deadass.

I don't know about all that.

You ain't got to know shit. Nigga, I'm telling you what I know.

I look for waves in the ocean, for the white frothy foam in the wake. But all I see is the blanketed bodies, the chorus of hands pushing at the fabric, hoping for a tear.

Seen the same look today when you lost it on Brandon. He ain't seen it because he was off somewhere else. But I seen it. You was pretending the drink getting a hold of you was what made you leap out your body but I seen it. Seen it since before he passed you the bottle. Reason I had my gun out before you swung on him. So tell me this. How in the hell did the nigga that flexed on death become so obsessed with it?

Finally, in the distance, I see the swirls of froth atop the skim running up the shore.

I ain't that dude no more, I say. Ever since I left—in college, in New York—I been fronting like I ain't speak with a accent before I got there.

Like you ain't never seen dirt roads.

Like my mom's car ain't sit in the driveway for weeks after hurricanes, I say. Been fronting so long, I done forgot everything. Then Aubrey died and I started thinking about home. Started talking to my mom and she told me all these stories about our family. How she grew up on a dirt road. Ain't even have a fridge, bro. Used the river to keep their cheese cold. We was real country people. And just like that, one generation later, we gone from rivers to fridges, dirt paths to roads, and I'm up there in the biggest city on Earth, running around and I ain't know if I'm country or I'm city. Had me wondering why I was up there, if I learned anything.

Des lowers his cigarette from his mouth.

You seen snow? asks Des.

I turn my head and look at Des. His eyes shine in the moonlight. They're glassy from sleep and liquor. I begin to chuckle.

Country boy ain't never seen nothing seem funny to you? asks Des.

It ain't that, I say. Just thought you were about to ask something deep.

The waves patter on the shore like feet pounding the pavement.

So you seen snow?

Yeah, bro, I say. Yeah I seen snow.

The wind picks up.

Me, I ain't never seen snow. All the water I seen is, Des gestures to the ocean and the inlet, running.

✕

I remember when this place felt like all I would see of the world. My only keepsake from back then is a family picture that was taken a few months after Junior got locked up. Junior never liked cameras and he never smiled for them, but he asked Mom to pay to have the picture taken when we visited him. An inmate ran the studio with the permission of the guards. Junior chose the pale-blue backdrop scattered with white clusters. Mom was in the middle, frizzy hair streaked with gray, arms crossed because the guards didn't allow touching, not even between the free. I stood to Mom's right, hands at my side, lips pursed the way they did at the beginning of a race. Junior stood to her left, gray dusting his hair, unintelligible ink lines peeking out from his blue jumpsuit. The smiling mother and her two unsmiling sons with the blue sky and the white clouds behind them, we look like a triptych of a family just arrived in heaven, the closest the three of us will get to an afterlife.

✕

I pull the picture out of my wallet. It's faded now from years of friction. Then I put it away. It's late. The waves are still far, but they're getting closer. Beyond them is the horizon where, in a short time, the sun will begin to blot out the night's stars. The skim covering the sandbar that separates the Atlantic from the Intracoastal has progressed on both ends, the brackish waters and the saltwater meeting and mixing. Small rivulets run in both directions from tide pools. With time, the skim will deepen, the sand will disappear, and the daily struggle between the inlet's current and the ocean's tide will begin. But for now all I see is Des's silhouette, blurred in the foreground.

You just about out of here, Des says. You going to be all right up there?

I'll be all right. And when I'm not, I'll call y'all. Call my mom. Thinking about flying back to Jamaica to see her. Definitely going to fly down more and see y'all.

Even if you don't, Des says and then shrugs. You always going to be Florida.

Three-eight-six till I die.

And if anyone runs up on you and wants smoke, you just let them know you got an army of no-good, Southern-drawling Florida niggas at your back.

Des chuckles and nods. I smile. Then we turn away from each other.

Des says, You going to teach them kids what you learned down here?

Couldn't avoid it if I tried.

You going to call old boy?

Think so. Don't know if he'll take me back.

You still got to try.

Des is quiet again, and I know exhaustion is coming for him, but I don't want to give him up to sleep just yet.

Thinking about moving back for real, I say.

You bullshitting.

Deadass. Don't know when, don't know how, don't know what I'm going to do if I make it back, but I don't know how much longer I can live without all of this.

Look who done finally grown up, he says.

Took me long enough.

Des opens his pack of cigarettes. He shifts and the remaining two rattle around in the near-empty box. He picks up the bottle and squints at it. A few inches of dark liquor remain. He perches a cigarette between his lips, lights it, and then says through the smoke, Getting late. Almost killed the whiskey. Almost out of smokes. What you trying to do?

Send Aubrey off, I say.

Des passes me the bottle. The Atlantic's getting closer. The Intracoastal's fighting to meet it. A pair of headlights rushes over the bridge, passing the gas station's insistent glow.

Rest in peace, I say.

Big ups to one of the realest, he says.

I tip the bottle on its side. The dark liquid rushes down the neck and a thin stream waterfalls into the sand. It pools and bubbles. I expect to see the saltwater rushing through the sand's pores to meet the whiskey. I hope to hear the voices of ancestors whose names I have never known, the baritone voice of my great-grandfather beneath the lime tree, the quiet sound of my grandmother telling her daughters she will send for them soon, Mom telling me and Junior we're starting over in the States, and Junior telling me about the cars he'll buy when he gets out, joining a voice unmistakably light and shrill and airy: Aubrey's. But instead all I hear is the waves crashing on the shore.

Their sound transports me back to the moments after Aubrey and I finished gigging and we had traveled back to where we shoved off. We spent hours that night talking about her dreams, ones she described in such detail that, instead of the dark night in front of us and the unchanging river, I saw her make her way through her life. She was still skinny and her face still smooth in my mind, but her hair and the clothes she wore were different, the image of her a mishmash of the Aubrey I knew then and the signs that I imagined showed maturity. As I watched her move and start new jobs and travel, I smiled then, as I am smiling now, the memory of her no longer an intrusion pulling me away, but a visit from a friend I have not seen in a long time, a much-needed excuse to step away from all the scheduled affairs of the day to talk with someone I miss. I let my cheeks widen and open my mouth to show my crooked teeth because I don't fear what Des will think when he sees them. He smiles back and claps a hand on my shoulder and we nod.

Glad I knew her, I say.

Des nods and then says, Should we head home? Egypt's going to kill me if I let her sleep in that car all night.

One last race?

You know I ain't never turned down a challenge, Des says.

Last one to die?

Des laughs into a cough, and then spits phlegm onto the beach.

Too old for that shit.

He takes off his shirt, throws it into the sand, and hoists up his shorts. I do the same.

Where to? he asks.

Where the river meets the ocean.

Fuck am I supposed to know where that is?

I imagine us, two shirtless boys racing across the flat plane of the beach, the ocean waves rolling in beyond us. We'll run upright, shoulders bent slightly over our hips, raising our knees just shy of ninety degrees, the balls of our feet spraying sand behind us. We'll sprint like young men again, speeding along without fear of death until we feel the cool of the thin film of water where the brack meets the fresh. We'll race until we feel the wetness where the natural tides that they forced my ancestors to cross meets the man-made channel where I fished under the quiet cover of night with the girl I loved when she lived and again after she died.

You'll know, I say.

Des drags his heel across the sand to make a starting line. I place my left foot just behind it, lower my body, lean over my knee, and look down. He does the same.

Want to call it? he asks.

On your marks. Get set.

Before I can say go, Des leaps in front of the line. I shake my head and take a short, terrifying step forward with my left foot. I let the lean proceed into falling. My right foot catapults under me, trying to catch my weight. The loose sand sprays outward as I try to raise my feet to land on their balls, but I keep striking the ground at midsole. My legs are heavy. My knees push forward but I struggle to raise them, let alone kick down with any real force. I'm falling more than I'm flying.

By the time my body has straightened out and I look up, Des is in front of me. The ridges that once indicated his shoulder muscles are gone, replaced by pockmarked acne he didn't always carry. His shoulders turn out awkwardly, arms stiff at his sides.

Though there's no way I can reach top sprint mechanics when I'm this out of shape—though I fear the pain I'll feel when this ends—the familiar cold, the coarse rush of air through my nose tasting like iron or blood when it hits my tongue, awakens something in me that I haven't felt in a long time. I breathe as deep as I can, which is far more shallow than it once was. I repeat to myself that I must keep breathing and everything else falls into place and pace. The distance between me and Des narrows. He bobs up and down in the rolling sand and my vision shakes and still I see that he's getting closer. The sand stiffens and cools; the water was just here. My step lands closer to my toes. Des's shoulder is just in front of mine.

Though I cannot close the gap, our legs begin to move in sync. We lift and kick at the same time. We cannot escape the other's stride. We do our best to hang on, swept away less by a desire to win than by the pace that neither of us has set but that neither can escape, when finally I hear the patter of water beneath my feet and feel the spray of cool droplets from Des's stride and know that he has won.

Nigga, where you going? Des yells as he slows down and I keep sprinting past him. I charge ahead, leaning over my shoulder now the way we leaned over the track's curve, turning toward the river to join a cool breeze rushing toward the inlet. I won't look back but I know Des is there, following me. I run into the water that's climbing now to my ankles, the sand suctioning my feet to the floor from the moment they strike the ground until the moment I wrest them free. I hear him yelling, Nigga, where you going, as the water climbs to my shins, cold now, much colder than the ocean, a kind of cold that reminds me of the piercing-blue sky on winter days in the Northeast city I now live in.

The chill wrests whatever sleep there is from my body and I

picture the smile on Des's face as he follows me into our brackish, unclean river. I cannot hear him speak, but I know he's
muttering under his breath, This nigga, as the water climbs
all the way to my knees. And I don't need to ask to know that
he'll do as I'm doing now and leap headfirst into the river, the
water so cold for a moment that I can feel nothing else. I know
that he and I, who ran across Flagler County the whole day and
then sprinted across this beach in the stone's throw between
night and dawn, returning to this murky river like amphibians
who need it to live, will swim upstream. And when I finally
resurface to see Des, perhaps behind or perhaps in front, I know
that I will scream that word that I have avoided since I touched
down, that word that speaks to us in a way no other does, that
word that means as much for what it does not say as for what
it does, that word whose difference from its parent Des and I
have fought for, that word in which the absence of one sound is
the presence of something else entirely, a presence somewhere
between a story and a history, between fate and fatal, between
an inlet and an ocean, and I will say, That's my nigga.

And when Des arises and I claim him at the top of my lungs,
he reciprocates and the wind flares with an intensity that
wicks the spray off the meeting currents into the air, droplets
shining for a moment in the dying moonlight. The breeze is
cool but warming, an afterlife of this North Florida winter, its
speed and temperature something like the one I imagine was
supposed to carry my dead ancestors back to Africa, like the
one I hope caught the women of my family when they buried
their people, and like the one I hope will be there to greet my
brother when he finally makes it out. And finally the weight of

all the stories about my family and of walking their well-trod trails no longer feels like an anchor but like a buoy, keeping me afloat where the river meets the ocean.

Another flare of the wind and a rush of the current makes Des and me stumble and we steady our feet, our hands clasp, and we dap each other up in all the motions that came so easily but felt so foreign earlier today, the same ones that feel like a bed long slept in now. And when our arms circle each other's backs, we do not pull away as quickly as we had this morning, our bony, tough bodies pressed against each other, firm and unyielding, stable as support, and we're young together, we're boys together, we're boysboysboys.

Egypt Sings of Droughts and Floods

These trifling niggas. Daniel and Desmond. Left me in the car. Acting like I was just going to sleep the whole night. Like they don't know no better. Rolling around in the water. Like it's their home. Like the moon don't know they're wandering.

It's about three in the morning. The dark sky's gray-blue. Morning's coming soon. It's later than late. It's later than I've been out in a long while. Twig's still sleeping in the back seat. He drank so much he could sleep in a ditch if he found himself one. I drank too much too. The liquor and lingering sleep make it hard to remember what I'm doing here, how long we've been doing this.

Tati loved the night stretching longer than we thought it could but moving so fast we thought it short. She said as much the last time we were together, the night of the almost-fight at the Lion. After Aubrey jumped in, apologized, and ran off, Desmond dropped me at Tati's. It was around four in the morning, but Tati was going to be deployed in Afghanistan the next week, so we spread the night out as far as we could. I sat down on her back porch and watched the trees sway in the breeze through the screen. She went to the kitchen, returned with a tall glass of water, said I couldn't leave till I finished it.

I ain't drink that much, I said.

If you say so.

I gulped the water down. Tati turned to the backyard. Since her mom passed, we could be as loud as we wanted. We didn't say anything. The house felt empty. The frogs droned steadily, but they'd been out for so long that I couldn't distinguish them from the static of wind-tossed trees.

You see the way Desmond was looking at that white girl? she asked.

Who you telling? I said. Way he was talking on the drive home, you'd think Aubrey saved everyone's lives tonight.

Wasn't nothing going to happen anyway. Scared old boys. Way they was jawing at each other, wasn't nobody going to hit nobody.

I don't know, I said. Thought for a second you were going to hit Brandon.

Thought you might too.

Tati stood up and walked to the edge of the porch. She ran her nails along the screen. They made a rattling sound like a can rolling down the street.

Thought I might, she said, but I wasn't going to. At least, not unless he hit me first.

He might've.

Then we really would've had a problem.

Desmond might've pulled out his gun, I said.

You might've jumped on Brandon.

You might've hit back.

We would've gone to jail. Tati chuckled. How you like that?

Army comes to get me but they can't because they done locked me up for fighting these rednecks.

Tati opened the door and walked out into the backyard. I followed. The loose dirt was soft and cool against our bare feet. I dug mine in until my toes were covered.

You scared? I asked.

Yes and no.

What you scared of?

Tati walked to the magnolia tree, pulled a branch down, and plucked a flower from it. When she put her nose to it, she smiled.

You think soldiers go to heaven? Tati asked. Like if I kill someone, is that going to keep me from getting in?

Last I checked, you ain't been to church in a minute. Thought you ain't believe.

Might not, Tati said, or I might just be mad at my mom.

Tati dipped her nose into the magnolia again and breathed deep. This time, as I watched her, I could almost smell its sweetness, though I knew she was thinking about her mom. She spent so much time grooming that magnolia tree and this garden, despite the armadillos trying to run off with her vegetables and petals, despite this soil too loose for plants to set down roots. Tati, thinking of her mom, and me, thinking of her.

I don't think I believe, she said. But if I did, I don't know if soldiers would get in.

Most of us wouldn't get in anyway.

Tati walked to me and ran her hand behind my ear to pull my hair, which was long and straightened then, from my face. Then she placed the flower in the space behind my ear. A sweet smell fell like a soft blanket draped by a parent tucking a child in for the night, and I couldn't tell if the scent came from the flower or from Tati's hands, until she pulled them away. Then she said, Hope that made up for that white girl reaching for your hair.

The nerve, I said.

That look you gave me when she touched you.

The amount of time I spent in the bathroom after, fixing my hair. I couldn't tell if it got messed up because we was getting wild or because she fucked it up.

We laughed and then I pulled the flower out from behind my ear. I ran my fingers over its soft petals, put my nose to it, breathed deep the almost-too-sweet scent, and then exhaled. When I looked up, Tati was looking at me, a small grin on her face.

I'm going to miss this, she said.

Staying out too late with these trifling-ass niggas?

Rednecks damn near shooting at us.

Riding home together.

Sitting on the porch.

Trying to keep from getting hungover.

Running our feet in the dirt.

The magnolias.

The warm nights.

The nights.

What about the nights?

The mornings come, and also the nights.

We lived together in those early morning late nights. We learned the fullness of our lives, talking about all the small glances that the boys did not see and all the words the boys did not hear. We forgot things that they wish they knew and we knew things they would never remember.

Sometimes, we knew that when they woke up, they would not remember what happened, like at Daniel's going-away party, the day before he left for California, in late August or early September. After Daniel went to a party with Twig and the white boys, where he got drunk, he met us at J-Boogie's house around midnight, about an hour late. He stepped onto the back porch wearing a sleeveless hoodie, cargo shorts, and flip-flops. Sweat shone from his forehead and he smelled like the pineapple scented body spray he bought at the Daytona mall. He gave me a hug and kissed me on the cheek, and then did the same to Tati, who pushed him into the group of boys, all of whom dapped him up.

These boys is too much, Egypt, Tati said to me. Always getting drunk so they can pretend they ain't remember getting handsy with us.

They too scared to when they sober.

Rightfully so. I'd smack that nigga six ways from Sunday.

Then someone handed out shots that nobody needed. Everyone but me downed them and it was quiet for a moment. Then Daniel said, Now, I ain't no faggot, but I love all of y'all niggas.

He tried to give a speech, as though he could command a room, but people kept talking. When Daniel devolved into repeating himself quietly, I took his drink and told him I was taking him home. Then we got in my car with Desmond and Tati. Along the way, we stopped at Taco Bell, and Daniel mentioned that he was queasy. We pulled over and he knelt in the grass. When I stepped out with him, the dew climbed past my flip-flops and wet my feet as Daniel barfed. He wiped his mouth and started talking about how much he would miss us and then he started crying. Desmond helped him up and Daniel kept crying and talking about how he couldn't even stand up without us. He didn't know how he was going to survive in college.

As we ushered him back into the car, Tati shot me a look, surprised Daniel was a sad drunk. I certainly didn't expect it. He kept talking about all the things he would miss as I drove him home. We sat in his driveway until he quieted down and then I took his keys and opened the front door as quietly as I could, but Daniel tripped and fell loudly enough to wake his mother up. After she came out of her bedroom, Daniel started vomiting again. We dragged him to the bathroom and he kept crying as he puked up everything, even the water we made him sip between rounds. When he finished but was still breathing heavy, he said he had a secret he's been keeping from us for a long time that he didn't want to keep anymore, and he said his dad beat him when he was a kid. Ms. Henriquez and Desmond got real quiet. Daniel cried.

He beat me, Daniel said, and I loved him.

Then he talked about how Aubrey didn't want him but he loved her too, at which point Tati kneeled down next to him, grabbed a tissue, and wiped the mucusy spit from his mouth. She gathered that boy playing at being a man into her arms, rested his head on her shoulder, and patted his back until he stopped crying. A while later, she pulled him away, his tears staining the shoulder of her pale-blue shirt, and we put him to bed. Ms. Henriquez walked us to the front door, where she said, I don't think he's going to remember this, but now you know.

Then we drove to Desmond's. I stepped outside to say good night and Desmond said he had to talk to me. Tati returned to the car. When we were alone, the night lasting so much longer than I thought it would have and Desmond swaying like the liquor turned his legs to Jell-O, he said, It ain't fair. Ain't fair Baby D's dad beat him. Ain't fair my dad walked out on me. Ain't fair niggas is shitty fathers.

Even though he and I both knew I was a Daddy's girl, he was too drunk to hear me, so I let him talk for a while, thinking it would calm him down. Instead, he worked himself up until he cried and I held him. When he finished, he tried to get me into his bedroom. I said no. He kept trying. I waved to Tati, who came outside, said good night, and pulled me back into the car.

As we drove away, I asked Tati, You think they cry when we not around?

You mean with each other? Tati asked. I nodded. Them niggas? If they did, they wouldn't know what to do with us.

Tati laughed and I rolled my eyes. She nudged my shoulder and I laughed.

I don't trip too much about it though, she said. Just leaves us more time to ourselves.

Them niggas can't handle they own feelings. How they supposed to handle us?

Right, Tati said. We a whole lot to handle.

In the quiet of the late night, finally alone as we drove home, we rehearsed the events of the night and all the things that we thought but did not say because the boys were around. That night, rare because Daniel was with us instead of with the white boys, and rarer still because he unburdened himself the way he did, was one that Tati and I never spoke about to the boys again.

We two secret keepers always found each other in long nights with the boys. We did so after the Brawl at the County

Fair. After Aubrey pulled Daniel out of the fray, as Tati swung on a boy that Desmond tried to hold still, someone yelled cops. Desmond ran back to his car with his boys and Tati and I ran back to my car. We sped down US-1 and Tati watched the road behind us for what felt like miles. When we came to a red light and finally figured we were free, Tati cracked a wide grin and started laughing.

Can't believe we got away with that, I said.

Them boys lucky, Tati said. I was fucking them up left and right before them cops came.

I'm saying though, I said. Thought we couldn't scrap because we was girls.

Forgot they was dealing with some knocking niggas out on the way to the school bus,

Earrings off, weave snatching, nail breaking,

Three-eight-six till we die,

Florida bitches.

We laughed until we were quiet. Then, the adrenaline wore off and I said, Hope Baby D got home safe.

Daniel? Tati said. Man, that boy peeled out before shit even got started. Don't know what he was doing out there anyway.

Acting like he tough.

Dragging that white girl all up in our business.

Him and Desmond, I said. Them boys better learn to take care of themselves.

After we laughed at the two of them, we retold the story of that night to each other, beginning with meeting up at my house without the boys and arriving at the county fair just the two of us. We told each other the story again at practice on Monday, when the brawl came up and Daniel and Desmond talked over us, bragging to the boys about all the damage they did. But the ways they looked at each other and the ways they finished each other's sentences were different from before. When Desmond punched the redneck for calling Daniel out his name, that was probably the first time anyone had ever hit someone for that skinny Jamaican boy who grew up as his father's whipping post. When Desmond shoved Daniel out of the crowd and told him to get home, that was the first time I ever saw Desmond, who expected all his boys to jump into scraps with him, try to keep someone safe, to keep someone's future alive. That day at practice, as they spoke, I gave Tati a look and she smirked, and then all the girls on the team watched us and smiled. When the boys lined up for their heats, providing the privacy to share stories not to be repeated, we shared all the details the boys couldn't know.

I doubt those boys romping around on the shore have the good sense to figure out what questions they need to ask to learn what they don't know. I can't imagine Desmond told Daniel much about life after graduation. The meals he missed working two jobs and helping his unemployed mom pay the mortgage and the car loan. The hours of sleep lost after he quit one of his jobs to enroll at community college and did his homework in the late hours. The lies he told to try to impress me when we first started going on dates. The times he was lying on my bed and asked me what I thought Daniel was doing. There is so much that has happened that turned our life into the monotonous habits that fill the time between work, into imagining the wild nights a friend is having in a Northeast city, and into drinking too much and throwing hands with your chosen sister at a bar. There are so many fragments they take for whole.

Remembering me and Tati speaking in those quiet hours in this night turning to morning makes my eyes ache and water until I open them once more and wipe the moisture from their corners. When I dry my hands on my pants, I step out of the car to see Daniel and Desmond climb out of the water on the shore like primordial life taking its first steps, one of them hobbling along from overexertion, their skins glistening from the slimy waters catching the blue moonlight, which makes them look like they are made of onyx. As one wraps his arm around the other to stabilize his limp, though I cannot tell which moving statue is Daniel and which is Desmond, I remember that the shore on which they walk will all be underwater, not just when the skim turns to tide but when the sea levels rise and the ocean drowns the land. The image of this flood overwhelms me, the shore turning into ocean, the rocks ascending from the sand becoming reefs, the car in which Twig still sleeps rusting, and I imagine some far-off future, when we live on stilted houses above the land we refused to abandon when the United States declared it no longer a part of the nation, when smoking finally kills Desmond and Daniel returns for the first time since tonight, and Daniel and I will place Desmond's cloth-wrapped body in the boat that we'll shove off from the home that Desmond and I will raise our children in, and Desmond's coffin will follow the trail of the Intracoastal to this point where he and Daniel bathed in its waters.

My eyes wet thinking about our future and, not wanting to miss this opportunity, I scuttle down the rocks, slipping on a loose one near the bottom but catching my footing on the shore, and run myself into stability, toward Daniel and Desmond, who smile from ear to ear. Before I have neared, they see the purpose in my pace and direction, and they stop to wait for me. My arms extending wide, my bones clank into their sides as I wrap my hands around them and my feet slip in the shifting sand, throwing my weight onto them, who try to lean on each other but cannot, and we all fall down. A tangle of limbs on the shore, sand cast above us by our impact and then the wind, I say, Y'all niggas always leaving me behind, at which the two of them laugh, until Desmond says, We here now. When Daniel asks if we should wake Twig up, I tell him no; this is our time.

It's unlikely, so unlikely, that we found ourselves here in the Earth's history between the emergence from the ocean of this land we call home and its eventual reclamation by the water when the tides rise, this short time in our long lives after we befriended each other and then gave ourselves to work's routines and still somehow returned to each other. In our minutes before the sun rises and we have to drive Daniel back to his car, before he flies home and cannot be counted on to call us or to return, we do not retreat from touch the way that Daniel and Desmond once did; we linger here, looking something like a multi-limbed monster, in this moment that the land is not yet the ocean's floor.